A NEW BEGINNING WITH YOU

A YORK BEACH NOVEL

NICOLE VIDAL

COPYRIGHT

DEDICATION

I would like to dedicate this book to my better half. Without your support and encouragement, I would not have pursued this dream. You are my anchor and the best partner a girl could ask for.

TABLE OF CONTENTS

GENEVIEVE

I can't believe I'm back here. Ten years have passed but nothing here seems to have changed. I'm looking at the ocean from the best spot on the planet. To my right sits the chair where my grandma – we called her Memére, the French equivalent – doled out her sagest advice.   Mrs. Jones, our caretaker and Mem's best friend, must have stopped by. It's the offseason, and Mem's chair should be in storage. I wish she were still here. She always knew what to say, and she never told me what to do. She listened, pointed out all angles of the problem and offered suggestions. What are you going to do? she would ask. Even when I chose wrong, she was there to pick me up, offer more solutions, or just listen.

So much has happened since I was last here. There have been so many memories at this cottage. Some were amazing and some well - life is filled with bumps and curves like the rollercoaster at the amusement park in the village. Time to move forward from the last bump - it was more like a ditch, but forward is where I need to go. Forward to forget about him - the reason I'm not married and have a huge debt from a wedding that didn't happen.

Might as well get started now. I grab a hoodie from inside and start down the beach. I will stop at Mrs. Jones's cottage to thank her. It's a beautiful early fall evening. I pull my hoodie on as I slowly walk in the shallows, carrying my tennis shoes. The water is already cold. The soft sounds of the water lapping at the shore is something I've always found calming, ever since I was a girl. It's as if time slows down to a turtle's pace on the shore. Hopefully, if I spend enough time here, I can bring that serenity back home with me. It's a short walk, but soon I lose myself in old memories.

Summer was the best time of the year for me. It meant we pack up the car with everything we need including our dog, Coco (What can I say? We named her when I was only seven) and headed to the cottage. She had tan fur and spots like chocolate chips. I was the oldest. My brother, Pete was four. He was a baseball fanatic. He slept with his glove even in the offseason. My sister, Maggie was two. She was only two so not much to report.

My mom, Joanie, was a secretary at the elementary school in the next town over, so she had summers off. Dad worked as a car salesman, so he was coming and going from the cottage all summer. Now that every possible thing was packed, we crammed into the car and took off. It was crazy early. My dad, Robert, seemed to think the earlier we left, the better. All I knew was I hoped to sleep most of the four-hour ride to the cottage. If this were a normal family vacation, we would have nowhere to check in until three in the afternoon. Luckily, my grandparents owned the cottage, so off we went at this very early hour of the morning. We wouldn't have been able to afford this cottage for the entire summer if it didn't belong to them. Money problems were high up on the list of my parents' issues.

We are about halfway there and through my sleepy fog, I heard, Pete screaming, "I have to pee! Like, now!"

We waited and hoped Dad would find a rest area or restaurant, knowing that Pete's definition of now is actually more like within five miles. Thankfully, we found a cute little diner, and Pete was all set. We got back on the road to my summer in the sun. We didn't make it very far before an awful smell started coming from Maggie's side of the car. "Yuck," I thought, "no kids for me! I'm not changing that ever!" So much for a sleepy ride to the cottage on the beach. Dad pulled over to the side of the highway and Mom jumped out to change Maggie. The good news was that Maggie was clean and not crying. The bad news was that there was nowhere to leave the dirty diaper, so it was sitting in a baggie by Mom's feet. So much for getting rid of the smell.

The cottage was my favorite place on earth. It was a quaint two-bedroom, one-bath house with barely enough room for the five of us and Coco. Thankfully, there was an enclosed lower porch with a door, so I had my own space while we were here. There was a medium-sized yard with a fire pit and an outdoor shower. While the house does have some kid required amenities like TV, we weren't allowed to use it unless it was after 5 pm or pouring rain. Even then, Mom tried to discourage it and attempted to force family game time or reading. "I never minded the reading, but family game time: ugh!" I was much better off left on my own to read, color, or write stories about how I wish my life were.

Finally, after what seemed like forever, we arrived at the cottage. I rushed to my room and started to set up my things. Summer is a long time for a seven-year old. The beach was calling my name; I went as fast as I could. I gathered necessities in a bag - nothing fancy: a blanket, a book and a water. Things were different at the cottage. At home, Mom was very strict. She had to know where we were, who we were with and that we would be safe. Here at the cottage, it was no holds barred. We could come and go as we pleased, and that included walking down to the beach. I did a quick check to see if the Cavallaro family had arrived yet. They spent their summers here too. No such luck. I was on my own for now.

I took off down the rickety wooden staircase to the beach straight into the shallows. I wasn't thinking and I stepped right into the water. It was still cold. Our winter had been an easy one in Rhode Island, so we got out of school on June fifteenth this year. I leapt back out of the water and set up my blanket. I sat down and simply stared at the ocean. It was so peaceful and serene on that day. Some adults had told me, I had an old soul because I understood the calm of the sea and carried on conversations above my level. Call it what you want, I loved it here. It wasn't long before Pete interrupted my peace. My time alone on the beach for the day had passed. Here comes the entire family, I thought, *"Oh goody! Forced family time.* Hopefully, if I just stick my nose in this book, no one will bother me. I highly doubt that my mom believes I have not finished Harry Potter and the Sorcerer's Stone, but a girl can dream."

I realize now how fortunate I was to spend my summers here. My parents were always fighting about money. I'm sure if the cottage had belonged to them, it would have been sold years ago to cover some expense or another. Thankfully, this place belongs to my Memére and Pepére. They worked their whole lives to get this place and would never sell it. Tears fill my eyes as I think of Memére and Pepére. What will happen to their cottage now?

I'm so lost in my memories that; I reach Mrs. Jones's cottage without realizing it. Her cottage is similar to ours, well, maybe not "ours." Who knows who will get the cottage? Mrs. Jones sees me approach and wraps me into a great big hug.

"Oh dear, look at you. You're so thin! Are you feeling well?" she says.

"Hi, Mrs. Jones. Thank you for setting out Memére's chair. I truly appreciate it. How did you know I would be here?" I ask.

A grin crosses her face. "I heard about the wedding - well non-wedding - and figured you would be here sooner, rather than later. It's been three days. What took you so long?" she says with her hands on her hips.

I laugh. She means it has been three days since I chose not to marry Daniel. Despite all the current upheaval in my life, it's nice to know Mrs. Jones is her usual blunt self.

"I had a few things to wrap up," I respond.

"Would you like some tea? Perhaps something stronger?" she says winking.

"Something stronger," I reply.

Mrs. Jones walks into the cottage and promptly returns with two glasses. After taking a sip, I don't know what's in the glass, but it's certainly stronger than tea. If I can't have Memére, Mrs. Jones is the next best thing. When her only daughter was ten, she died of leukemia. Her husband, Stan, died about five years ago. At that time, she sold her house and moved to her cottage permanently. She has watched over the neighborhood ever since.

The cottage I'm staying in belonged to my grandparents until they died six weeks ago. Both of them passed away in the span of seventy-two hours. Memére died in her sleep and the next morning, Pepére collapsed. I truly think Pepére died of a broken heart. They were supposed to be at my wedding to Daniel. Instead, we had a small service for the two of them together. It may have been a sign.

I sit with Mrs. Jones for nearly an hour before heading back to my grandparent's cottage. We catch up on various local goings-on and chat a bit about my life. Mrs. Jones isn't Memére, but she listens to every word without judging me at all. When I finish explaining the reasons why I'm there she offered me her wisdom.

"You're the only one who can decide what's best for you. You have a lot of thinking to do and a lot of big decisions to make. Whether it's going back to Rhode Island, moving here, or starting over somewhere else; those are your choices to make and yours alone. You will make the right choice, dear. You certainly did by not marrying Daniel," she says.

"How did you know I shouldn't marry Daniel?" I ask.

She snorts. "I've known you your entire life. Not once in the two years you were with Daniel, did I ever see you look at him like you did Joseph."

"But . . . "I sigh. Deep down, I know she is right. I have never felt even a sliver of what I felt for Joey for Daniel. On the other hand, who meets their true love when they are seven years old? No one does. No one.

"Take your time, think about what is best for you, and go get it. I love you, Gen."

"I love you too, Mrs. J." I get up and hug her. "Thank you. I think coming here was the first smart thing I have done in a long time," I say and start down the stairs towards the shoreline.

Along the short walk, I can't help but think about Joey, the true reason I couldn't marry Daniel. I met Joey when we came here for the summer when I was seven. That year the snow had been heavier than usual, even for Rhode Island, so we had a bunch of snow days to make up. By the time we were able to head to the cottage, it was already late summer.

I didn't even take the time to unpack. Grabbing a towel, I took off out the door to the beach. This was my favorite place to be. The smell of the ocean air surrounded me as I ran down the beach. I was completely lost in my thoughts when I ran smack-dab into a boy playing football on the beach.

"I'm so sorry. Are you okay? My name is Gen. What is your name?" I asked as I surveyed my victim.

"Joseph. I'm Joseph. I'm fine. You were running very fast for a small girl," he said as he looked me up and down.

"Thanks, I think. Where are you staying?"

"We're staying there in the blue one. You?" I looked up at the largest cottage on the beach, the one with an amazing deck stretching towards the ocean. I thought that Mem's cottage would fit in it twice over.

"We are in the white one two doors over." I said avoiding his eyes.

"Great! I'll see you every day then. What is Gen short for? Do you not like your name?"

"Genevieve, my name is Genevieve. Most of my friends and classmates stumble on it, so people call me Gen. Do you only go by Joseph?"

"My mother says Joseph is a strong name, but only she calls me that." He looked towards the blue cottage where his mother had stepped onto the deck. She was waving him in. I was stunned by how beautiful she was - tall and lithe. I'd never seen anyone so glamorous before. "Well, looks like I have to go. See you around."

"Okay, bye Joey."

"Bye, Genevieve." He grinned and took off running toward his cottage.

We became inseparable. My parents always thought I was out with Joey's sisters, Norah and Kelly, but that wasn't always the case. Joey and I ran on the beach, played hide and seek and talked for hours that summer. As we got older, we spent more and more time alone together. Once, we found this cavern down the beach. . .

I snapped out of my stroll down memory lane when I suddenly hear his voice. I have to be imagining it. There is no way that glorious sound is real. Looking up the beach, I see the silhouette of a tall, fit man. My body recognizes him instantly. What is he doing here? The last I heard, he had a child on the way and was getting married. A little boy comes rushing towards me chasing a ball. I bend over and scoop it up before it can roll past me.

He points to the ball and says, "Hi, my name is James and that's mine." Smiling, I hand him his ball and he runs away. I'm not ready to see Joey yet so I keep walking trying to avoid him. There's no way he knows I'm here. I need more time. I fail miserably as Joey heads right for me.

At first, he looks just as stunned to see me as I am to see him. Neither of us speak but then James says, "Daddy, say hi to the pretty lady who gave me my ball back!" Joey gave a low chuckle and takes the ball from James to clean it off.

"Thank you, James," I reply.

"Genevieve, how are you?" Joey asks. He is the only person I let call me that. Even though I'd been about to marry Daniel and spend the rest of my life with him, I never - not once -let him call me by my full name. That probably should have been my first clue something was wrong.

"You know her, Daddy?" James asks with a curious look on his face. *James is his son?*

"Yes, buddy. I have known Miss Genevieve since we were about your age." he says. "Here, go play while we chat for a minute." He hands James the ball.

"Okay!" James runs off towards the shore. I'm still in shock that Joey is right here in front of me when he pulls me into a bear hug. The scrawny boy with pale blue eyes he had been is gone. Joey had been my first kiss, first love, first . . . everything. His eyes are the same piercing blue color, but he isn't scrawny anymore. College and beyond have been very good to Joey in the body department. Standing in front of me is a man with an athlete's body - strong and lean but sculpted in the right places. His eyes bore into my soul as he lets me go. Immediately, I was cold all over and shivered.

"How are you, Genevieve? What you are doing here? It's the offseason. How have you been doing? What have you been doing?" He pelts me with questions. Before I can answer any of them, he looks embarrassed and adds, "Sorry, that was a lot. Let's start with what you're doing here?"

I simply stare at him. I came here to move on from Joey and yet here he is. I hadn't even considered the possibility he would be here. Deep down I knew I wasn't over him, but I'd been lying to myself for so long that I'd almost convinced myself I was until this very second.

"Joey, you've known me for twenty-two years. I'm not going to lie to you. I never have and I won't start now. Memére and Pepére are gone. I came here to see their cottage again and sort through their personal items. I came here to forget about you. I was supposed to get married three days ago, but standing there at the altar during rehearsal, staring at my future husband, I only saw you." I look down at the sand away from his piercing blue eyes. He reaches out to lift my chin and fire flows from his fingers over my entire body.

"Genevieve," he says, leaning down so his lips are mere inches away from mine. I can't help but close my eyes, willing this to happen, when the sudden shock of cold water on my feet makes me pull back in surprise. Opening my eyes, I look down to see James.

"Daddy, I need to use the bathroom," he says. "I can't hold it much longer."

"Okay, bud. Let's go," Joey says. Shooting me an apologetic grin, he adds, "Genevieve, I want to finish this conversation later. It's long overdue." Scooping up James, he runs off toward his parents' cottage two doors down from mine.

I let out a slow exhale, so thankful that we were interrupted. I don't know if I could handle him touching me again. Confusion clouds my heart, but one thing is certain – I'm not ready to be near him. How is my body reacting to him like this? I haven't been anywhere near him in ten years. I know nothing about Joey anymore other than he has an adorable son.

After staring at them until they disappear into their cottage, I force my feet to move. James is the most adorable little boy I've ever seen. He has his father's coloring and hair but most notably, he has his father's pale blue eyes. I focus on James only to avoid focusing on Joey.

If he had touched me again, I don't think I could have handled it. I have been thinking about his touch since the last time we were together. I remember him and our time together randomly at home. I would like to say it was all his fault that we broke up, but I know deep down, that isn't the case. I completely believed him when he said his parents would not allow him to marry me. Did it hurt to hear him say those words? Absolutely. Did I blame him? At seventeen definitely. Now, not so much. I completely understand why his parents with their country club membership and fancy cars would not want their golden child, their only son, marrying someone like me. Honestly, it wasn't really about me, per se. More about my parents and their issues. But during our last summer together; I knew it wouldn't last and I jumped in anyway. I gave Joey everything and I don't regret it. I regret not chasing after him when he drove away. Every time I think about that moment, I hear that Rascal Flatts song "Cool Thing" in my head.

I find myself sitting in Memére's chair staring at the ocean and thinking about Mrs. Jones's advice. What do I want to do with my life? Well, I have three weeks to figure it out. While Daniel is lounging on a tropical beach in St. Kitts on our honeymoon; I must get myself together.

How do I move forward when being here takes me back down memory lane? Seeing Joey and his carbon-copy son brings up so many more questions than answers. What about James' mom? Did he ever get married? What is *he* doing here?

JOSEPH

"I'm done," James yells from the bathroom.

"Do you need help?" I ask.

"Nope, all set."

"Good, get ready for bed. You have school tomorrow morning."

"Ok, Dad. Three stories, please?" James asks.

"I will be up in a few bud. One story today. You were out playing for a while."

I sit down in my chair. Earlier on the beach, James was wrong, very wrong. The lady isn't pretty. She is more gorgeous than I remember. The girl I last saw over a decade ago was thin and awkward. This woman staring at me with wide green eyes and flowing auburn curls, is stunning with curves in all the right places. I was floored by her back then, even more so now. Sad and withdrawn but stunning. I imagine the loss of her grandparents is difficult for her. I should have made my presence known at the service. I couldn't bring myself to add to her burden then. Now, six weeks later, my son brings her back to me. James is the best thing that has happened to me since I last saw her. It was one of the worst days of my life, walking away from her. I realize that shouldn't happen when you're eighteen, but it did. Not even when Stacia died was I so distraught and I was going to marry her. Well, I was going to marry her because of James. It was the right thing to do. Archaic, maybe. What my parents expected, absolutely. That was four years ago. Since then, I have been trying to find the best routine for James and myself. Now, we're here living in the cottage by the beach for the foreseeable future.

Genevieve and I need to have a talk. Set a few things straight. I don't know anything about her last seven or so years and the same goes for her with me. I need some answers. The most pressing question is whether or not she felt it too. The second I pulled her into my arms earlier, I was transported back a little more than a decade.

"What kind would you like, young man?" Mr. Smyth at Old Tyme Ice Cream had asked me.

"I would like chocolate soft serve on a sugar cone with chocolate sprinkles, dipped in chocolate sauce," I said.

"Coming right up. You are only the second person to ever order that," he said.

"What do you mean?"

"The older Harpin girl orders her ice cream exactly the same way. You would be wise to hold on to her if you can. It isn't every day that two people are ice cream aficionados with the exact same taste."

"I will see what I can do. Thanks, Mr. Smyth. See you next week."

I left the shop with my ice cream and headed back to the cottage. I planned to ask her the next day if she would like to go to Old Tyme next week. In my mind, I saw the two of us sitting on the bench outside the shop eating exactly the same ice cream. Maybe I should have listened to Mr. Smyth after all.

I get up from the kitchen island to go read to James. Once I reach his room, the very same one I used when I was a boy, he is sound asleep with three book choices lying out on his bed. I tuck him in and put the books away. I head back downstairs to set up for the morning. James will need a lunch and at least two snacks. He seems to be coming home starving. It's still early so I decide to sit on the master balcony and read. That was something she and I used to have in common. I wonder, if we still do. I glance to the left and see her porch lights are still on. I decide to go talk with her now rather than waiting until morning. I grab the baby monitor I haven't used in years and switch it on. I'm out of the house before I can think much more about what I was going to say.

I follow the path in front of the house near the street. I keep checking to see if the monitor is still working. What am I thinking? I should go back inside with James. No, he is fine. I tell myself. Before, I know it, I'm standing at the bottom of the stairs to her porch. If memory serves, Memére never used the front door - too much sand in the living room. So, I follow the porch around to the rear of the house towards to shore. I turn the corner and there she is curled up in Memére's chair, hoodie pulled tight around her head. She is probably freezing and doesn't know it yet. I stand there for a solid minute pondering the right thing to do, just leave and come back tomorrow after drop off, wake her and help her into the house, or what?

Here goes nothing. I place the monitor on the railing, grab Genevieve's phone, and put it in my pocket. I reach down and lift Genevieve, walking toward the back door. As I lift her, she puts her arms around my neck, and I hear a small little snore. Now I'm not sure what to do; I'm holding the one that got away in my arms, and she still fits perfectly. She smells amazing. Lavender and vanilla surround me. *Focus!* I tell myself. I gently lower her onto the couch and remove her sandals. I lean down to cover her with Memére's quilt.

But before I walk away, I hear, "You still smell amazing, Joey. Thank you for taking care of me even after all this time. I love you, goodnight." I take a few steps away from the couch and place her phone on the counter. I shut off the lights and head for the door. I look back in and wonder at seeing her by the little light of the moon. Could she really mean that? Do I still have a chance to have her in my life? I have so much to make up for, so much to apologize for. I don't know how long I stand on Memére's porch, but I will be back. I don't want Genevieve to forget about me. I don't want her to move on. I don't know the whole story that brought her here, but I want to remind her of us.

GENEVIEVE

How did I get in here? I don't remember moving. Oh, right. Joey was here last night. Wait, What!?! Joey was *here*. I try to replay it all in my head. I remember wrapping my arms around his neck as he lifted me up. I told him he still smelled good. Did I really tell him that I love him? Oh no! Well, it isn't untrue. I just never planned on saying it again. What do I do now? Kels will know. I get up from the couch and look for my phone. I find it on the counter. Didn't I have it outside with me? Joey. I sigh. Oh boy! I am still in deep and I haven't spent any real time with him in over ten years.

I text Kelsey. It isn't too early.

Me: You up? I'm in big, deep, oh my god.

Kelsey: Yes, what are you babbling about? Too early, not enough coffee.

Me: Don't you need to be at work in, oh, 30 minutes and it takes 15 to get there?

Kelsey: Shit! F$%@ I will call you when I get to the bakery.

Me: Okay.

Since Kels is going to work. I decide to get moving. Kelsey was my college roommate. She is the only other person besides Memére and apparently Mrs. J. who knows anything about my relationship with Joey. Was it even a relationship? I mean we were kids, then we were stupid teens spending every single gorgeous summer night together.

Since college Kelsey and I have been complex neighbors. She lives in the next building over. We have girls' night every Friday.

I run upstairs and take a quick shower. I'm supposed to be on my honeymoon, so I don't have any work scheduled right now. I should probably set up a few things while I'm here. I will take a walk to the village along the shore and grab some coffee. Dressed in yoga pants and a light hoodie, I set off for the village. A few days ago, when I was driving in, I noticed a new coffee shop. I think it caught my eye for two reasons. One, I need coffee to survive and two, it was called Village Perk. Kels and I are *Friends* junkies. We have a marathon at least twice a year. We know those episodes inside and out, but we still love them. She always rooted for Ross and Rachel. I truly wanted Joey to find love. Yes, I absolutely see the irony there.

I decide to walk the whole village first and, then get my coffee. A little backwards from my normal routine but nothing about me being here is normal. The village is a quaint area with gift shops, souvenir shops and even a restaurant that makes saltwater taffy in the window. The flavors range from Maine blueberry to chocolate. They come individually wrapped in a white box. I will have to get some before I go home. Unfortunately, "home" is just another issue that I will need to solve. I don't have my own place anymore; I was set to move in with Daniel and my lease expires tomorrow. I add it to the list of things I will need to conquer. Just not right now.

Some of the shops I remember from my childhood are still here like Old Tyme Ice Cream and the Candy Shoppe. As I continue walking, I see the amusement park straight ahead. Funny, I remember the walk around the village taking longer than this. I suppose everything is a very far walk when you're young. I guess two trips around will do it for now. I realize halfway through my second trip around that I have left my phone at the cottage. Kels is going to kill me. I text her with drama and don't answer when she texts back. I turn the corner just ahead of Village Perk and just my luck, Joey is walking out with a large bag of goodies.

"Hey there! Good morning, sunshine," he says.

"Hi!" I say as I look away.

"Hey, don't look away from me."

"I'm embarrassed about last night," I say.

"Don't be. I was just about to head to your cottage with these delectable goodies anyway. We need to talk. Will you join me on the beach?"

"Sure, I just need a coffee. I'll be right out." I rush into the coffee shop and wait in line. I realize that I'm wearing workout clothes, while Joey is dressed for a casual workday. Khaki pants and a striped polo with the perfect colors to go with his tan. Just another reason that rekindling youthful love isn't going to work. I stare at the coffee shop's exhaustive menu. It has everything from a cappuccino to a triple expresso mocha chai latte. The case has more pastries and baked goodies than should be allowed. My hips should probably skip the goodies, but I think this will be a place to visit regularly while I'm here. Rather than figure out which specialty drink to try, I order a venti Columbian coffee with milk and sugar. While I'm waiting for my coffee to be prepared, I look outside toward Joey. He is watching me from the sidewalk. It isn't in a creepy way, more protective if anything. I give him a small wave and turn back to the barista.

"Here you go! Have a great day," she says.

"Thank you," I reply and walk away. We shall see how this day goes.

"All set?" Joey asks.

"Yes, let's go. I should go back to the cottage and change first. I need to get dressed and put on some makeup"

"Why? You look as amazing as always. It doesn't matter what you are wearing," he says. I blush and we continue walking.

"I have so many questions for you, Genevieve. What are you doing here? Yesterday, you said you were here to forget about me. There has to be more to that story."

"So much has happened since I saw you last. Your choice to walk away that summer hurt more than I ever thought possible." He places his hand on the small of my back to guide me across the street and I forget what I'm talking about. I would like to say; I have no response to him but that would be a lie. He removes his hand once we safely cross the street, I feel instantly cold and wish his hand was still there. What is wrong with me? I shouldn't still feel this way. I was supposed to marry someone else a few days ago. But isn't Joey the reason I didn't get married? That Daniel had never made me feel the same and Joey had barely touched me.

"Hey, Genevieve. You still here?" He inquires.

"Sorry, I just got lost in my thoughts for a second."

"Are you ok?" Joey asks.

We have just arrived at the beach. We are about a half mile down the shore from our cottages.

"No, I'm not. I can't do this right now. I'm not ready to spill all the things that have gone wrong since you left me standing at the cavern and walked away." I look down at the sand. Joey and I sit on one of the benches along the edge of the beach. He stares at his clasped hands.

"I understand if you are not ready to talk but will you at least listen to what I have to say? I owe you an explanation. I'm so sorry for leaving. I'm sorry for how my parents treated you. How I treated you. I was a stupid kid who only saw what I was going to lose if I didn't do what they said. They weren't going to pay for college, they were going to cut me off from my inheritance. The only problem with believing them was, I lost the most important person in my life that day – you." He looks up from his hands and takes mine. Seeing our hands together, I feel like the last ten years haven't happened. Despite knowing I would immediately feel a loss; I pull my hands away.

"I appreciate that, Joey, and I understand that you thought you were doing the right thing. We're from two different worlds, and maybe it should stay that way. Thank you for breakfast but I have to go."

"Genevieve, please don't leave. I have more to tell you. I want to hear about what you have been doing and learn how I can put a smile back on your face."

"You can't," I reply. "So much has happened. I'm here to clean out the cottage and prepare it for sale. Perhaps we should leave the past in the past."

"Don't go. I know I wasn't there for you before, but I would like to be now." As if I can just let him back in. He broke my young heart into a million small pieces. Apparently, they are still not back together, even though I thought they were.

"I don't know if you can or if I want you too. Have a good day." I stand and walk down the beach towards the cottage. I barely make it a few steps before Joey is next to me.

"Please, let me try," he pleads.

"I can't, I just can't." I continue down the beach. Tears threaten as I walk farther away from the one person I have ever truly loved.

JOSEPH

I watch her walk towards her cottage. I want to stop her and try to explain, but she doesn't want to hear what I have to say. I can't blame her. A weird twist of fate has brought her back to this idyllic place and it was a good one. Memére and Pepére aren't here anymore and I know that is awful for her. They were the rock she laid her foundation on. Yes, she has parents, but they didn't really hold her up like her grandparents did. I understand grief, believe me I do. While I wasn't in romantic love with Stacia, I loved her for bringing James into my life. I'm quite certain, Genevieve is still grieving, but is there more to it? There has to be. But what is it?

I wait long enough for her to get ahead of me, so she won't think I'm following her. I mean, we're neighbors and I do need to go the same way. Once I arrive home, I head to my office to work while James is at school. I'm a marketing consultant for the regional soccer team. I travel to the office once a quarter to meet with the players and management with occasional fundraising events. Otherwise James and I live here at the cottage. I hope he learns to love it as much as I always have. I would like to say I will be productive today, but I highly doubt it. That flexibility is certainly one of the perks of being your own boss, but it isn't one you can use often. Luckily, my schedule today happens to be light, only one conference call at eleven thirty.

GENEVIEVE

I barely make it back to the couch where I slept and I'm balling. The true question is why. There are so many possibilities – Mem and Pep, debt from my failed wedding, Joey, the cottage. I don't know if I can handle all of this. I hear a faint beep from my phone. I should check it. I am sure Kels is pissed. I have two missed calls, one from Kelsey and one from Mom and some missed texts from Kelsey. I decide to text Mom instead of calling. She will know I'm upset if she hears my voice.

Me: Hey mom. I was out walking in the village. Is everything okay? Did I forget to handle something?

She replied quickly.

Joanie: No, I was just checking in to see what your plan is for the cottage. We assume that Corinne left it to you although we don't know for sure. Are you going to keep it? Are you going to sell it? Perhaps your father and I could buy it from you to keep it in the family. Especially since you need money now due to that miserable failure of a wedding or lack thereof. I am sure that your grandparents would be rolling over in their graves if they knew that, you of all people would sell their home. We had so many great memories there. Too bad, you didn't appreciate any of them.

At first, I think to respond with something tart, terse, and downright disrespectful, but I decide to let it go without an answer. Her statements simply go to show that she knows nothing about me anymore, and I wonder if she ever did. The cottage is the only place I have ever felt at home, which I think has more to do with Joey and the times I spent with Memére than my parents and siblings. If I have learned anything from my non-wedding, at least I learned to say what I feel and let go of what I cannot change. I call Kelsey back but get her voicemail, so I leave a message.

I'm the queen of procrastinating when I want to. I only brought a few things with me as far as food was concerned but I have all the ingredients for my specialty dessert – cheesecake. I set to preparing it for a late-night binge for one before moving on with this cleaning and figuring out my life.

I guess now is as good a time as any to get started on organizing Memére and Pepére's personal items. At least I will be starting on that list of things to do. They spent a lot more time here in recent years. I grab a few boxes from the office and head upstairs. I decide to tackle the guest bedroom first because it will be easier. I stand in the middle of the room and I can still hear Memére and Pepére, sitting at the kitchen table, talking about the day's events. I open the closet to grab the clothes, but I'm not prepared for the scent that arises from there. Even though this is the guest room, I can smell Memére's perfume as if she were standing next to me. Oh, how I miss her. She would be who I'd want talk to about this. I start combing through the closet. There are items from each aspect of her life from her early days as a hairdresser to when she decided to stay at home after Dad was born. Surprisingly, she was the same size for most of her life and her closet likely rivaled that of any Kardashian. She had evening dresses and matching petticoats as well as suits for church in this closet. Her casual clothes and house dresses were in their bedroom. I went through them one by one, remembering the best times when she wore them. I separated them in piles by style and boxed them up. I will drop them off at the consignment shop and donate the causal pieces to Goodwill tomorrow.

My phone is ringing, I hear it, but I can't find it. I rush downstairs just in time to see it was Kelsey but miss her call. I immediately call her back.

"What's up, Gen? You didn't sound good this morning," she asks.

"He is *here*. He has a son and he hugged me, and I felt like I was on fire . . . oh, Kels," I say.

"Who is there? Wait, Joey is there, and he has a son? Wow! Did you see him? Did you talk to him? Where is the mom? Is he married? I have so many questions, Gen."

I respond by replaying the last eighteen hours or so. I even tell Kelsey that when he carried me inside, I said I still loved him. To which she says in true Kelsey fashion, "Do you? Do you still love him?"

"Yes, I do, and I'm scared out of my mind. I literally just walked away from the altar. It is wrong for me to still feel all this, and he just hugged me. I can't even imagine what a kiss would be like."

"You need to talk to him and lay it out there," she says, "Tell him how you feel."

"What if he doesn't want me, Kels?" I ask.

"Then you will know for sure. I must get back to work. I can come up on Friday for a girls' night if you want. Love ya."

"Thanks, Kels. That'd be great. See you then. Love ya too."

I always feel a bit better after I talk to her. I don't know what to do just yet, but at least I have said something. I continue to wallow in my thoughts while trudging with the boxes to the foyer. The doorbell rings. I'm not ready to see Joey yet; please let it be something else. I open the door to find James standing on the porch soaking wet. When did it start raining?

"Oh James, come in, come in. Are you alright other than having wet clothes?" He simply looks at me with his father's eyes.

I say, "Stay here, I will get you a towel to dry off." He nods slowly and I walk away. I grab a towel from the linen closet and head back to the foyer. The poor little guy hasn't moved, not even an inch.

I hand him the towel, and he starts drying off.

"Thank you, Miss Genevieve," he says, stumbling over my name. It is quite endearing though.

"You're welcome. You can call me Gen, if that is easier. What is going on? Are you lost or hurt?"

"No, I got home from school and the door was locked Dad usually meets me at the door. I don't know anyone else, so I came here."

"Ok, do you know your Dad's phone number, sweetie?"

He rattles off Joey's number. I start to walk towards the kitchen to call Joey and James follows me.

"Why don't you sit at the table. Are you hungry?"

"Yes, I am. Thank you," he says in a low voice unsure if it is okay to be here with me and accept food. I turn to grab some cookies out of the cabinet, and I hear pounding on my door.

"I am guessing that is your Dad," I say.

"You're probably right."

Just as I start towards the front door, I see Joey standing in the pouring rain on my back porch. He must have remembered that Memére never used the front door and ran around the porch. I sigh inwardly. I nod and he comes in. He rushes to James.

"Oh James, are you okay? You scared me."

"Dad, you weren't there, and I didn't know what to do so I came to see if Miss Gen was home. I just got here. Where were you?" he yells, shaking from the wet clothes.

"I'm so sorry I worried you, James. I was in a fender bender after picking up my dry cleaning. I just wrapped up with the police. I tried to get back as fast as I could."

"Is the car okay, Dad?" he asks, unsure if that is the right question.

"It is a bit scratched up, but we can have it fixed. It's just a car."

I stand there watching this unfold in my kitchen as if I belonged there. I start to step away, but Joey stops me. He comes around the table and pulls me into a bear hug. He speaks softly to me as he holds me.

"Thank you so much for taking care of him. I'm so grateful he felt safe enough to come here especially considering he only met you yesterday. I'm glad I told him about you this morning." I try to push away, but he only holds me tighter, as if I was his lifeboat. I gently push back again so I can look him in the eye. I can see his genuine concern for James and his gratitude that I was home. I also see something else. I have seen that look before. It is pure desire with a dash of sorrow due to our unknown status, if I had to guess.

"You're welcome. What did you tell him?" I reply, softly.

"I told him that you are the love of my life and that I messed it up awhile back. I also said I am not ready to give up on us yet." Joey steps back and looks at me, pining for an answer to the unasked question; *Will you take me back?* as James asks for a snack.

"I can get you one at home" Joey says smiling at James. "Let's get going. Thank you again, Genevieve. Have a good night."

"She said her name was Gen, Dad," James states matter-of-factly.

"That is a nickname, bud. I'm the only person who calls her Genevieve and hopefully, one day again, she will let me be that person again."

"Goodnight, Miss Gen. Thank you for your help."

"Goodnight, James. You're welcome anytime," I reply.

I stand dumbfounded in my kitchen for what feels like forever. I don't move until my stomach growls and I realize that I haven't eaten since yesterday. Yes, I went for coffee and breakfast, but I didn't actually eat while

I was chatting with Joey at the beach this morning. If the feel of his arms around me during a chaste hug with his son nearby is any indication, we are still attracted to one another. Would he still want me if he knew everything?

I decide to fix a Pepére special. While mine is not the same, probably because I make it myself, the sentiment is there. The perfect grilled cheese, brown and toasty but not close to overdone, with potato chips and gherkin pickles. It has always made me feel better. When I was younger, I would have had a can of cola but today calls for wine. What kind of wine goes with grilled cheese? Who cares? Wine goes with everything.

The rain has slowed, and I stand on the porch staring towards the ocean. She is pissed off at the moment, rough and choppy. The storm probably isn't over yet. I watch for a bit longer. As the fog rolled in, my view is obscured. I decide to call it a night. I refill my glass, grab my tablet and head to the sunporch to read. I can't bring myself to sleep in their room. I know in my head that; they're gone but my heart is not prepared to take over their room. I hope that they left this cottage to me. My mother is acting as if that would be the wrong decision, not sure why. She didn't even like to be here. We only came because it was free. Otherwise, we wouldn't have been able to afford a vacation much less one that lasted all summer at a beach front cottage.

My tablet is full of things to read, from smutty romance novels that might make some people blush to thrillers and even the classics. Instead of starting a new book, I re-downloaded a classic: *To Kill a Mockingbird*. I loved it the first time I read it in eighth grade and every additional time since. I don't get very far into the book before sleep starts calling my name. It is probably the wine. I set everything aside and go to sleep.

It doesn't take long before I'm dreaming of Joey and the way things were our last amazing summer.

At this point, our parents weren't paying attention to us. We met at the amusement park in the village after Joey's day shift. I had just finished the lunch rush at the Pizza Palace.

"How was your shift?"

"It was fine."

"Good tips, today?" he asked.

"A big group of college girls equals a good tip when Daddy is paying." he chuckles.

"Are you ready?" he asked.

"Yes, let's go."

We started walking towards the cavern we found a few years ago. It was a hollowed-out cavern about eight blocks down the beach from the Cavallaro's cottage past Mem's. It started out as somewhere for us to escape the forced family time in our houses, but it ended up being our spot to be alone. We had many deep conversations there about topics ranging from colleges to death and to what color was the best for a sno-cone. At least we had priorities. It was where we shared our first kiss. I think I was fourteen at the time.

"Genevieve, look at me," he had said. I wasn't sure why I was nervous. We had kissed before on the cheek and shared a peck on the lips.

"Joey, I'm nervous."

"Why? It's just me. I'm your best friend, and I will never hurt you. You know that, right?"

"Yes, I know," I whispered.

I lifted my head to look him in the eye and he was so close that, I smelled the cologne he put on this morning. "I should probably learn what that scent is," I thought. He was inching closer to me. He puts one hand on my cheek and his other held my hand. Before I knew it, his lips were on mine. His lips were soft and warm, and I felt like there was no one else in the world. At first, it was weird kissing Joey because he was my best friend but as time went on it was as if we were always meant to be together as a couple.

He looked at me after a bit and asked me if I was okay. I said yes in a small strained voice. I was more than okay. I just wasn't sure what to do next. Unfortunately, we were interrupted by a passersby and we leapt apart like we were doing something wrong. I hadn't really thought about my first kiss like most girls. I was awkward and somewhat shy when I was at school but here with Joey, I was more outgoing because I was comfortable with him. There were no secrets between us. I told him everything, no reason not to.

When I wake the next morning, the sheets are all tangled, and my tablet is dead. Did I even read anything? Probably not, but a certain gorgeous blue-eyed man was in my dreams again. I get up and immediately prepare myself to get started on the master bedroom. But first, coffee. I head to the kitchen and look at the clock. It's ten in the morning, I guess I needed some rest. Armed with coffee, I grab more boxes and my music and head upstairs. I pause at the threshold and take in my grandparents' room one last time, as they left it. They had been living here full time for about five years now. They would visit us in Rhode Island at least once a month, which you would think explains my absence here. It doesn't. I couldn't come back here, not after the accident.

The room is simply furnished with; a queen size bed and night tables, likely antiques, considering their age. The quilt is a patchwork of each blanket she made over the years, a four-by-four square here and a strip there. There is a rocking chair near the bay window where Memére like me gazed at the ocean. The only thing missing was a private balcony. Maybe I should put one in. Who am I kidding? I owe so much for the wedding. A wedding that was so much more over the top than anything I ever wanted. Daniel had wanted the big fancy wedding. I would have been happy with a justice of the peace on the beach outside with a dozen or so people. I see Daniel's reasoning that I should pay for the wedding, I did cancel it, but he was okay marrying me even if it was just an okay fit. That isn't how I want to start a marriage.

Despite the small size of the house, there are two closets in this room. I tackle Pepére's first. Will it be easy? No. Easier than Mem's, certainly. Pepére was a simple dresser. Casual items for every day, coveralls for work, and two suits for dressy occasions. I box them up and carry a box downstairs. I trudge back upstairs to grab the next box. I hear the mailman go by but head back up to finish the clothes. This is going to be much harder than the guest room. This is their bedroom. I feel like a thief going through their personal items. I shake my head; no, I need to get this done. I put in my earbuds and start working. I think the music helps to ease this process. I'm so caught up that I don't hear Kelsey arrive at the cottage. She taps me on the shoulder and scared me half to death.

"Holy Crap, Kels! What are you doing here?" I ask.

"It's four-thirty on Friday. Girls' Night remember?" she says.

"Wait, it is already four-thirty? Wow! I have been up here for six hours. Grab a box and let's head downstairs."

"It's so good to see you! Did you bring provisions because I haven't shopped yet?"

"Nope, but I brought those in from the front porch. Who is sending you flowers?" she asks.

I look at the gorgeous purple dahlias and calla lilies, and I know immediately, Joey sent them. I'm instantly taken back to when I first said they were my favorite flowers.

We had snuck off around lunch to get away from our families and I had dragged Joey with me. We were walking in the village and we were probably sixteen and the chamber of commerce was holding the annual flower show on the green.

"Do we really have to waste time walking through all these flowers?" He pleaded with me like a grown man, knowing he didn't have a choice. He sighed and resigned himself to the flowers, knowing it would make me happy.

"Yes, we will be quick. I love flowers but we can't afford to have them so each year I walk here, usually with Memére, and take them all in. Today is your lucky day, you get to come with me." I said. He grumbled something under his breath but held my hand as we walked.

We wandered around to display after display. There were roses, tulips, camelias, and lilies of every color. Just as the 'make-it-stop' look appeared on Joey's face, I saw the most gorgeous arrangement of dahlias and calla lilies. I looked at Joey and said,

"These are amazing! Spectacular. I will use these for my wedding someday." He smiled and we walked back to the cavern.

It isn't lost on me that I did not choose those flowers for my bouquet in my wedding with Daniel. That should have been a clue for me months before I called it off.

I must have been lost in thought for a little too long. Kelsey is standing in front of me jumping up and down like a buffoon.

"Who are they from, Gen?"

"They're from Joey. He is the only person who knows those are my favorite flowers," I say. Before she can ask, I continue,

"Why? I don't know."

I carry the flowers to the side table on the sunporch and come back to the kitchen. Luckily the cottage has Wi-Fi now, so we're set with some Netflix episodes of *Friends* if we can't find a sappy movie to watch. I tell Kels there is no food or wine, so we need to go shopping for girls' night.

Off we go to the store to get the necessary provisions. We load up the cart with so much bad food. Not one healthy item in the cart. We include dark-chocolate chocolate-chip ice cream, Reese's Peanut Butter cups for Kels and

Swedish Fish for me, cool ranch tortilla chips and onion dip, Moscato and a sweet red blend as well. We are just about to head to the check out and I feel a tug on my sweatshirt.

"Hi, Miss Gen. How are you today?" James asks.

"James, I'm well. How are you?"

"I'm good too. I'm here to grab snacks for my trip to Grandma's." I'm confused for a moment, since I know, thanks to Mem's updates, that Joey's mom passed away from cancer, but James continues on "She is my mom's mom and I spend a lot of time with her so I know her."

"That's lovely. Where is she, sweetie?" I ask. James nods towards the end of the aisle. I see the smirk on Kelsey's face as I approach the woman. She appears young for her alleged age. If I have to guess, she must have had James' mom, when she was a teenager.

"Hi, Miss?"

"Mrs. Munroe. Gwen Williams Munroe. My little James says you are his neighbor and you helped him out after the fender bender a couple days ago."

"Yes, I own the cottage two houses down the beach. He came to my house when he arrived home before Joey -I mean - Joseph." I reply.

"Miss Gen, can you check on my dad while I am gone? I don't like that he is alone when I visit G-ma but I like visiting," he says.

"Yes, of course, James. I will check on your Dad."

"Thank you," he says, "See you later. I will be back in a few days or so."

"Bye, James." Just as I'm about to turn away, James tugs on my sweatshirt again. I bend down to his level and he launches himself at me. We nearly fell over. He gives me one of the sweetest hugs I have ever received.

"Bye, Miss Gen." He turns, waves, and walks towards Mrs. Munroe.

As she is walking away with James, I hear her say "She is lovely, James."

He replies, "I like her, and I think Dad still does too."

I wonder if James knows something I don't. Maybe the flowers, Ugh! I need to thank him for the flowers. I give Kelsey cash for the provisions and step outside. I think I will start with a text to Joey.

Me: Thank you for the flowers. They are gorgeous. How did you remember?

Joey responds as if he is waiting for my message.

Joseph: I remember everything. Can I see you tonight?

Me: I can't. I'm picking up snacks with Kelsey and we are having a girls night in.   Does tomorrow morning work for you? I promised James I would check in on you while he is gone.

Joseph: When did you see James? He is with Gwen for the weekend.

Me: I just saw him at the market with Gwen. She is beautiful. You will have to tell me more about her. Does eight thirty work at the cavern?

Joseph: Perfect! I will see you then. Have fun with Kelsey.

By the time we get back to the cottage it's already six-thirty pm. Kelsey starts laying our snack spread out on the counter. It is well into the acceptable time to have a drink or two. I pour two full glasses of the red blend. Who am I kidding? I pour half of the bottle into each glass. Kels grabs the chocolate and we get comfy for a *Friends* marathon. We don't need a rhyme or reason to watch the episodes as long as we are laughing. We watch the moving episode with the guys yelling "PIVOT" to move the couch, the episode when Phoebe has her babies, and any episode where Janice laughs just piles on the fun. Kelsey falls asleep at nine-thirty pm. I get up and go sit on the deck.

I notice a small box near Mem's chair. The box is wrapped in golden paper. I have never seen a box like that before around here. The only place to get that box is near home. It is from Helen's Bakery. There is no way Joey knows about it, but here it is. Just like any other bakery, there are so many amazing confections to choose from, yet somehow, he managed to pick my favorite cookie. The box is lined with nine macaroons. At least six of them are tan or dark-brown colored. I would guess those are chocolate flavored. The other three are purple, pale pink, and red. I grab the first chocolate one. It tasted like Nutella. I don't recall ever mentioning my favorite cookie when I was younger. I don't think I even knew what a macaroon was then. I set the box aside and walk inside to get my phone. Kelsey is snuggled up on the couch snoring like there is no tomorrow. I appreciate that she came all the way here even though she was tired. I head back out to the porch and start to text Joey.

Me: Are you awake? Thank you for the macaroons. How did you know?

Joseph: Yes, I am. Mem told me at one point during one of our talks. Can I stop by and see you? I don't want to interrupt girls' night.

Before I can answer, Joey is standing at the foot of the beach steps. I watch him slowly climb the steps like he thinks being here is a bad idea.

"I don't want to intrude on girls' night, but I've wanted to kiss you since I left here after the accident." Joey stands before me and places his hand on the nape of my neck, threading his fingers into my hair and staring me in the eyes. He moves in slowly to make sure I don't object. I don't have time to process what was happening before his lips are on mine and he is kissing me breathless. I reach up to touch his cheek and he pulls away.

"I'm sorry, I don't know what came over me. I have no right to assume that you want me to kiss you," he says.

"There is a lot you don't know, but I . . . well, I am free to kiss whomever I want right now."

"And how would you feel about only kissing me from now on?" he asks.

"Joey, I . . . I came here to forget about you, I left my fiancé at the altar during our wedding rehearsal a week ago. I owe so much money from my non-wedding, my grandparents are gone, and I have to deal with this cottage and the lawyers." I say. I blurted all of that out before I could even think that there is still so much more and he says,

"I will be here for you every step of the way. I have so much to share with you and apologize for myself. After I saw you on the beach and saw how James came to you, I can't let you go again. For right now, can we just sit here like we did when we were young?"

I just start to answer, and Joey moves away from me. He looks for the furniture that should be on the side porch.

"Where is the furniture?"

"I haven't taken it out yet. Mrs. J. brought this out for me when she heard about my non-wedding. She figured I would come here to sort things out."

"I'm very glad she was right," he whispers.

Joey reaches for my hand and leads me down the steps to the beach. Our hands still fit like they were molded together. It is as if my hand is set on fire when he takes it. I feel warm over my whole body. He grabs the blanket off Mem's chair before we head down the steps. He spreads the blanket on the beach and motions for me to sit. I sit down and Joey joined me. We sit in silence staring at the ocean just like so many nights when we were younger. The tension was much different then. I can feel the heat radiating off of him and he isn't even that close to me, except for our hands intertwined on the blanket between us. How could I still want him so much? I was just a young woman when he left for college.

I'm not sure how much time has passed as we sit here before Joey says,

"Can I talk first? There is so much I want you to know."

"Not tonight. Just hold me, please."

"No place, I would rather be." Joey turns to face me and pulls me closer. I can smell the same cologne he wore when we were young and a freshness as well. Probably fabric softener. I sigh at being so close to him again. He kisses my forehead and tucks me under his chin. I feel safe and as if nothing else matters despite the mess my life is in. I don't know how long we are there before I fall asleep. At some point, Joey carries me into my room under the porch.

During the night, I wake a bit startled. How did I get here? Joey. I sigh inwardly. He always took care of me when we were younger. Still wants to apparently. I take stock of what is happening. We are lying on my bed like spoons nestled in a drawer. Joey is behind me, with his arm draped over my side and our legs intertwined. I try not to move, but I want to check the time. I craned my neck a bit to look at the clock. It was five-thirty in the morning. I slowly move my head back and nestle closer to him. I don't know if he is awake, but he pulls me closer. I could wake up like this every day. No, that can't happen. There is no way he could forgive me if he knew everything.

"Stop thinking so hard. It's too early," he says into my hair.

"How did you know?"

"I felt you tense up. Want to talk about it?" he asks.

"Yes, but coffee first, please."

"Noted. Why don't we go to Rick's?"

"Coffee here before we go. Are they really still open?"

He laughs. "Coffee first, noted. Yes, they are still open."

We move to get up, and I see Joey out of the corner of my eye. Is it possible he is more gorgeous half asleep?

"What is going through your head, sweetheart?" He places a kiss on the nape of my neck.

I blush and reply, "I was thinking you look pretty amazing half asleep."

He smiles, "You're as beautiful as ever yourself, first thing in the morning."

"Liar." I say.

"I will never lie to you."

"Okay. Let's get some coffee and head out."

I head upstairs and find Kelsey standing on the porch, coffee in hand. "Morning, Gen. I'm so . . . "She pauses seeing Joey following me up the stairs.

"Morning," I say. "Joseph – Kelsey; Kelsey – Joseph" They shake hands. Joey excuses himself to make coffee in the kitchen.

"I was going to apologize for falling asleep, but I see you were not bored last night," she says in a low voice.

"Nothing happened last night - well almost nothing. I texted him a thanks for the macaroons."

"Wait, macaroons from Helen's. Wow, he does his homework. How on Earth did he know that?" She asks surprised considering she knows everything about Joey and me.

"Apparently, I wasn't the only one having heart-to-hearts with Mem. Also, I was the topic of conversation pretty regularly between them."

"What else did you talk about last night? Did you even sleep?" She peppers me with questions.

"We didn't talk very much. We sat out on the beach and then I fell asleep. He brought me inside and we slept in my room. Just slept. Now, we are headed to breakfast.

"Genevieve, what would you like in your coffee?" Joey interrupts.

"Cream or milk and one sugar, please," I respond.

"Sorry, we are headed to breakfast. Would you like to come check out a local haunt?" I ask her.

"No, thanks. You go. I am going to go for a run. I will be here when you get back."

"Are you sure?" I ask, secretly hoping she won't change her mind.

"Of course," she says. "Is there are park or trail around here for me to run? I'm not a fan of running in sand."

I'm about to answer but Joey joins us on the porch and hands me my coffee. He says, "I didn't mean to eavesdrop but there is a rail trail that starts four blocks to the right of Mem's front door. It goes in a loop and is a total of four miles. There are markers so you can turn back if you want a shorter run."

"Thank you, Joseph," she replies. "I will see you later, Gen. Love you."

"Love you too, Kels." Kels walks away to get dressed. I turn and look at Joey. He is staring at me again.

"What?" I ask.

"Nothing, just studying you. I need to re-learn the curves of your face. Are you ready to go?" I'm stunned into silence and my brain is mush. I don't recall Joey being so romantic. Then again, we were just young teens.

"I need ten minutes. Why don't you go change and I will meet you at your cottage," I suggest?

"Sounds good," he says. He lightly kisses me and heads down the steps. I stand there and watch him head home. I'm lost in the feel of his lips on mine yet again. If he makes me feel this much with a peck, how will making love feel? Are you out of your mind, Genevieve? You can't go there? Can you? I'm apparently lost in thought for a while as Joey is heading back towards me instead of waiting at his cottage and I haven't changed yet.

I rush into the cottage and grab a few things. I head to the bathroom to brush my hair and fix my face. I hear the door open and Joey calls out,

"Genevieve, it's me. I will be in the kitchen."

"Okay, I will be down in a few minutes," I respond. "I just need to change my clothes." I step further into the bathroom and quickly shuck off my yoga pants and tee. I put on a pair of capris and a shirt. I take a quick look in the mirror and turn to head to the kitchen. I slam right into a wall of muscle as I turn into the hallway.

"I'm sorry. Are you okay?" Joey asks as I place a hand on his chest to catch myself.

"Yes. I'm fine. I'm ready, let's go," I say, rushing ahead to avoid the thoughts in my head about what is under that shirt and the trouble it could get me into.

"Let's take my car," I say. I grab my keys and head onto the porch. We get to the car and Joey opens the driver door for me.

"Thank you."

I could get used to being this close to him again. I shake the thought off as fast as it came. There is no way he will forgive me. While I'm lost in thought, Joey has walked around and settled into the passenger seat.

"Do you remember how to get there?" he asks.

"Yes, let's go. I'm starving." I reply and smile at him and he smiles back. It lights up his whole face. I recall that joy and the shine in his eyes. It's amazing to see it again. We drive to Rick's in comfortable silence. I think he is shocked that I remember how to get there, to be honest. When we arrive, Joey jumps out of his door before I even park to open my door for me.

"Thank you," I say as he takes my hand. His hands are soft and as our fingers intertwine, I realize they still fit perfectly. As we approach the stairs,

Joey lets go long enough to motion me to go first. After holding the door, he takes my hand again and the hostess leads us to a table in the corner.

We are immediately approached by our server. We both order more coffee and pick up our menus. I look at the menu even though I don't have to. Although the menu itself is fresh and new; all the meals are the same. When Katie, our server approaches with our coffee, she asks if we want to order.

"Yes, I will have a Rick's slam with bacon and wheat toast, a large orange juice and a water, please." Katie looks over to Joey who is clearly oblivious to the fact that she is staring at him like he is on the menu.

He says, "I will have the same, thank you."

As she walks away, Joey takes my hand again, and he is gently rolling his thumb in circles.

I ask, "How long have you been visiting Mem? I mean how long had you been visiting? Ugh, that's still so hard."

He looks at me as if the answer would hurt me. "I went to see her at least once a week since we moved here." I must look shocked because he reached out for my other hand.

"You live here? When did you move here?" I ask quietly.

JOSEPH

"I will tell you everything you want to know, Genevieve. But first, I want you to know that I'm so sorry for my actions when we were younger. They told me they would cut me off if I ever saw you or spent time with you after our last summer together. I believed I needed their money and connections for my future. I have very little contact with my father since my mom passed away. I thought I needed their money to get ahead in life. That isn't the case."

"Does it help? Absolutely, money makes everything easier. But I didn't realize what I was giving up until it was too late. I should have never left you. Would it have been extremely difficult for the two of us to make it without our parent's support? Definitely. Would it have been worth it? Most definitely."

She starts to say something, but I cut her off. "Please let me keep going, or I won't get it out. It has taken me a long time to muster the courage to come find you again and then my son leads me to you. The only good thing that has happened in the last ten years is James. The last ten years have been filled with less than smart choices and heartache for me. I wasn't strong enough to stand up for you – for us. After I left you, for which I am truly and deeply sorry, I went off to college and earned my degree. I immediately started working for my father as a marketing analyst in his firm. I was making more money than I needed, and I had so many fancy things. I had the fancy car, posh condo and memberships to all the places - the golf club, the country club, etc." I look up and Genevieve is staring me straight in the eye. She has a straight face and she nods. I press on.

"I wasn't happy. I was going from event to event with the flavor of the month my father would arrange. That was part of the deal, find a suitable wife - suitable by their standards not mine and I could keep my job and inheritance. The majority of the women were airheads looking to be a trophy wife and that was certainly not what I wanted."

Katie returns with our food, places it down and silently walks away as if she can tell we are in a deep conversation. I continue barely touching my food. "This went on for about two or three years. Around that time, I met Stacia, James' mother. While Stacia looked the part; blonde hair, blue eyes, and paid for assets - she wasn't an airhead. In fact, she paid her way through Johnson and Wales for restaurant management and development using her assets in a local club. I have no doubt she fooled my father into thinking she was someone that she was not when he set us up." At this point, I'm afraid to look up at Genevieve but decide I need to see how this is affecting her. I lift my eyes from the table to find she is looking at me with genuine concern, for which I am grateful.

She asks, "Do you want to eat before it gets cold? We can keep going with what you need to say after we finish." She always put other people before herself.

I look at her and slowly respond, "Yes." We continue to eat our breakfast. We talk about other things, mostly current events and some football and baseball, as the season is starting for one and ending for the other. I am glad to hear she still loves the same teams as I do. Once we finish eating, we get Katie's attention and ask for our bill. Genevieve reaches for her wallet to pay the bill at the same time I reach for my own.

"This isn't a date, Joey. I need to pay for my breakfast," she says in a matter of fact tone.

"I invited you to breakfast, Genevieve. I will pay whether you consider this a date or not." I reply. "Would you consider dating me again, Genevieve?" Katie approaches and takes my credit card. She returns quickly,

I sign it and we stand to leave. I reach out for Genevieve's hand. I notice a small hesitation, but she takes mine and we head for the door.

"You are ready to ask that, even only knowing the little bit of information you have from the last ten years about me?" she says as we walk up the stairs towards her car.

"Absolutely. There is nothing you could say or do that will change the fact that I love you, Genevieve. I have loved you since I was eight and I still do." As if there is nothing else to say, I pull her close to me, smooth the stray hair away from her face and kiss her as if my life depends on it. I hear a small sigh as she kisses me back. I slowly pull back and we stand there in an embrace deciding what to do or say next. I can see the wheels turning in her head about what I just confessed but decide not to press her on it right now. I hadn't expected to tell her now how I feel, but I did, and now we have to move forward.

Genevieve reaches into her purse and unlocks the doors. She hands me the keys and walks to the passenger side. I take them and hurry around her to open her door. I swear I hear her say, "How could I feel this still?" under her breath as she gets in. I walk around the car with a grin on my face and get in. I drive back towards the cottages smiling to myself, hoping I have a chance to fix my mistakes.

"I should head back to the cottage to catch up with Kelsey. I think she is heading home tonight ahead of her shift tomorrow," Genevieve says.

"She is a great friend to drive here only for one night," I offer.

"Other than the young boy whose cottage was a few houses down when I was on summer vacation as a child, she is my best friend. I know you are not finished telling me everything you want to tell me, and I have to share so much with you but . . ."

"I understand. I need to call and check-in with James. Can I see you later tonight after Kelsey goes home? I would like to finish our talk," I say.

"Yes, I will text you when I know more details."

The drive to the cottages seems shorter than before breakfast despite the heaviness of our conversation and my confession, or partial confession. I park in her driveway and walk her to the door. We stand there just staring at one another.

"I will text you in a little while," she says.

"Sounds good." I lean in and place a tender kiss on her lips and turn to walk away. This walking away business should not be this hard. I have only been near her for at most forty-eight hours since James brought her to me again. I feel like I never left her. I should not want to lock her in the cottage with me and spend the day in bed learning the curves she now has. The few times we were together what seems like ages ago were awkward and nerve wracking.

I didn't know how she takes her coffee until this morning. That is crazy. I didn't even know she drank coffee until this morning. But the feel of her in my arms makes me feel like it is only us; as if the past ten years didn't happen. Maybe it's this place, maybe it's fate but I will not let her walk away from me again.

Suddenly, I'm back at my cottage again. The walk isn't far but I had been so lost in my thoughts that I don't remember doing it. I grab the mail and head inside. I place the mail on my desk in the office and make myself another cup of coffee. It is only nine in the morning. I sit on my deck and think about one of my conversations with Mem about two years ago.

"How is she?" I had asked as if I had the right now that Stacia was gone.

"I don't think that is what you want to know, Joseph. You want to know if she is happy, if she is with someone, if she has moved on with her life." I nodded. "Right now, she just started dating someone from work. I think she said his name is Daniel."

We spent so much time talking about Genevieve. Every week since Mem moved back to the cottage five years ago, we talked about the good times during those summer breaks. I learned everything I could that has changed about Genevieve since I went to college. Mem shared stories about her and Kelsey in college and even some stories about Genevieve and her sister Maggie. Somehow through those chats, I learned her favorite cookie and her penchant for Del's lemonade.

"Go to her, Joseph. Tell her how you feel. Time doesn't make a love like yours fade away. It only makes it stronger." Mem reached her hand to me and handed me Genevieve's address. I took the card and I rose. I gave Memére a hug and went for a walk on the beach. I found myself at the cavern, but I couldn't bring myself to walk in. Genevieve and I spent so much time here when we were young, just hiding out from our parents. I reminisced about our friendship and courtship with different eyes. I would go to her, I decided, and I set off for my cottage.

The sound of a notification on my phone brings me back to the present. I look at my phone and see her name on the screen.

Me: Do you want to have dinner tonight? I can cook something. Say six at the cottage?

Joseph: Sounds good. Can I bring anything?

Me: No, I have everything I need here. Thank you.

Now I may have a chance, and I will not screw it up. She deserves all the information about Stacia before I can be with her again.

GENEVIEVE

I turn towards the door and head inside. Kelsey is eating after her run.

"How was the trail run?" I ask.

"Good," she says. " It was flat and fast. How was breakfast?"

"Oh Kels. A good start, I guess. He told me about how his parents made him leave for college and that they would only pay for it if he stopped seeing me. There must be some history that I don't know about between his family and mine. He started to tell me what happened all those years ago and how he met James' mother. The restaurant was not the right place to continue that conversation so we will finish it at another time. I don't think it truly matters what he has to say. When he kisses me, all of that stuff just melts away. I don't care about his parents, their money, their attitude towards my family, or Stacia."

"What about James?" she asks so quietly I barely hear her.

"What about him? I only met him twice. He seems like a great kid with the same compassion in his eyes as his father," I reply.

"Are you ready to be a mom? I recall you stating you did not want kids with Daniel. Is Joseph different?" Kelsey always gets to the point. It is one of the things I love about her.

"As long as I can remember, the only baby I wanted to carry was one where Joey was the father. I don't even know if Joey wants me, Kels. He doesn't know that my uncle, Leo, was the drunk driver who killed Stacia. Even if I wanted to invite Joey and James to share my life, I don't think he will want me if he knows the truth despite the off the charts chemistry when he barely touches my hand. I never felt any of that with Daniel."

She looks at me "Don't think I don't realize that you didn't answer my question, but I will let it go for now. I'm going to shower and get on the road. I have a date tonight."

"You do? With who? Do I know him?" I ask.

"I don't think so. His name is Michael. This is our second date. Well, first real date. We literally bumped into each other at the coffee shop on Wednesday and we chatted for two hours. We have been texting ever since."

"Ok. Be safe. Text me when you get home."

Kelsey heads to the shower and I get more coffee. When in doubt, bring coffee and you will be my bestie for life. I check the fridge to make sure I have everything I need for dinner. I only know Joey's teenage favorites so I will just have to make my specialty and hope it works. As I finish up my cup, Kelsey is ready to head home.

"Thank you again for coming all this way for just girls' night." I say.

"Anytime, that's what besties are for. I will text you when I get back. I brought your forwarded mail. I left it on the desk."

"Great, I will take a look later. I still need to clean out the office anyway. Could you pick up Charley from the kennel sometime this week? We can arrange for me to get her and bring her here. No reason for her to stay boarded if I'm not on my honeymoon."

"Sure. I will let you know. Gen, if you still love him, tell him. Forget about Daniel and get your first love back. Let him decide about your uncle. Don't decide for him."

"Love you, Kels. Have a great time on your date."

"You too," she adds.

"Not a date, Kels."

"If you say so. Bye, sweetie." Kelsey walks towards her car and backs out of the drive. I wave and she waves back. I hope Michael is a nice guy. She could use some fun in her life.

After Kelsey leaves, I head upstairs to freshen up. I still need to cook so getting dressed up is out of the question. While I can cook and cook well, if I do say so myself, I am very messy in the kitchen. I pull my hair up into a messy bun, pull on a white tank, a grey thread-bare tee and denim shorts. I'm not sure if I'm ready for this. I mean spending time with Joey is amazing. Different than it was before, but he gets me, and most of the time, I don't even have to say anything. He knows when I'm lost in my head and how to pull me back. I hear footsteps on the porch. Did I lose that much time? I thought I had another hour. I check the clock. It is only five fifteen pm.

"Sweetheart, it's me." Joey enters looking around the cottage. "I hope you don't mind I'm early. I wanted to help you prepare dinner or at least keep you company while you do."

Sweetheart. I could get used to him calling me that again. He has been calling me that as long as I can remember. I do another quick check of my appearance. Hair up, fresh clothes and light makeup. What is wrong with me? This is Joey and it isn't a date. We are just catching up, that's all. Who are you kidding? You're still in love with him. I shake myself out of my thoughts to answer Joey.

"No problem. I will be right down. I am happy to have the company and help." I take a deep breath and head downstairs. Get it together, I scold myself. You can do this!

As I walk down the stairs, Joey is standing at the landing with a gorgeous bouquet of calla lilies. Maybe this is a date, I think to myself. No, no, it's not. However, the flowers are in sharp contrast to his clothes. He is dressed comfortably like I am in workout shorts and a tee. The shirt is tight enough to make me want to touch his chest again; I think my earlier impression of his chest was spot on - he clearly has kept up his running over the last decade. His legs are lean and sculpted muscle. I can only imagine what his abs look like. *Focus, Gen, Focus.* He hands me the flowers as I reach him at the bottom of the stairs, and he places his hand on my cheek. Immediately, goose bumps run down that side of my body and I immediately shiver. Although we have history to sort out, I don't think I can walk away when a simple gesture makes me want to drag him to my bedroom. He kisses my forehead and turns towards the kitchen. I stand still for a moment regaining my composure. As if he could read my mind, he turns back and grabs my hand and led me to the kitchen.

"Do you have a vase for those?" he asks.

"Yes, I will get it." I place the flowers on the counter and go in search of the vase. I look in the cabinets down below and have no luck. I go to get the stool and almost crash into Joey. This kitchen is small for two people and being this close to him is turning my head and my heart to a gooey pile of mush. He steps out of the way and I stand on the stool and bring down the vase. He reaches for it and places it on the counter. It shouldn't shock me that when his fingers graze mine, I felt electricity pass between us. If this cottage were mine, I would reconfigure the kitchen to make it larger and maybe add a third-floor master suite. I could never use their room as my own.

"Hey, you there? So, what're we eating? Do we need red wine or white wine?" he asks as if that would break the tension in the room. It just keeps getting steadily warmer when he is around.

"Shrimp Alfredo with garlic bread and I have already made dessert but no peeking." He looks at me with those pale eyes as if to say, I have ways to make you tell me. He is right, I would break and tell him.

"So white wine?"

"Sure, white works."

"Alright, where do we start?" he asks as he is washing his hands. He reaches up into the glass front cabinet for the wine glasses. He starts to open the wine and fill the glasses.

"Ummm, the recipe is in my head so . . . Could you grab a pot and fill it with water to cook the pasta and preheat the oven to 350, please?" I ask.

"Sure," he turns to get the pot from the cabinet beside the stove.

"How did you know that was there?" I ask, wondering how he didn't even think about where it was.

"I already told you I visited Mem at least once a week after they moved here. She was a very wise woman and I enjoyed spending time with her. We talked, mostly about you, played cards and sometimes I would assist her with cooking."

"Mem let you cook with her?" I say. "Wow, that's surprising. She didn't usually share her kitchen with anyone."

"Well, I'm a special guy." He smirks.

"Modest too!" I reply swiftly.

We keep working to cook dinner and fall into an easy, comfortable rhythm. He asks what to do next as I grab the ingredients around the kitchen. There are a few close calls with us nearly colliding. I turn to get the colander which is above the stove while Joey was washing the shrimp in the sink. As I reach up on my tiptoes, Joey comes behind me and reaches over me to get it down. The moment I feel his entire body behind me like when we were sleeping, I need to get some air. I duck under his arm, turn off the boiling pasta and bolt for the porch. I'm taking deep calming breaths facing the water when Joey joins me on the porch. He stands perpendicular to me looking at my profile.

"What just happened, sweetheart?" he asks quietly.

"I have never lied to you. We still haven't finished talking about Stacia, the accident, and Daniel and so many other things. I don't understand it; I was supposed to marry someone else a week ago but . . .. I"

"You what, sweetheart? Tell me. I know there is so much more to say so tell me what is going on in that gorgeous head of yours."

"I feel like I did all those years ago like I can't breathe without you and I want to spend every single waking minute I can with you. And yet, I'm still angry with you for leaving me. None of it makes sense. I should not want you to kiss me again, but I want that and so much more. I should not want you to be here when I wake in the morning. I came here to move on from Daniel whom I couldn't marry because of you and to forget about you and yet here you are making me feel so much. It's amazing and it hurts all at the same time."

"Genevieve," he whispers but I keep going.

"I want to get married and maybe have children but the only person I ever truly wanted any of that with is you."

"Genevieve," he whispers again, but just as I'm about to keep going, he grabs my waist and turns me into his body and crashes his lips to mine. I'm lost in the scent of him surrounding me and the taste of him on my lips. We continue to kiss and explore each other until the smoke detector goes off in the kitchen. Joey rushes away from me to turn everything off. I turn back to the ocean, my solace for a moment. Joey returns to the porch and wraps his arms around me from behind. He gently kisses the nape of my neck immediately making me shiver all over.

"Let's go sit and talk, okay? We can figure all of this out together," he says while pulling me even closer.

I turn to look him in the eye, and he moves his arms to the rail behind me. I feel safe and protected and in turmoil all at once. I reach my hands to his cheeks and kiss him gently on the lips. "Okay." I respond quietly. He takes my hand and leads me to the living room.

JOSEPH

It crushes me that I hurt her that badly. In my defense, I would like to say I was a dumb kid and when I made the choice to leave, I was. However, I had plenty of time to correct my mistake over the past few years and couldn't bring myself to interfere with her life, the timing was just off, way off. I lead Genevieve to the couch, and we sit facing one another. I'm holding her hand while gently making circles on it with my thumb.

"I will apologize to you every day for the rest of my life, if you will let me. Looking back, I felt like I had no choice but to leave you. Over the last five years, I have been spending time with Mem and vicariously getting to know you better through her while working up the courage to ask for forgiveness with her blessing. As you know, I met Stacia through my father. She clearly bamboozled him into thinking she was a gold digging, trophy-wife candidate. She wasn't. She looked the part, but Stacia wanted to work for the things she got. She was putting herself through school when she learned that she was pregnant. She worked as a dancer at the club until she was showing too much to continue. Despite her job, Stacia was faithful to me and I knew she was telling the truth about James. I would like to say that my parents pressured me into proposing to Stacia but I felt it was the right thing to do. I was never in love with her. We both knew it. I believe that is why we never actually got married." I look up from our hands into Genevieve's eyes and see that they are glistening, but I don't acknowledge it yet. I keep going.

"This is the part where our lives become twisted together again. I knew leaving you meant we couldn't see one another again. Fate had other ideas. Stacia took a year off from school after James was born but she was driven to finish her degree. She was determined to do so even with a new baby. We worked out our schedule to make sure that James was with me while Stacia was in class. Stacia was heading home from a study group late on a Friday night. The drive was long, but she was determined to see James. It was raining but not dangerously so." My voice catches in my throat. Tears well up in my eyes. I can do this; I can get through this for Genevieve.

Bringing a hand to my face, Genevieve says in a muffled voice, "I know the rest. My uncle killed Stacia while he was driving drunk; he survived, she didn't. You don't have to relive it again."

I pulled her into my lap and murmured, "Are you sure?" She nods.

"Thank you," I say into her neck. After a few silent moments, I lift my head to look her in the eyes. The tears still threaten to fall.

"Don't cry," I say to her. "There is nothing else to say other than I gave my inheritance to Johnson and Wales for a scholarship in her name and I wish I came to you sooner. Mem urged me to go to you right after Stacia died but with a child, I wasn't ready. I was trying to figure out how to be a single father. Now, a few years later, he brings you to me. Say something, beautiful." I plead.

I turned placing Genevieve down on the couch and slowly climbing over her so I'm looking down at her.

"I love you, Genevieve. Would you go on a date with me?" She stared up at me and laughed.

"Of course, I will, but I think the love part is supposed to happen later."

"Can't go back now," he says leaning down and placing my soft lips on hers. We lay there exploring each other, our hands gliding over each other.

GENEVIEVE

Is this really happening? I literally pinch myself to make sure this is real. Joey looks down at me and places his lips on mine and heat starts to pool between my thighs. His body is reacting to me as well. I reach for his shirt and start to tug it up over his head. Oh lord, his abs are amazing! It's not only a six-pack he even has the muscles on the sides which leads to the V at his hips that drives all women crazy. I run my hands down his chest, taking it all in. I place kisses across his chest and up to his lips. He reaches to take off my shirt. We sit up and he tosses it to the floor. Immediately he reaches for the tank too.

"Fair is fair," he says. "I don't have a shirt on". The tank joins the tee on the floor. I lie back down on the couch feeling slightly self-conscious. Joey must be in my head again.

He says, "You're more gorgeous now with these curves than before." I blush as he looks me in the eyes and asks, "Is all of your lingerie like this?"

"What do you mean like this?"

"Sexy as hell and covered in lace."

"Yes," I reply in a raspy voice. His demeanor intensifies as if he is wondering what else I'm wearing. Joey reaches down towards the waistband of my shorts and dips his hand underneath. He lightly grazes the top of my barely there thong and must feel me tense a bit.

"Are you okay?" he asks.

"No, Yes, but I need to tell you something," I say.

"Anything."

"I haven't been with anyone in a very, very long time."

Joey lifts off me enough to look at me with concern.

"What do you mean?" In a low voice, I respond, "I haven't been with anyone since I was with you."

"Say that again. Did you just say, you haven't been with anyone since you were with me?" he asks as if that is impossible — as if there was a long line of suitors waiting for me.

"Yes, I have only been with you. I got close with Daniel a few times, but he decided we should wait until after the wedding; a wedding that never happened. So . . . "

"Oh Genevieve," he says while sitting up. "Why didn't you tell me before?"

"It isn't exactly something to blurt out in conversation, is it?" I sit up and reach for my shirt, but Joey pulls me back into his lap.

"I'm sorry. I have messed this up, haven't I?"

"No, no you haven't," he says, "We will just take it slow. We haven't even been on a real date yet." His stomach growls and reminds us that we haven't eaten.

"I recall you said dessert was already made. Any chance you are willing to have dessert for dinner?"

"Yes, let's." I pull my tee on over my bra, put the tank on the chair and pad towards the kitchen. Joey joins me, interested in what sugary dessert I have made.

"Have you learned baking skills in the last ten years?" he asks.

"Why, yes. Yes, I have. All the time I spent at home while Kelsey was out on a date, I tried out one of her new recipes. I would say I am a better baker than cook but you can be the judge as time goes on." I pull the cheesecake and the sliced strawberries out of the fridge. I line the top of the cake with the strawberries while he grabs the plates and forks.

"That looks delicious!" Joey says licking his lips. "Oh boy! That will get me into trouble. I continue to stare at his lips, and before I know it, they are on mine faster than I can get my thoughts back to the cake.

After kissing me breathless yet again, Joey pulls back and says, "I saw you staring and figured I could plant one on you."

"Anytime, you want to kiss me, you go right ahead. You will get no objections from me," I reply while trying to steady myself. I can't imagine how having sex with Joey will be if I'm tingling all over from his kisses. I grab the plates and serve the cheesecake. He takes the glasses and spoons and leads me to the porch. I take the blanket off Mem's chair and we head down to the sand. We sit on the blanket and eat our dinner. We chat about Mem and the cottage and how I hope it is mine. We talk about James and Gwen. Joey talks about Gwen with such reverence. Along with Mem, Gwen helped him deal with Stacia's death and learn how to care for James, especially in the early days. Around one in the morning, we leave the beach and go to sleep. We lay in each other's arms as if it were the most natural of things to do.

I haven't slept this well since . . . ever. I slowly get up, trying not to wake Joey. I stand there at the threshold staring at him. I could get used to this. Then everything comes rushing back. You can't stay here in Maine, can you? What about your job? What about a place to live? You don't have anywhere to go at the moment and you only have two weeks to figure it out. Ugh!

I shake my head and move slowly towards the kitchen. A girl needs her coffee. After it finishes brewing, I sit on the porch to enjoy the morning air. I could get used to this every day. Can I work from here? Why not? There is only one monthly meeting I need to be present for. I don't need to be present daily. I will contact Jessie and see if it could work. If she allows that, I can fix two of my problems with one 'yes'. I grab my phone before I lose my nerve and email Jessie with my request. It's Sunday so I don't expect an answer right away. There are some texts from Kelsey.

Kelsey: Hey, girl! I made it home.

Kelsey: Are you there? I'm headed out on my date. I was able to pick up Charley before my date. She is such a cuddle bug.

Kelsey: How was your night? My date was fantastic! We are going out again on Thursday to the game. Text me back when you get up.

Me: Morning, Kels! I am so happy for you. Thank you for getting Charley. I will come get her as soon as I can.

Charley is a great dog. She is a shepherd mix I adopted from a rescue about three years ago when she was seven weeks old. I look at the time. It isn't too early but Kels is probably still sleeping. I set my phone aside and enjoy the peace of the waves crashing and the salty breeze.

I hear Joey talking. When did he get up? I try hard not to eavesdrop, but I hear him say, "Yes, I will see you after dinner, buddy. Have a great day with G-ma. Love you too." Awwww, my heart just melted a bit more.

"Morning, sweetheart," he says, as he leans in to kiss me. I'm at a loss when he pulls away, but he hands me a fresh cup of coffee. This man is smart. He already knows coffee soothes my soul in the morning. Well, anytime of day, actually.

"Morning." I grab his outstretched hand. "Where are we going?" I ask.

"Nowhere." He sits in Mem's chair and guides me into his lap.

"We really should get the rest of the furniture out. We might be more comfortable for our morning coffee."

I look at him and slowly nod.

We. Yes, he said 'we'. Why does that scare me? Scared isn't the right word. Nervous is more accurate. Could this really workout? What about

James? What will he think of this whole relationship, potential stepmom? Wow, me as a mom. I hear Joey talking to me.

"Genevieve . . . sweetheart . . . are you there?"

"Yes, sorry. I was just thinking about us."

"Oh, good or bad?" he asks.

"Both. I have a bunch of concerns that mostly center around James. I have no business asking this so soon, but how many relationships have you been in since Stacia died?"

Joey looks me square in the eye and replies, "You can always ask me anything, no matter how difficult it may be to answer. None. I haven't introduced James to any woman since his mother died until you."

"A lot has happened since the night I arrived here. We just decided to date again last night. What are we going to tell him? What are the rules here?" I continue to ask questions. I can't stop myself sometimes when I am nervous.

"I hadn't really thought about it much. I love that you are concerned for James and his feelings. We will have to take it slowly. No overnight visits for a while, at least when James is home. I think it is fair to say you are my girlfriend, right?" he asks.

"Yes, that is fair to say. Then you can join us for meals and day outings like going to the village amusement park next Friday. It's the last Friday of the season."

"I would love that. Thank you." I look off towards the water. He takes a sip of his coffee. I wonder how he takes it. Isn't that something a girlfriend should know? I will learn eventually. I decide I should just ask now.

"How do you take your coffee?" I look over at him as if it's the holy grail.

He grins and says, "Like you do, cream and one sugar, two if the cup is large or venti." I smile. He lifts me off his lap and heads into the cottage to place his cup in the sink.

"I'm going to head home, go for a run and do a few things." Joey says.

"Ok, I need to get a few things done around here. I have to tackle the office today, but it should only take an hour or so."

"Would you like to come over when you are done?" he asks carefully as if I could or would say no.

"Absolutely. Do you have any good movies?" I inquire.

"I'm sure we can find something to watch," he says as he pulls me into his arms. I immediately have flashbacks of last night and how insane his body is. I could just gawk for hours if he would let me. For now, I will relish his arms holding me close. He kisses the top of my head, slowly releases me, and heads out the door, saying "I will see you later."

"Bye," I reply and set off to clean the office.

I feel a shower will serve me best before getting started on the office. The smell of my favorite lavender and vanilla shampoo always perks me up in the morning. Once dressed in my daily vacation uniform of yoga pants and a tee, I head to the office. The office is modest. There is a desk and a chair as well as a reading corner. If Jessie allows me to telecommute, I will live here, and so the books belong where they are. Pepére's carved box sits on the shelf as well. I don't have the heart to move it just yet. I'm not surprised to find the desk is in meticulous order and doesn't really need any cleaning. I only need to shred the old statements in the closet. Pepére was an efficient and organized man. The boxes in the closet are labelled by year dating back five years and inside each is separated by month. I start shredding with the oldest box first. I have filled three large black bags and decide to take a break. In the kitchen, I grab a water and wash the coffee cups from this morning. I see that I have some messages on my phone.

Kelsey: Hey girl! You're welcome. I like having her around.

Me: You swore off dogs since that fiasco with Brutus.

Kelsey: Yes. I know I swore off dogs but she's great company. I got home around midnight. She didn't bark at Michael, but she was really loud last night around 1 am barking for about fifteen minutes. I don't recall her barking that much at your place.

Me: She doesn't really bark at my place.

Kelsey: Anyway. I hope you have a great day. See you soon. xoxo

Me: See you soon. xoxo

Just a few more boxes to shred. I'm about to start the last box when I see a gold embossed letter on the desk. I reach into the top drawer for Pepére's letter opener. He was the only person I knew who still used one. Just underneath it is another envelope addressed to me in Memére's handwriting. I sigh and slowly open the letter just a bit terrified as to what it might hold. Immediately, I see the date. Just a few weeks before she died. The page is filled with her gorgeous script. They don't teach that anymore; I steel myself and start to read. Unfortunately, it's only a few sentences.

03/28/2019

My dearest Genevieve,

If you are reading this letter, I am no longer with you. I wanted to tell you that I am so proud of you and the young woman you have become. Not once have I ever told you the right choice to make and I hope you appreciate that. To date, that has served you well. Offering advice to guide you and watch you grow was my greatest joy.

I have two confessions to make and a few things to share with you.

The letter stops there. Why didn't she finish it? What could she possibly have to confess? She must have started writing it right after I talked to her about Daniel. I recall that heart-to-heart vividly.

"How did you know Pepére was the one for you?"

"Oh, darling, our love has spanned fifty-nine years. I had two amazing sons and three fantastic grandchildren. I knew the moment we met that he would hold a special place in my heart. What is this about? Are you having doubts about Daniel?" she asked.

"Yes, I am. I said I would marry him, but something is just off. We are supposed to be spending the rest of our lives together, but it feels like this is all about the party. As long as the wedding is costing insane money he doesn't care about the minutiae like the color of the napkins. They just have to be top of the line." I continued to list all of the necessary preparations and Mem in her usual fashion just listened intently.

"Do you love Daniel?" she asked. I paused too long, yet another clue that it wasn't right. Flashes of Joey went through my head.

"Of course, I do," I stammered.

"Do I?" I whispered mostly to myself.

"Can you see yourself with him in twenty or thirty years?" This one hit me in the gut. I had only ever seen myself with Joey.

Despite all the debt, I was smart not to marry him.

I gaze back at the desk and see the gold embossed letter again. It pulls me back into the moment. I reach for it – Stein, Cohen and Hughes, PC with an address in Providence. I open the letter. It reads:

08/20/19

Dear Miss Harpin,

You have been listed as the Executrix and a beneficiary in the Estates of Corinne and Edmund Harpin. Your presence is requested at our office on Wednesday September 3, 2019 at 11 am. This time slot is to discuss your role as Executrix, should you wish to accept it. Please be advised that all named beneficiaries and heirs at law will be present at an appointment at noon the same day for a reading of the will.

Thank you,

Collette Hughes, Esq.

Before I can register what I'm doing, I grab the letters and run over to Joey's. I pause in the driveway to catch my breath. I don't know how long I'm standing in the driveway staring at his Navy BMW before he comes outside. I had seen this car at the cemetery during the funeral.

"Sweetheart, what's wrong?" He is standing so close to me we are almost touching. He places his hand lightly on my arm. I can smell his cologne and it was messing with my brain. I don't answer his question.

"Is this your car?"

"Yes, why?" he replies slightly defensive.

"Were you there?"

"Oh, sweetheart. Of course, I was there. I wouldn't have missed it. As I told you, we have been chatting quite a bit since they came back. I loved them as if they were my own grandparents."

"Why didn't you say something?"

"I saw you with Daniel and didn't want to intrude. That was not the time for me to tell you how I felt or that I was a fool for letting you go. I'm not the steal-your-fiancé type of guy, you know that, don't you?"

I grab his arm tighter to steady myself. Joey scoops me up and carries me onto his screened front porch. I'm still clutching the letters in my hand. Soon thereafter, it starts to pour outside and the most wicked thunderstorm we've had in a while follows. I cry while he holds me without asking why. It is as if the weather knows my feelings. He smooths my hair as I lay my head on his chest. I listen to his heart beating as I calm myself down. I have never felt this way before both the grief and dare, I say, love. How could I have fallen in love with this man already? Again? Was I in love before when I was seventeen, and just didn't know it? After some time passes, Joey asks, "Why don't we go in and find a movie to watch?" I nod and we stand and walk inside.

When we were younger, I never made it past the front porch. Mrs. Cavallaro was very clear that people like me, were not allowed in her home. I had always imagined what it looked like. How the other half lived.

I take in everything around me. The space is open and airy. A gorgeous light fixture hangs in the living room area. The ceilings are high with exposed beams. The floors are pristine hardwood. He must have redone the kitchen because it is amazing with stainless chef's appliances, granite countertops and gorgeous cabinetry in a perfect grey. I took a few more steps to see that the back of the cottage is all French doors leading to the back porch. It is gorgeous.

"Joey, your parent's cottage is amazing. I'm sorry, your father's cottage. I always wondered what it looked like inside." It was not meant as a jab at his family, but I swear I saw him wince at my words.

"I bought it from my Father for James just after Stacia died. I have a life use, but it belongs to James. I hope he loves it here as much as I do. The only things I updated were the kitchen, the French doors and the master bedroom and bath. The rest is the same as it was."

He hands me a glass of Riesling and gestures towards the sectional. We sit there in silence before he asks, "What got you so worked up that you ran over here other than you couldn't stay away any longer?" He smirked. I hadn't realized I hadn't told him about the letter or Mem's draft of a letter.

"I was going through the office and I found this letter in an envelope." I hand Mem's letter to him. He takes it and lifts his brow asking if he can read it. I nod and he reads the letter.

"Oh Genevieve, that's all there was?" he asks.

"Yes, did she not finish it? Was it on purpose? I have no idea what she needs to confess." I inhale deeply.

"We will figure it out." I hand him the other letter from Atty. Hughes. He tells me that he got one as well and that we will make a plan to go together. He also indicates that he has no idea what Mem could have left him.

"What about James? Doesn't he have school?"

"When he gets home later, I will ask Gwen if she is available to take care of him. I think she is off on Wednesdays."

He takes my glass and places it on the leather ottoman. I rest my head on his chest while he looks for a movie.

"Do we have time for a movie before James comes home?" I ask. He informs me that Gwen will bring James back around six in the evening. We curl up on the couch and watch *The Ugly Truth* with Gerard Butler and Katherine Heigl. It has just started on a national network. It's a fun romantic comedy; I have seen at least five times. We are lazily laying on the couch all tangled together. He is behind me with his hand splayed on my stomach. Gerard Butler's accent gets me every time. I think Joey may have heard me swoon a bit.

"Seriously, Gerard Butler?"

"Umm, yes. Absolutely. That accent, oh my. Those muscles don't hurt either. Don't be offended, your body rivals his just fine." Joey kisses the nape of my neck and I get goose bumps all over. I turn my head and he kisses me.

After a bit, we turn our attention back to the movie. The last part I recall seeing is the date with Katherine's bosses and the vibrating underwear.

I feel a nudge on my arm.

"Miss Gen, Miss Gen. Daddy, Daddy. Wake up." It takes me a few seconds to register that Gwen and James had arrived home. How long have we been sleeping?

Gwen calls James over to the kitchen to wash up giving us enough time to gather our composure. Thankfully, we are fully clothed and innocently fell asleep during the movie. I attempt to get up from the couch but James plops himself between us before I can. He asks some questions and shares his entire weekend's activities with us.

"Hi Daddy. Hi Miss Gen." His head swiveling between us as he asks, "What did you do this weekend? What are you doing here, Miss Gen? We went to the park. We saw some strange looking birds at the avi?" he pauses, then looks at Gwen.

"What is it called again, G-ma?"

"Aviary, the birds were at the aviary," Gwen replies from her position in the kitchen. She is watching this all play out.

"After that we went to dinner with Uncle Scott. I went to sleep late last night Daddy. Today, I rode my bike on the trail with G-ma and now we are here."

"That sounds wonderful! I am glad you had a great time with G-ma. Could you go unpack your bag in your room?"

"Sure, be right back." He says as he rushes off.

Joey turns to Gwen. "Thank you for bringing him home. I'm glad you had a good time this weekend." James shouts from his room, "Miss Gen, could you come here, please?"

I look to Joey, he nods and says, "Top of the stairs, first door on the right down the hall." Gwen seems to realize that I haven't been upstairs yet.

I knock on James' door. "Hi James. What can I help you with?"

"I wanted to give this to you. G-ma helped me pick it out at the avi . . . "

"Aviary," I say, assisting him.

"Yes, there. It's for you." I look down and James has handed me an ornament with two doves on it. "It reminds me of your Memére and Pepére."

"You met my Memére and Pepére?" I ask him knowing that he has.

"I visited them with my Daddy sometimes. I miss them."

"Me too, James, very much. Thank you. I will put this on my tree this year."

"I was thinking maybe you could put it on ours here so we can share it," he suggests.

"I will talk to your Dad about that. Let's go back to the kitchen and ask him now." I say.

"I'm not finished, I will be down in a bit."

I turn to head towards the kitchen and I overhear Gwen and Joey talking.

"You're smitten, Joseph." Gwen says as if she's an expert.

"I always have been. I should've never left her all those years ago but on the other hand, if I hadn't, I wouldn't have James." Joey replies. Gwen nods as if she completely understands the complexity of who she is and moving on with Genevieve.

"James hasn't stopped talking about her all weekend."

Joey replies, "That is surprising. He only met her last week."

Gwen continues, "James is a smart and intuitive boy. He knows when his father is happy and when he isn't. Take it from me, don't make the same mistake twice. Hold on to her, you deserve to be happy and James adores her.

I clear my throat, so Joey and Gwen know that I'm coming back towards them. Gwen and I exchange pleasantries. James joins us in the kitchen to escort Gwen out.

"Goodnight, Joey and Gen. It was a pleasure seeing you again." she says while walking to the door with James.

"Goodnight, G-ma. I love you."

"Bye, James. I love you, too."

After Gwen leaves, Joey indicates to James that it is time for bed. James heads to his room and gets ready for bed. "That was a little dicey." I say to Joey.

"Why? We fell asleep watching a movie, sweetheart, nothing nefarious was going on . . . not yet anyway." He smiles at me.

"Are you worried about Gwen? Gwen is an amazing grandmother to James and was helpful right after Stacia died. I'm allowed to date and I'm choosing you. Well, if you will have me, have us. Gwen likes you, she said as much while you were upstairs with James."

"By the way, what did James want to talk to you about? If you aren't sworn to secrecy, of course."

I laugh. "He and Gwen bought this for me at the aviary. He said he missed Memére and Pepére and that the doves reminded him of them. It's an ornament for a Christmas tree. I told James I would be honored to have it on my tree. He asked if he and I could share it and put it on your tree here instead. I told him; I would ask you."

"Dad." James calls from his room. Joey lowers his head. I make my way to my sparkly flip flops to go home.

"Please wait until I come back out. It should only take fifteen minutes or so."

"Okay, I will wait." I head into the kitchen for a glass of water. I sit at the island admiring the gorgeous kitchen. I hadn't known Joey knew so much about remodeling kitchens. I have never been upstairs until today, but I can only imagine what the master suite looks like. If I have my bearings correct, the balcony above the back porch is attached to the master bedroom. The view must be amazing. I start to thumb through the newspaper on the kitchen island while waiting. I soon realize that it has been forty-five minutes since Joey went to say goodnight to James.

I quietly climb the stairs and turn towards James' room and find the two of them snuggled in the bed sound asleep with books strewn everywhere. I stand there looking at their faces. James' looks exactly like Joey's did when he was seven; it's surreal and disarming at the same time. I sigh deeply and wonder if I could fit into the life that Joey has created for his smart, giving and gracious son. I don't have the heart to wake them. I turn back towards the foyer and find some paper. I leave Joey a note to call me in the morning. I quietly slip out the front door and walk to my cottage. I stand on the porch for a few minutes and enjoy the sounds of the ocean. I can hear the soothing waves crashing on the shore. It may be the best sound in the world. Aside from wanting my own space during our summers here, I think that is why I chose the porch as my room.

The next morning, I wake refreshed and ready to take on the day. I hear from Jessie. She has set up a conference call for Thursday. I would have liked to have it sooner but with the lawyer's meeting on Wednesday, I would like to hold off any more bad news until after. What if Jessie says no to my request? I will have to leave here and go . . . go where? I have only one more week until I have to go back to work in Cranston. I will have to talk to Kelsey and see if I can stay with her until I find a new place. While I love her, we aren't good roommates. We got our own space after college for good reason.

I think Mem said it best after one of our chat sessions during college, "You can be best friends but not be able to live together."

Around eight thirty in the morning, Joey asks me to dinner at his place with James. I accept and ask if I can bring anything. He says no. I finish up cleaning the office and drop off clothes to Goodwill and grab a coffee from Village Perk. Keeley, the owner and barista from earlier in the week, remembered my order. She has already started it when I walk in.

"Your usual?" She asks.

"Sure."

"Are you from around here or just vacationing? I have only seen you once." Keeley was as Irish as her name, with gorgeous red curly locks and piercing green eyes. As a young girl, I hated my curls while my sister, Maggie would have killed for them.

"I used to come here to my family cottage on Lighthouse Road every summer when I was a child. This is the first time I have been back in about ten years." I tell her.

"Do you live near Joseph?" she asks. The twinge in my chest makes me pause. Jealousy, really, Gen? You still love him, don't you, the words whip around in my head. Yes, I do but am I ready to forgive, forget, and be with him again? He crushed me. Yes, he has apologized more than once since I arrived, but I'm so raw. Knowing I couldn't marry Daniel was the easy part. Paying for a wedding as well as a honeymoon, I didn't go on is a lot to handle.

"Gen, Gen?" I hear in the recesses of my consciousness.

"Sorry, Yes, I know Joseph."

"He's gorgeous. The whole package: gorgeous blue eyes, muscles on muscles. I would love to get to know him so much *better*." I cringe inwardly at the way she says 'better'. "Do you know if he is single? I didn't see a ring.

He only comes in here once in a while. I considered asking him out when he was here last week, but he bought breakfast for two so . . . maybe he had an overnight guest."

"I have only been here for a little over a week. I don't know the status of his love life. Is my coffee ready?" I say wanting to get out of this conversation as quickly as possible.

She hands me my coffee. I don't want to get into my history with Joseph - Joey with her at this coffee shop. While I don't know for sure he truly wants me, what I do know is my heart and my head are not on the same page. My heart is telling me to jump into the deep end, but my head is screaming, "He has a son! He left you once, he will do it again!"

I slowly walk down the shore with my coffee and sandals in hand. The beach is deserted for the most part. The last big summer weekend is Labor Day then all the summer residents head back to their winter homes for the school year. Both our family and the Cavallaro's always stayed until the very last moment all those years ago. We would miss the first two days of school to soak up the ocean just a bit longer. In my head, I see Joey and I playing on this very beach, building sandcastles, and throwing mud at one another when we were about ten. I can smell the salty air and feel the crunch between my toes. Could we really work out all these years later? The question just hangs there in my mind as I see Joey on his deck on a call waving his hands very animatedly. He doesn't look happy with whatever the caller is saying. I don't think he sees me, so I turn left up the path towards the street. I barely reach the street side of the path when Joey bursts out his front door.

"Good morning. Why did you take the path to the street?" he says out of breath. He looks rumpled, like he just rolled out of bed but that is impossible because James has school today.

"Hi. You didn't look very happy on your call and I didn't want to bother you."

"You wouldn't bother me," he mumbled. "I'm so sorry, I fell asleep with James last night."

"Don't be. I'm sure he missed you while he was with Gwen. Are you sure you don't need me to bring anything later?" I ask again because, if anything, I'm a gracious dinner guest.

"No, I'm - Ugh!" He looks at the caller ID on his phone. He quickly kisses my cheek and says, "I have to take this, it's a work call. I will see you later, love you."

He answers the phone and slips back into his home. I stand there stunned, not because he took the call but because he said he loved me. I head back to the cottage. I set up a few calls for when I return to work. I need an illustrator for one of the children's books I'm editing. I have a classmate from grammar school who writes and illustrates comic books. Maybe he would be interested in branching out into children's books. I send him a message on Facebook and head to the deck for a bit. It isn't particularly sunny today; mostly cloudy in fact so I am glad I grabbed my worn and comfy hoodie. After a while, I check the time, freshen up and head to Joey's for dinner. When I arrive, I approach the French doors and Joey waves me in. James is doing homework on the island and Joey is cooking.

"Hi, Miss Gen. How are you?" James asks. He hops off the stool to hug me.

I bend to hug him and reply, "I'm well. How was school? What are you working on?"

"School was okay. I'm working on my Math homework. It is pretty easy for me and I could do it on the way to school in the morning, but Dad says it needs to be done right away when I get home. No, procrast . . . what's the word again, Dad?"

"Procrastinating." Joey says, grinning.

Joey comes around the island and hugs me as well. "Hi. How was the rest of your afternoon?" Then he whispers in my ear, "You smell amazing." Just as I am relishing his arms around me and the compliment, he releases me.

James says, "You were here already today, Miss Gen.?" Smart boy, listening to each word carefully.

"No, I was walking on the beach, your dad was taking a call on the deck and we talked for a bit. Is that okay?" I ask carefully. While deep down, I hope that James is okay with me being around and spending time here, I am scared to find out how he really feels.

"More than okay. I think Dad could use the company while I'm at school even though he's working." I blush and Joey winks at me.

James finishes his homework and leaves to wash up for dinner. Joey has a clear system for James, and it seems to work. I moved closer to Joey and he pulls me in for another embrace. I look up at him and he gently kisses me on the lips. I feel like the whole world disappears when he touches me and wonder if it's the same for him. I sometimes forget where I am. Even though I relish his kiss, I'm at a loss because we haven't really set any boundaries other than no overnight visits. We should probably talk more about that later tonight. Joey makes Pesto chicken with asparagus and garlic potatoes. The three of us ate and talked about normal things including Joey and James' annual final Friday trip to the village amusement park. James asks me to join them and I tell him I will check to see if I'm free. We clear the table and fall into an easy flow of cleaning the pots, pans and dishes. I wash, Joey dries, and James puts the dishes away. It feels perfect like I belong here not in this house, but with Joey and James.

James and Joey head off for bedtime. I sit at the island. Joey is reading James a book. I am pretty sure; James can read on his own. I hear them talking but can't make out the words.

JOSEPH

"Dad, can I ask you something?" James says in a low voice almost hard to hear.

"Of course."

"Is Miss Gen your girlfriend?"

"I would like her to be my girlfriend. I have known her for a very long time since I was about eight years old. The day we met her on the beach was her first day back here in about ten years or so. As you already know, Memére and Pepére were her grandparents. Miss Gen and I were very close before I left her . . .here for college." James listens intently nodding his head. I press on, "Miss Gen came here for some time away from home. She lives in Rhode Island."

While I ponder what to add next, James asks, "Do you love her like you loved my mom?" I sigh and pause to carefully answer this delicate question. I have never discussed the true nature of my relationship with Stacia with my son.

"James, I loved your mom very much for bringing you into my life but my love for Miss Gen is different. I believe there is one person who is our perfect match. For me, not only is Miss Gen my best friend, she is also my perfect match." I take a beat and hope that is enough of an explanation for tonight.

"I like her, Dad. She is very pretty and nice to me. I was very scared when you were not home, and she took care of me."

"Yes, she is very pretty. I agree with you. I know and I'm so sorry, I didn't make it back in time." I looked at James.

"I don't want her to leave us. Will she leave us?"

I have had this conversation about my future mate in my head a few times with James, but it never went like this.

"I don't know how to answer that, buddy. Miss Gen is here on vacation. I'm sure she will go home at some point, but she will not leave us like your mom did. I hope that helps." Hoping once again that this tough chat was ending.

"It does help. Goodnight, Dad. I love you." He snuggles into his bed more. "I love you, James."

I head back out into the living room and find her watching *London has Fallen*.

"Really, another Gerard Butler movie?" I ask. She smiles and it lights up the whole room. I sit next to her on the couch and hold her.

"It was on, and what can I say? - the accent gets me every single time." During the commercials, we discuss our plans for Wednesday. Gwen has agreed to stay here with James until we get back. The guest room is made up for her to stay whenever she needs too. Genevieve leaves around eleven. I try to read a bit but fail miserably, and I head to bed wishing I had her next to me, even if we were just sleeping. I miss her in our home already.

The next evening goes pretty much the same but we prepare James that Gwen will be here after school to meet him on Wednesday. I tell him I have an important meeting to attend and will be home late probably after he goes to sleep. Genevieve casually mentions she has to pick up Charley at Kelsey's as well.

"Is Charley your pet?" James asks.

Genevieve nods.

"Charley is a dog."

"You have a dog? You have a dog!" James exclaims and leaps up to hug her. "I have always wanted a dog, and Dad keeps saying no. Can I borrow yours sometime?" Before answering, Genevieve looks at me over James' head and I simply smile at her.

"I'm sure we can work out some dog visits for you." He squeezes her tighter and heads off to bed.

"You probably just made his year with that promise!" I grin.

"I plan to keep it," she replies and smiles back. Her smile just makes the room brighter. Now, I need to figure out how to get her to stay. I know it's absolutely unrealistic. She has a job, an apartment, and a life away from here. She is here on vacation more or less but I can't imagine her not being here with us.

First thing the next morning, Genevieve rings the bell ready to head to Providence. I reach for the knob as she is stepping inside the foyer. She looks amazing in a navy sheath dress with a matching jacket over her arm. Her heels are sexy as hell and it will take some work not imagining what's under that dress all day. After all, she did say that her lingerie were all sexy. Her signature scent of lavender, vanilla and something I still can't put my finger on surrounds me as she stands next to me. She gently kisses my lips as she steps inside. Despite my desire, she looks sad about this meeting.

"You look gorgeous. Are you ready for this?" I ask, knowing full well she is not prepared for this. I think she will be fine during the meeting but will fall apart afterwards.

"Thank you. You clean up well yourself." I 'm wearing charcoal suit pants with a crisp pale blue shirt and matching tie.

"I won't lie to you. No, I'm not ready at all, but I need to handle the estate and move forward," she says, looking towards the floor.

I reach for her chin and lift it so that she is looking at me, "I happen to know something about grief. There is no set straight line for handling it. I know there are days where you feel like you have a handle on it and other days it grabs your heart like a vise. Some days start out fine and turn on a dime with a random memory or image you see in the street. I'm here for you, to listen or hold you, anytime you need me."

"Thank you. How long does it take?"

I think carefully about my response. "I don't miss Stacia as my fiancée, but I see families sometimes and wonder what she would be like with James and how James would be if he had her influence the last four years. Honestly, I believe, grief stays with you always but the space it takes up in each day decreases as time goes on though you never forget the love from that person. I also think it changes a bit over time more to remembrance than heart-aching hurt."

Genevieve steps closer to me and wraps her arms around me. After what feels like an eternity, she looks up, goes onto her toes and kisses me. Even with those sexy heels, she is six inches shorter than me. While I would like to scoop her up and take her upstairs; we have an appointment to get to. Also, I promised I would take it slow, but that promise is getting more difficult to keep as the days go by.

I walk to the kitchen island to grab my jacket and keys and we head to the car. I put my arm out and she takes it. I walk around with her towards the passenger side and open her door. I tuck her safely into the seat and gently close the door. I glance at my watch, a gift from James for Father's Day just before Stacia died, and hop in and we are off to Stein, Cohen and Hughes, PC.

We both start talking at the same time and she indicates that I should go first. I replay my conversation with James last night to her. She listens intently. There are a few times when she looks out the window but says nothing. Once I finish, I ask her, "What is going on in that gorgeous head of yours, sweetheart?"

"Thank you for being honest with me and James. I still love you, but I don't live here. I have to go back to work in about ten days or so. I did contact Jessie, my boss, to see if I could work from home. At the moment, I'm homeless. I don't know what I was thinking. I knew something was off, but I didn't renew my lease because I was moving into Daniel's. Damn him." I don't say a word. Instead, I reach over and take Genevieve's left hand and gently rub circles on it.

She continues, "Jessie didn't respond about the work from home, but scheduled a call for tomorrow. I have no idea what she is going to say. Hopefully, I can crash with Kelsey until a unit opens in our complex. I love Kelsey but we are not meant to live together. We are completely opposite; I'm neat, she is a slob. She waits until she runs out of clean clothes and I wash each week.

"Can we make this work if I live a few hours away?" Genevieve asks not expecting me to answer. It's rhetorical.

"We will absolutely make it work. I work from home except for once a month."

"What about James? He has school. I don't want to impact him adversely."

Even though I'm driving, I look at her and say, "If we want to make this work, we will."

"I'm sure Jessie will say yes to your proposal and then you can work here sometimes, and I can visit you on weekends with James." I keep listing reasons we can pull it off and finally she laughs and shakes her head.

"Okay, I give. We will make it work." I feel her tense up when she sees the sign for Downtown Providence. I simply continue rubbing circles on her hand as if it will help.

"It is going to be fine, sweetheart. We will tackle this together." I exit the highway and head into downtown. The offices of Stein, Cohen and Hughes, PC are located near the Providence Place Mall. Maybe we can get a great meal before getting Charley.

The offices are what you would expect. Dark mahogany paneling, leather couches and fake foliage line the lobby. A bubbly brunette in a business suit sits at reception answering a bunch of phone lines at once through a headset. She glances up as we approach her, raising a finger for us to hold on. She answers one more call and then asks our names. We tell her and she asks us to take a seat. I point for Genevieve towards the couches and we sit. Although I have never seen this behavior before, Genevieve is nervously tapping her toe on the carpeted floor. I reach over and take her hands angling her towards me so I can look into her beautiful green eyes.

"Breathe," I say. She nods, closes her eyes, and takes a few deep breaths. She opens them only to find our respite is short lived as we're called into Atty. Hughes's office.

GENEVIEVE

Atty. Hughes emerges from the hallway, hand outstretched in our direction. She is wearing a suit which is perfectly tailored for her and this office, except for the color. It is pink; bright pink. She has strappy heels with bows at the toe to match. She reminds me of Reese Witherspoon as Elle Woods in the *Legally Blonde* movies.

"Good morning, Miss Harpin and Mr. Cavallaro. Thank you for coming all this way. Miss Harpin, I'm very sorry for your loss. Corinne and Edmund were wonderful people. I will miss them as well."

I speak quietly, "Thank you, Atty. Hughes. How long have you known them?"

"Colette, please call me Colette. Your grandparents were my clients for about fifteen years. I saw them last in late March when they updated their wills. Please have a seat."

I feel Joey guiding me into her office. Joey and I sit in the two chairs across from her desk. Her office is the standard office of a named partner - large space with a great view of the city, sitting area with a chaise and a bookcase. Her desk is neat and tidy. I note two small frames with photos of children but no husband. I glance at her ring finger. There is a tan line but no wedding ring. Atty. Hughes sits and offers us a beverage.

In unison, we replied, "No, thank you." I took a moment to glance at Joey who looked steady and calm. I'm not sure if his façade matches his emotional state. Mine certainly doesn't. I'm doing my damnedest to keep it all together right now. Little did I know what Atty. Hughes would drop on us in the next two hours.

"Miss Harpin."

"Gen, please," I suggest as a way to soothe my psyche.

"Gen, as stated in my letter, your grandparents both nominated you as the Executrix of their wills. I have to ask if you would like Mr. Cavallaro to be present for this meeting or if I should escort him out. Please understand that is not meant as a slight but to protect the confidentiality of Corinne and Edmund."

"No, I would like him to stay, if he is willing to do so." I state looking over at Joey who looks sad and stoic. I wonder if this brings up memories from Stacia's death for him. Atty. Hughes looks to Joseph who nods in an attempt to keep things moving.

"Could you give us a minute, please?" I ask.

"Of course." She excuses herself from her office and tell us to open the door when we are ready for her to return.

"Are you okay?" I ask. "If you want to go because this brings up feelings about Stacia; I can do this myself."

"I'm fine. I wasn't allowed to be part of any of this for Stacia because we weren't married. Gwen handled all of it. I didn't realize what Gwen went through or I would have pushed harder to be included. I would like to stay. I want to be here for you."

I place my hand on his cheek and place an emotion-laced kiss on his lips. It takes a moment after pulling back for us to gather ourselves and stand to open the door.

Atty. Hughes returns shortly thereafter and continues, "As I stated, you were nominated Executrix for both estates. If you are willing to accept the position, I will get the filings started for you right away. If you are willing, I will assist you in the administration of the estate based on your grandparents wishes. Their wills are mirror images, so the order of their deaths does not impact the bequests. You and Mr. Cavallaro are the main beneficiaries after a few smaller bequests of cash and a few furniture items. The only difference between the wills are letters left by Corinne – one to each of you." She places a copy of the wills and two envelopes graced with Memére's elegant script on her desk.

"I will give you some time. We have about thirty minutes until the rest of your family arrives. They were notified because they are heirs at law. Please let me or Kimberly know if you need anything in the meantime." She politely excuses herself.

I looked over at Joey and took a deep breath. "Where should we start?" he says in a strained voice.

"I'm shocked and I haven't read anything yet. They left us everything?! Why?"

"Me too," he chokes out.

"I think I want to start with the letter. You?"

"Makes sense," he says as he reaches for the envelopes. He hands mine to me. I glide my fingertips over my name on the exterior. Oh, how I miss her. She was my rock. As if being in the cottage without her wasn't clear enough, seeing her handwriting makes my stomach drop to my toes. I slowly flip the envelope over and open the flap. I'm straining to keep the tears from falling and I don't even know what the letter holds. I start to read her final words to me while Joey reads his.

03/28/2019

My dearest Genevieve,

If you are reading this letter, I am no longer with you. I wanted to tell you, I am so proud of you and the woman you have become. Not once have I ever told you the right choice to make and I hope you appreciate that. To date, it has served you well. Offering advice to guide you, being your sounding board and watching you flourish has been my greatest joy.

I have two confessions to make and a few things to share with you. I'm going to die. I was diagnosed with cancer about a year ago. I decided not to share my illness with anyone nor seek treatment. I considered sharing it only with you, but I did not wish to burden you with my secret. Please forgive me.

I had hoped I would not be the bearer of this next piece of information however, your mother has forced my hand. About two years ago, Pepére and I decided to have DNA tests done for our family tree to learn the exact lineage of our family from Canada. The testing came back with some shocking results. We learned our son; Robert is not your biological father. Your Uncle Leonard is your biological father. I have not shared this information with anyone other than Pepére. It is unclear whether your mother has shared this information with Robert or not. I will leave you to handle this information as you wish. After you process your anger towards your mother, please know Peter and Margaret are still your family regardless of their parentage. I suspect Joseph may have a hard time with this information and I regret not telling both of you sooner. Please don't run from him and be patient while he handles this information as well.

Now, I will stray from my normal advice giving only stance. I hope you did not marry Daniel. I almost indicated this when you came to me questioning your decision last month. I have never once seen you look at him the way you looked at Joseph, despite your young age then. I realize you do not see the larger picture yet, but you will. Joseph, James, and I have been meeting regularly since Pepére and I moved back here. There is so much you need to know. Joseph will tell you in his own time. Please hear him out. May you and Joseph find your way back to one another. He is your greatest love, Genevieve.

Je t'aime plus que tu ne le sauras jamais,

Memére

I read the letter through once and hoped I misread it. How could it be? How could she do that to my father, to Robert? A host of disgusting names float through my head regarding my mother. While she is not my biggest ally; I don't hate her. She was an okay mom; she did the bare minimum. Robert, on the other hand, went above and beyond. Did he know about this? I hear my name as tears start flowing down my cheeks.

"Genevieve, look at me." I slowly lift my head from the tear stained pages and realize that Joey is crying as well. I have never seen him cry until now and I can only imagine what his letter says.

JOSEPH

I thought I should wait until Genevieve finished reading her letter first but decided to read mine at the same time. I wasn't expecting the information this letter holds.

03/28/2019

My dearest Joseph,

If you are reading this letter, I'm no longer with you. I was diagnosed with cancer about a year ago. I decided not to share my illness with anyone, and I have opted against chemotherapy. Please forgive me.

I wanted to tell you I am so proud of you and the father you have become. In the past few years, you and James have gained a special place in my heart. I cherish the time both you and James spent with me. Thank you for sharing him with Edmund and me. Edmund and I would like you to have a few personal items. We left a letter with a key and instructions in the office of the cottage in Edmund's carved box. Genevieve knows which box I'm referring too.

About two years ago, Edmund and I decided to have DNA tests done for our family tree to learn the exact lineage of our family from Canada. The testing came back with some shocking results. We learned that our son, Robert is <u>not</u> Genevieve's biological father. Our son, Leonard, is her biological father. Genevieve is learning this information at the same time you are. I understand this is a difficult fact to learn and may cause some grief to resurface regarding Stacia. I have considered sharing this with you over the last year but could not find the courage to crush the progress you were making with James. After you process your renewed grief, please know Genevieve will try to run from you. Don't let her go again.

There is so much you need to tell Genevieve on your own. You must tell her the truth about your parents, Stacia and James. May you and Genevieve find your way back to one another. She has held your heart since you were eight years old and you have held hers. If she is not already there, she will come to the cottage for solace, and she will try to shut you out. Stand firm in your love for her and do not let her go again.

Je t'aime,

Memére

"Genevieve, look at me," I beg. She shifts to face me. I pull her up to her feet and wrap my arms around her to hold her tightly. So tight, that I'm sure she can hear my heart beating fast in my chest. Despite the news, I have just read, I am comforted in this moment. She didn't run; at least not yet.

"Do you want to talk about it? I understand if you need more time to process all of this but please don't do it alone," I plead with her. "Please don't shut me out. We're a team and we will always be a team."

She nods against my chest slowly stepping away from me but keeps her arms around me. "I won't run but I'm not ready to talk about this yet, but I will have to in about ten minutes when everyone else arrives."

"No, you won't. Let's have Atty. Hughes come back in and ask her some information about the next meeting with your family." I suggest as if I'm calm, cool and collected. I grab her hands and gently kiss them and walk towards the door. Kimberly acknowledges me indicating she will get Atty. Hughes. I return, move my chair closer to Genevieve and reach for her again.

"Talk to me, sweetheart. I gather the letters aren't exactly the same, but I would think that the information about Leonard is." She simply nods but doesn't utter a word. Her tears have slowed. I don't know what kind of tears they are though. Is she mad, sad, shocked, all of the above? For me, the information about Leonard doesn't change the fact that Stacia is gone and it shouldn't for her, at least in my mind.

Atty. Hughes rejoins us in her office. I inquire about the next meeting. I ask if the same information will be relayed to Robert, Joanie, Maggie and Peter. She indicates Corinne and Edmund requested Robert and Joanie be presented with the DNA results; who they share the information with is up to them. She also states that we do not have to be present for that portion. However, Genevieve must be present as the Executrix for the reading at Memére and Pepére's request. Atty. Hughes stands and indicates Robert and Joanie are here. She goes to speak with them. I thank her and she leaves. Shortly thereafter, Maggie and Peter will arrive for the reading. Joey thanks her and she leaves.

We sit in her office in silence. I assume the attorney is meeting with Robert and Joanie at this point. I wonder what Robert knows. Does he even have a clue that Joanie cheated on him with his own brother? The silence is broken by Joanie wailing at Atty. Hughes at the revelation about Leonard and Genevieve. Joanie goes on a tirade about Memére and how she could bring all this up now; ruining her life from the grave.

"How dare she get a DNA test?" she screams. I hear Robert ask her to calm down and be respectful, but Joanie storms out of the conference room. I feel Genevieve start to tremble as she realizes that her mother is headed her way.

Genevieve stands and sees her mother through the glass partition, but Joanie continues past the office without saying a word to her. Due to Joanie's reaction, Atty. Hughes escorts Peter and Maggie into her office with myself and Genevieve to give Robert some time alone in the conference room. We exchange hugs and pleasantries and wait until it is time for the reading. After some time passes, Atty. Hughes escorts the four of us into a large conference room. The table has six identical folders placed around it except for one specifically labeled for Genevieve. Robert is standing near the sideboard preparing a cup of coffee. He raises his head and acknowledges his children and me as we enter. He looks as if he has been hit by a truck. Joanie hasn't returned yet from wherever she stormed off to.

Atty. Hughes motions for us to take a seat. We sit there in silence waiting for Joanie to return. I'm not sure how much time has passed, but Kimberly escorted her to the conference room. She took a seat at the far end of the table.

GENEVIEVE

I sit next to Atty. Hughes, with Joey right next to me as close as the chairs will allow. I don't think he realizes the comfort I am taking from him in this moment. Despite our history, I feel like we were never apart. He can read when I need him, he backs off when he should and presses when he should. I can't imagine going back to work and leaving him and James. While we are waiting for my mother to return; I thumb through the folder before me. I started reading the details of the estate and am a bit shocked by a few things. Atty. Hughes is about halfway through the reading when she was callously interrupted by my mother.

"Not only did she leave me out of her will, her sole surviving son got nothing! You get it all!" she says glaring at me. Peter and Maggie have not been clued in yet, so they don't understand her anger.

"How dare she do such a thing! It was not her place to get those tests done. I buried this secret long ago and never planned on sharing it with anyone. Damn her!"

I see Collette reach to the phone and push a yellow button. While my mother's rant continues, two imposing men enter the room. I wouldn't say they're security guards but more likely two male lawyers who happen to be the size of NFL linebackers that Colette had on standby after Joanie stormed out earlier.

I did my best to keep it together, leaning into Joey for strength. He simply looks at me with compassion in his eyes and holds me up. I do not plan on engaging my mother in this setting regarding the bombshell Memére dropped or the additional nuggets she just dropped herself. She had known Robert wasn't my father since the beginning. She knew Leonard killed Stacia. So many times, so many opportunities to come clean. Robert has been largely silent during this meeting. He clearly didn't know about Leonard and is handling the news in his own way. My plan to remain silent is crushed when my mother demanded I sell the cottage to her because I'm not good at handling money and I have so much debt to pay from the wedding. Thankfully, Colette jumps in to continue reading the provision.

"Mrs. Harpin, if you will take a seat, I can answer that question on behalf of Gen."

She stalks back to her seat and glares at me, "Buddy buddy with the lawyer, huh, Gen? How did you pull that off? Were you in on this too?! Of course, you were."

Colette looks over at me and I nod, knowing she will tactfully diffuse the attacks my mother just levied and tell her that I don't own the cottage alone. My mother takes her seat and Colette continues.

"Mrs. Harpin, I only met Gen today for the first time. The clauses in the Last Will and Testament of your in-laws were their choices and theirs alone. Regarding the cottage on Lighthouse Road, it has been bequeathed to Miss Genevieve Harpin a 75% interest and Mr. Joseph Cavallaro a 25% interest. Gen will not be able to sell the cottage without consent from Mr. Cavallaro. However, there is one additional request which specifically pertains to you. Both Corinne and Edmund expressly requested that the cottage never be sold to you. Additionally, they both requested Robert be allowed a life use of the cottage at the convenience of Miss Harpin and Mr. Cavallaro."

For a moment, my mother sits stunned in her chair. She rises from her chair, looks Robert in the eye and says, "You knew about this didn't you. You knew they were going to cut us off."

Robert stands and looks at her squarely in the eye, then turns to me and says,

"I love you, Genevieve. I didn't know your mother cheated on me with Leonard. In my heart, you're my daughter. I would like to meet with you at a later time to talk more but right now, I need to go." I nod to him, stand and hug him as he circles the table. As he approaches the door, he turns back, looks at my mother says,

"I want a divorce," and promptly leaves the room. A hush goes over the table as Maggie and Peter glanced at once another as well. They have just learned the family secret. They ask to leave as well. Both come around the table, hug me and Joey, and say they will call at a later time to talk this out. Collette excuses them only after she indicates what they are to receive from the estate and informs them I will be in touch to coordinate their bequests.

That leaves, Collette, Joey, my mother, the NFL linebackers and myself in the conference room. Joanie is fuming at the other side of the oval table. She addresses Collette first.

"I get nothing. I stood by Robert and raised his children and I get nothing! What about her jewelry? What about the car?" Collette stands and indicated as calmly as possible that she was not an heir at law and is not entitled to receive anything simply because she was married to Robert.

Next, she turns to me. I stand to meet her. Thankfully Joey is still seated between us. She starts to walk towards me.

"I hope you're happy. You ruin your life by not marrying Daniel, who I hear is going places at your office, and you're the daughter of a murderer." Her words sting. My mother takes two more steps towards me and Joey stands to block her from getting closer.

"Now you want to protect her, Richie Rich. It's a little late for that, don't you think? You leave her heartbroken because Mommy and Daddy are too hung up on your future to let you date a poor girl." I have had just about enough of her mudslinging today. I step to my left so that I'm only partially blocked by Joey's frame and speak to my mother.

"How could you? How could you lie to me for all this time? Why didn't you tell me? Don't you think I had a right to know who my biological father is? You know what, never mind, I won't trust anything that comes out of your mouth ever again." I turn to direct my next statement to Collette. "Is your office still free?"

"Yes, please feel free to use it as long as you need." I reach back and graze Joey's hand. He turns to look at me unsure what to do next, and I head back to Collette's office. I realize I left my folder on the table and turn back to the conference room where I overhear Joey speaking to my mother.

She is attempting to argue with Joey. He responds calmly with, "Mrs. Harpin, I understand you're angry with all that has transpired here today. I'm sure that Corinne and Edmund attempted to have you reveal this information on your own prior to their deaths. I see now that you didn't wish for Genevieve's parentage nor the true identity of Stacia's killer to be revealed. I also understand why you may harbor ill will towards me for hurting Genevieve. My reasons for leaving and an apology are not owed to you. I owe them to her and her alone. I will, however, tell you this. I love her. I always have. I will do everything in my power to gain forgiveness and restore her trust in me."

I quickly retreat down the hall towards Collette's office. The folder can wait. He just stood up for me to my mother, ignoring the fact my biological father killed Stacia. My heart aches for all three of us and for Robert as well. So many details flood my head. I own the cottage with Joey. Wow! I have somewhere to live. Maybe Jessie will come through and I can work from the cottage. I'm swimming in the revelations of the day when Collette returns to her office.

"You left this in the conference room. Atty. Stein and Atty. Michaels will be escorting your mother from the conference room any moment now." I look up to see them flanking her at the elevator. Once the doors close, they turn away from the elevator with one of them nodding to Collette as they walk by."

"Holy Moly, I wouldn't want to come across them alone," she laughs.

"They are both cupcakes believe it or not. They played football together in college, were roomies in law school, and joined the firm together as well. Every now and then a show of muscle is helpful around here."

"I'm sorry you needed them today although I'm not surprised by her reaction to the news.   So, what happens now?" I ask her, wondering about the ramifications of all of this. She looks at me.

"As far as the estate administration is concerned, I will need the items listed in the folder over the next two weeks. Then I will file the appropriate paperwork with the court. I have outlined the process in the folder. Regarding, the life insurance policies, I will start processing those later this week. The proceeds could take a month or so to be deposited. The values of the policies are significant. You may consider getting a financial advisor. I can provide you with a few names to choose from if you need them."

I shake my head afraid to ask, but with tears welling in my eyes I manage to choke out, "How significant?"

"Each of your grandparents had a policy in excess of 1.5 million dollars naming you as the only secondary beneficiary," She replies. I must appear like I'm going to faint. Collette guides me onto the chaise in her office.

"On a personal note, Corinne spoke very highly of Mr. Cavallaro, almost to the point where I thought you two were already together." She glides her hand over her ring finger where the tan line is and continues, "If you have a second chance, take it. I would give anything to have one myself."

She stands and leaves her office. I gather myself and head back to the conference room to look for Joey. He is gone. Where did he go?

I ask Kimberly if she has seen Joey. She indicates he was on his phone and entered the elevator. I exit the building into the abnormally hot September sun and find him pacing by the car.

"Why did you leave?" I ask.

"I got a call from Gwen and I wanted to make sure James was okay."

"Is he?" I ask.

"Yes, he's fine. Gwen wanted to update me. He was sent to the nurse with a fever and needed to be picked up." I look up at him. His blue eyes stare back at me as if I hold the world. Rolling Collette's advice around in my head, I feel like I could stare into those eyes for the rest of my life. *Wait! What? Really, Gen? You just started seeing him again.* It has only been a little over a week. *But, I feel like I never left.*

"Do you want to head home now? We can make it back for dinner if we hurry. I can get Charley another time." I offer. "Kelsey will be fine keeping her a bit longer. She likes the company."

"I recall you promised a little boy your dog would visit. I think that will be just what the doctor ordered. Plus, we're already here." I go up onto my toes and kiss him. He reaches around and pulls me to him. Our entire bodies are touching from lip to knee. He continues to kiss me on the mouth along my jawline up to my ear. The last thing on my mind should be how he feels against me, but there it is and I'm quite sure Joey is feeling it too. I realize we're in a parking lot and slowly break off the kiss. I look at him and nod. He sets me back on the ground, reaches for my hand and leads me to the passenger door.

"Let's go get Charley," he says and jogs around the car to drive to Kelsey's condo.

We arrive at Kelsey's with a lot of fanfare from Charley. So much so that Joey and I are covered in dog fur and slobber. He excuses himself to clean up as best he can.

I recap today's meeting with Kelsey. There is a knock on the door. I don't really think twice before I answer it. I'm shocked to find Daniel on the other side of the door.

"Daniel," I say. A bubbly blonde is latched onto his arm. Both of them are surprisingly tan.

"Who is she?" I ask, afraid I already know the answer.

"She is my girlfriend," Daniel says

"How long, Daniel, how long? Why are you here? She is why you wouldn't have sex with me not some misguided notion of waiting until marriage. I'm such a fool. How long have you been sleeping with her? Why did you even propose to me if you were sneaking around. How long?"

His girlfriend pipes up, "I'm Lindsay and we have been together for almost a year. I have been trying to get Daniel to come to his senses. He was just marrying you for the promotion because you're boring and stable."

"Why are you here? What promotion, Daniel?" I ask.

He quietly replies, "I'm here for Charley. The kennel told me that someone picked her up a few days ago but it wasn't you. Kelsey is the only other logical person as you don't have any other friends." I nod processing the words coming out of his month. He pauses hoping I will hand over my dog or go after him for that little dig about my friends or lack thereof.

"Go on," I say, a bit snarkier than necessary, "What promotion?"

"Jessie offered me a promotion, but it had strings attached. She said I had to look the part of a stable family man, not a young partying bachelor. So, I started dating you. You're pretty enough. I proposed as soon as I thought it would help me get the job. I learned two days before the wedding they are going to promote someone else to the position. I don't know who it is yet. Luckily, you called it off before I could stand you up at the altar."

I feel Joey enter the foyer before he speaks. His presence calms me, but I get edgy looking for Daniel's reaction. Joey has clearly heard all of this exchange. He places his hand on my shoulder knowing the comfort it would provide and asks if I'm okay.

"Yes and no. Give me a few minutes and we will get going," I reply. Instead of walking away, Joey stays by my side with his arms crossed on his chest, but he says nothing. I appreciate he is letting me handle this on my own but am also glad he didn't walk away. I see Daniel's eyes narrow. As if I have done something wrong, he asks, "Who is he?"

I grab every ounce of fortitude I have left after this long and turbulent day, "Daniel, while it is none of your business, Joey and I came here for the reading of Memére and Pepére's will in the city. I don't owe you an explanation ever again. You will not be taking Charley as she was mine before we started dating — if you want to call it that — and we've never lived together. Also, all of the remaining bills from the wedding and the balance of the honeymoon that Lindsay clearly attended instead of me will be forwarded to you for payment. If you do not pay them, I will sue you. Don't ever come near me or Kelsey ever again.

"You b@*#&! I want the ring back. It cost me ten thousand dollars!"

"The ring has been sold to cover the expenses from our non-wedding. However, the balance is still significant considering you wanted the best of everything. I'm sure Lindsay would appreciate a different ring and probably one that costs more considering that was the price you were willing to pay for a promotion-only fake wife. Can you imagine what type of ring she will want to be your real wife?" Daniel stands there dumbfounded by my words, my gumption, and the fact Lindsay is now stewing at his side.

I take a few steps, grab the doorknob, and twist, raising my arm towards the door and escort them out with Charley following at my heel.

As soon as the door closes, Joey scoops me into his arms. "I'm so proud of you! Today has been a tumultuous day. You kept your cool and stood your ground."

"Thank you. It was hard, both at Collette's office and here, but I did it. Thank you for standing beside me but also letting me handle Daniel myself. Even though it appears I have the money to pay off the debts, I'm not paying for a wedding and vacation he took with Lindsay."

"That's my girl!" He replies as he sets me down. He keeps me glued to his side. Kelsey is hopping up and down and smiles at Joey's need to keep me close.

"Yes, Girl! Yes! You let him have it! I can't believe he wanted to take Charley too! Charley doesn't even like him." She laughs and comes to hug me. Joey lets go reluctantly.

"Thank you so much for taking care of her," I say. "We will head home now. I hope your date with Michael tomorrow goes well. Love you."

She kisses me on the cheek and lets me go.

"Love you too, Gen. Good luck with your meeting with Jessie. Safe travels."

"Good to see you again, Joey," she says while we are grabbing Charley's food, bowls and doggie toys.

"You too, Kelsey."

JOSEPH

I call Charley and she follows Genevieve and I to the car.

"Are you sure you want her in your car? Look what she did to your suit." Genevieve points at the fur still all over me despite my attempts to remove it. I look at my pants and smile.

"I can have it cleaned just like I can clean the car. Let's go home. James is waiting to meet her." I wink at her as I close the back door for Charley and then the front passenger door for Genevieve. We decide to grab some quick food before we reach the highway.

We aren't on the road very long when we come to a halt with a sea of red lights ahead of us. I do a quick search and realize that we just drove into traffic after a corporate event at the Dunkin Donuts Center in Providence. I call Gwen to let her know that we will be back much later than planned.

"Take your time. We will be here when you get back. I assumed you wouldn't be back until tomorrow anyway."

"Thank you, Gwen." I end the call and eat more of my sandwich from when we made our stop. It seems like she is pushing me towards Genevieve. The complexity and selflessness of that notion is foreign to me. Yes, Gwen knows Stacia and I were not 'in love,' and she knows I was forced to leave Genevieve for college, but she doesn't know every detail. Maybe she is right, I love Genevieve and James adores her, but she has only been in our lives for a little over a week. That is really fast. However, if you look at it from an overall perspective; it doesn't seem so crazy. I have known her my entire life. I can't imagine her going home next week. I glance to my right and see her staring at me.

"What?" I ask.

"Nothing. Just looking at you."

"Why? Do I have something on my face?"

"No, I was just . . . gawking. I was gawking. You're insanely good looking. You have abs for days that most men would be jealous of, you dress well, you smell amazing and every time you kiss me you leave me so breathless, I forget where I am. The only thing you are missing is a Scottish accent." I wink at him.

"Let me guess, Gerard Butler. Seriously, woman."

"Of course! Are you really jealous of an actor I will never be in the same room with let alone speak to?"

"Apparently, I am. I want you all to myself." He glances over at me with his piercing eyes and I feel like I could melt into his leather seats.

"You have me all to yourself. Don't you have an actress or singer you lust over?"

"Never really thought about it."

"Uh huh, sure you haven't. We're going to get home after James goes to bed at this rate. Poor guy will have to wait until tomorrow to meet Charley."

"Yes, he will. What time is your call with Jessie?" I ask. I know deep down that call could determine how easy or how hard it will be to maintain our renewed relationship.

"Eleven."

"Not too bad. I was thinking, I know we just started seeing each other again and I know this might be awkward for you, but the annual Scholarship Dinner is on Saturday night in Providence. Gwen, her husband, Jeffrey and her son, Scott will be there. I completely understand if you don't want to attend." I keep rambling on about all the reasons this invitation is an idiotic notion, but she reaches over and places her hand on my cheek. Thankfully, the traffic hasn't budged. I turn to look at her. I can't really read the look in her eyes right now.

"Yes, it might be a bit awkward, but I would love to go with you and James. I, of course, will need to shop." I smile brightly.

"James does not attend this event yet. I feel he is too young to handle the inevitable questions from well-intentioned donors about his mom. My sisters rotate who attends. Norah is staying with James this year. Kelly will attend the gala as well. My father's presence is up in the air."

"Oh." She leans away from me towards the door.

"I will not pressure you, sweetheart, but if we are going to do this, you will have to see my family members eventually. I honestly wouldn't worry about Norah or Kelly. They loved you then and they will again. My parents didn't give them the same ultimatum as they gave me simply because they are girls. I had to be the provider whereas my parents were going to find my sisters suitable husbands. College was optional for them but they both went. Norah is an accountant and Kelly designs clothing."

"What kind of clothing? Cocktail dresses?"

"Yes, she does. Actually, here. Text her." I say as I hand her my phone.

"I can't do that."

"Of course, you can. She will think it's me texting her." She reluctantly takes my phone.

"Kelly should be in my recent texts," I say. She finds the text icon and pulls up Kelly's name. I start to dictate to her.

Me: Hi Kel. I need some help. Do you have any dresses in stock for the gala? I just asked Genevieve to join me as my date and she needs a dress.

Kelly: Yes, I do. Our Genevieve. Genevieve Harpin. It's about time! What size is she? Still a size six?

I can see her blushing reading Kelly's words aloud to me.

"You need to answer her," he says. "I have no clue what size you are other than perfect for me." She opens her mouth to say something but instead focuses on her response not sure what to say.

Me: For the most part, yes. You may need to tailor a ten for her.

Kelly: Okay. Is she in Maine? I thought she lived in Rhode Island. I can bring some by your cottage on Saturday, if she is free.

Me: That works. There is a lot for you to catch up on. What time?

Kelly: I look forward to it. I'll be there around ten in the morning.

Me: Fine, I'll be leaving for work around one in the afternoon. Mrs. Jones is watching James. Thank you. Love you, Kel.

Kelly: You will need to fill me in. See you then. Love you too.

"You can't change your mind now. Seeing Kelly beforehand will help with your jitters about seeing my family again."

"Honestly, I'm not worried about Kelly and Norah. I'm more worried about your father and a little bit about Gwen. It can't be easy for her to see you moving on."

"Gwen is amazing. She actually likes you very much and told me not to let you go again when we talked on Sunday." Genevieve stares at me as if I said something unfathomable.

"Wow, just wow." She looks out the windshield as if she is gathering herself. I know better than to push right now. She is a thoughtful woman, always putting others before herself.

"Yes, you deserve to be happy and I hope you will be happy with James and I."

"How do you always know? No one, not one single person can read me like you do."

"I may have taken a long break, but my skills are still intact." He brings my left hand to his mouth and kisses the inside of my palm. Finally, we are starting to move towards Maine. We should arrive home around nine.

"I don't want to disturb Gwen and James. Can we stay at your cottage? Our cottage, I guess until morning?" he asks me. As if I could or would say no.

"Of course. We still need to talk about all that transpired today."

"We do. Honestly, it doesn't matter to me whether Leonard was your uncle or your father. Either way, he was part of your family. Your mother played with your life and I will not make you pay for it. I have to say; she's not my favorite person right now."

"Mine either," she mumbles under her breath.

"How do you feel about it?" He asks.

"I didn't really know Leonard all that well and unfortunately, the only people other than Robert who could tell me about him are gone. I'm not ready to ask Robert about my 'real' father. I'm not sure I even truly want to know anything. Robert is an amazing dad, Joey." She sighs deeply. "My mother, not so much. I can only imagine the turmoil he is feeling right now. I will call him on Friday." Genevieve pauses there for a moment. "Other than that, the cottage and the money doesn't really matter to me. That came out wrong. I mean I'm grateful, but I would much rather them still be here."

I squeeze her hand tighter. "I know what you meant. Do you want a coffee or are you set until we get to your cottage?

"No, thank you. I can make one when we get there. No need to stop. It has taken long enough to get back."

GENEVIEVE

We arrive at my cottage a little after nine. Wow, *my* cottage. I guess I can make the modifications now. I will never want to leave. Do I want to live here in Maine? Yes, but can I? I guess I will find out tomorrow. I realize I'm setting aside that it is partially Joey's too, but I'm not concerned about it.

Charley jumps out of the car and runs around not sure where to go. Then she runs off. Before standing, I take off my heels and walk towards the shore and find her wading in the low tide. Joey approaches and chuckles.

"She likes the water." Charley is running and barking at the water as if the tide is running away from her.

"I guess she does." I call her to me and head up the stairs. Charley follows with Joey pulling up the rear. I go into the kitchen and set up Charley's bowls and fill one with water.

"Wine or beer?" I ask Joey.

"Beer for me." I grab a beer for him and pour myself a glass of Pinot Grigio. "Where shall we sit?"

"Downstairs in your room," he replies.

"Okay."

He follows me downstairs and sits in the chair near the corner of the room. It is a large papasan chair that every girl has in her college dorm room. He motions for me to join him. I carefully climb onto the chair hoping it will hold the both of us. I nestle myself into his side. He has his arm around me and starts slowly dragging his thumb up and down my arm.

"Will you tell me what else is in your letter?" he asks carefully, as if he has no right to know. I look up at him and I can tell that if I asked the same question, he would share with me.

"Of course. She asked for forgiveness about not sharing her illness or telling me about Leonard. She talked about you and James and how you have become a constant in her days since they moved back here." I feel the tears welling up in my eyes. One escapes and he gently wipes it away. He shifts just enough to kiss my cheek where the tear had fallen.

"She also mentioned you as it relates to me. I'm shocked that she saw us together all those years ago and still felt like it would work going forward. Frankly, I'm scared how much I feel and how the last decade falls away whenever you are near me. I'm nervous for James. I didn't know Stacia. I hope you will continue to be comfortable keeping the photo of her in James' room and on the mantle. She is part of your life and his whether she is here or not."

"You saw them?" he asks quietly and shifts to look at me.

"Yes, she was beautiful, Joey. I see some of her in James, like the freckles on his nose that you don't have. James should have as many reminders of her around as you feel he needs. I'm scared he will push me away when I try to discipline him at some point."

"Oh, Genevieve. James adores you already. I love you more than I ever thought possible. I know it's fast." I cut him off. I sit up and straddle him on the chair. My hair falls around our heads like a veil and I kiss him as if I will never have the opportunity again. I slowly unbutton his shirt and push it off his shoulders. He pushes himself forward and stands to carry me to my bed. I unwrap my legs from his waist and stand before him. I reach behind me and slowly unzip my dress. I let it fall to the ground and it pools around my ankles. I'm standing there in my bra and panties and his mouth gapes open. This set is red lace but is not lined like the last one. I'm sure he can clearly see my nipples are hard pebbles.

"You're gorgeous," he whispers to me before taking my mouth again. "You weren't kidding when you said all of your lingerie was sexy. I like this one better. The straps across your chest are insanely hot. I will always wonder what you have on every day." He guides each strap down to my elbow and unhooks my bra, letting it fall to the floor. I laugh softly and blush at the same time. I reach to unbuckle his belt, but he stops me.

"We are taking this slowly tonight. I won't make it very long if I lose any more clothes." He continues to plant kisses sensuously down my jaw and across my chest paying special attention to each breast. He is now sitting on my bed and I am standing in front of him. He looks up at me while reaching for the sides of my thong. He pauses, placing his hands on my ass, giving it a gentle squeeze.

"Are you ready for me to take this off?"

I look at him and nod slowly.

"I need you to say it."

"Yes, I am." My brain flashes back to our very first time together. It was much different than this. I was so awkward and afraid to touch him. Now, he won't let me.

He glides the straps of my thong down my legs to the floor. As he stands, he places several small kisses up the length of my body. I place my hands on the hard planes of his chest and inwardly sigh. His body is drool-worthy. He lifts my chin, so we're looking into each other's eyes. His hands slide down my back and up my sides. I close my eyes taking in the sensations. He cups the side of my breasts and lowers his head to lave one of my nipples. At the same time, his hand heads lower. I instinctively shift my feet outward. His hand covers me leaving a trail of fire behind. I have no idea what he is doing, but wow, it feels amazing! I start to lose strength in my legs; he turns us and lays me on the bed. He uses his thumb to put pressure on my clit while two fingers enter me. A flurry of sensations course through my body. It doesn't take very long for me to see stars. I have never felt this way before. I hear him talking to me.

"Sweetheart look at me," he commands. I open my eyes to see him staring down at me.

"Hi." I smile up at him.

"That was amazing. I feel like I have been missing out."

"Do you now? Well, we have all the time in the world to do that and more over and over again," he says.

"That isn't what I have in mind," I quickly switch our positions and unbuckle his pants. His erection springs out of his boxer briefs as I pull his pants off his legs.

"Genevieve, you don't have to."

"I want to." He stops talking as I take him into my mouth. I hear him moaning and smile inwardly. This is different for me too. I feel like all I had with Daniel was this. I flash back to how hard I came from Joey's fingers. I can only imagine how it will feel when we make love again for the first time.

"I need you to stop if you don't want me to."

I stay focused through his orgasm. I travel my way up his incredible body. I lie off to his side, closer to the wall, with my legs over his. We laid there taking our time to gather ourselves, gently caressing one another. At some point, I reach for the sheet and draw it over both of us. We fell asleep tangled in one another.

Despite the fact we only sleep for a short while, I wake refreshed. I glance over at the clock. It read five in the morning. I nudge Joey. He turns to look at me.

"Good morning, beautiful."

"Good morning, yourself. We need to get moving. We need to check on James and see if he is up to going to school. I'm going to take a quick shower. I would invite you to join me but that is more than I want to explain to Gwen just yet. Could you make coffee, please?"

"Your wish is my command, milady."

I grin. "You're too much." I attempt to get up, but he pulls me into his lap for the best first kiss of the day I have ever had. "Can we do that every morning?"

"Someday. Go," he says setting me on my feet and swatting my ass.

I grab my robe and rush into the shower. Charley is whining to go out. I'm not sure where she will go but I let her out. I head upstairs and stand under the hot water reliving last night in my mind. I have no words to describe it and so many at the same time. I shut the water off and almost jump out of my skin when I see Joey is standing in the bathroom with a cup of coffee. I quickly grab a towel to cover up. He raises an eyebrow as if to say, I've already seen you naked, no need for the towel now.

"You certainly know how to woo a girl." He smiles and heads back to the kitchen, knowing otherwise we will never leave. I quickly dress in jeans and a tee since I'm not going anywhere. I just have my call with Jessie. The nerves are setting in about my call. Now that I own this cottage, my desire to telecommute is even higher than before. Will I miss Kelsey? Absolutely, but Joey and James are here and I'm happy here. Ugh! Just a few more hours and I will know.

We walk hand in hand over to Joey's with Charley on our heels. Even though it's barely six, Gwen is already awake in the kitchen. Charley rushes over to her as if she owns the place. Gwen bends down to accept some kisses from Charley. She greets us, "Good morning. How was your meeting?"

"Good morning. The meeting was very contentious with a few bombshells one of which marginally pertains to you. Picking up Charley was intriguing as well." Gwen's eyebrow raises up. "How is James? Thank you again for staying with him."

"James was running a fever, as I told you yesterday, but seems fine. He hasn't eaten anything solid since he got home from school. Just an ice pop and some Gatorade. I guess I will finish getting ready and head home."

"There is no rush. I'm going to check on James to see if he is up for going to school today. I would like to share the information I learned yesterday with you."

As if she were his dog, Charley follows Joey up the stairs towards James. I hear the shouts of glee as Charley jumps on his bed. My heart squeezes. I'm glad James is happy. Gwen addresses me.

"How are you after your meeting? I'm sure it was difficult."

"I'm a bit shocked by all of it. It will take some time to process what my mother did and repair the damage but as far as running into Daniel, I think I handled that well. I felt something was off in February but didn't see the whole picture yet."

Joey returns to the kitchen and gets two cups of coffee. Holding one for himself, he hands the other to me. I swear that I see Gwen give a little smile as he hands it to me.

"James is going to stay home today. I may be getting swindled but he's asking for you, Genevieve."

"Okay." I nod, set my cup down and head towards James' room.

JOSEPH

"Thank you again for staying with him, Gwen," I repeat.

"Anytime. What do you need to tell me, Joseph? You look worried." I hang my head and draw my hands through my hair.

"I will just come out with it. As you know, Leonard Harpin was responsible for Stacia's death." She nods sharply. "What you don't know - we learned yesterday - is that he isn't Genevieve's uncle. He is actually her biological father."

Gwen's hand goes to her mouth to muffle a soft sigh. "Oh, that poor girl. How are you handling it?"

"We talked about it quite a bit on the way back and last night. I don't know your feelings, but he was her family before; what degree doesn't matter to me."

"I agree, but this must be tearing her apart. You two have found one another again and now her mother's actions are threatening to crush her. How much longer will she be here? Did you invite her to the gala yet?"

I smile, "I asked her yesterday, actually. Kelly is coming to fit a dress for her on Saturday. I'm nervous about bringing her, Gwen."

"Why? You deserve to be happy Joseph. She makes you happy. She makes James happy. I can see the way you two look at each other. You should hold onto her."

"Thank you, Gwen. You don't know what it means to have you in my corner."

"I love you, Joseph. You and Stacia gave me the most precious grandson. I'm grateful for him and you. Having Genevieve as part of James' life will make him happy as well." She rounds the island and hugs me.

"I have to head home. I will see you next week at the gala. The rooms are booked with early check-in if you want to get ready there. Which sister is staying with James this year?"

I reply, "Norah is staying this James this year."

Gwen lets herself out. I text Kelly.

Me: Good morning Kel. I'm so glad you will be able to dress Genevieve.

Kelly: I'm so excited for you! Spill all the details. Well, the PG ones please. I'm your sister after all. 🙄

Me: She came here to move on from a broken relationship. She didn't know James and I live here now. We are taking things slowly.

Kelly: Is she moving there? I can't wait to see her. Is her hair still a gorgeous auburn color? Does she really need a ten or were you just being a guy?

Me: Yes, her hair is the same color. She has curves now she didn't when you last saw her. Trust me, Kel.

Kelly: Ewwwww! TMI.

Me: What are you twelve? You filled that in on your own. I will see you Saturday before I leave. Love you.

Kelly: Love you back.

I sit at the island and finish my cold coffee. I hear some giggling from James' room. I love that they're laughing together. I set my cup in the sink and head upstairs. Charley is curled up next to James against the wall and Genevieve is sitting on the edge of the bed with her back to me. Charley notes my presence but promptly puts her head back down next to James.

"Miss Gen, can Charley stay here with me today? I know she is your dog but I'm <u>so</u> sick and I could use the company."

Genevieve laughs. It's one of the most amazing sounds I have ever heard. I hadn't realized until just now that I had been missing it all these years.

"As long as it's okay with your Dad, she can visit for the day." I decide now is a good time to tell her I'm here, but James addresses me first.

"Dad, can Charley stay here with me today? Miss Gen said it was okay with her if it's okay with you. Also, can Miss Gen come to the amusement park tomorrow night?" She turns to look at me standing at the threshold. I can see that she is fine with it and James is happy as a clam with Charley snuggled up with him.

"Yes, I invited her to come tomorrow. It's fine with me, but you are responsible for Charley, including taking her out when she needs to go."

"Yay! Thanks, Dad. I will take great care of her."

"Get some more rest. Miss Gen has to go to a meeting, and I have some work to do," I say.

"Okay. See you later, Miss Gen."

"Bye, James," she replies after telling Charley to stay and be good.

GENEVIEVE

Joey reaches for my hand and leads me across the hall. My eyes widen as if that's a very bad idea.

"I just want to show you around. That's all," he says with a small glint in his eye. "I want to see you in my private space."

"Wow!" I say, stepping into the master suite. The whole house is large, and the master takes up one side of the second floor. The other side has two bedrooms with a Jack and Jill bath. The room is traditionally furnished. Large king bed with navy linens with white accents and only two pillows. It's clear a woman does not live here because there are no throw pillows or blankets anywhere. There is as sitting area with cozy chairs and a fireplace with a TV mounted above. Although all of that is amazing, the view is breathtaking. Joey catches me ogling the view.

"Come here," he says.

He reaches for me and leads me out onto the balcony. It has a small area with two chairs and a side table but there is also a larger area with a small sectional. There are no words. While the view from my cottage is nice, it's set back farther from the water and the view is partially obscured by a few large trees. This one is all ocean, everywhere the eye can see.

"Oh Joey. This is gorgeous! I would never leave this porch." He is behind me now with his arms around me, kissing the nape of my neck. The ocean breeze is only intensifying my goose bumps. I slowly turn and stare up at him.

"Thank you for sharing your space with me."

"You can use it anytime you want." He leans down and kisses me. I will never get used to how I feel when his lips are on mine.

"I may take you up on that." I say as I pull back from our kiss.

"I like having you here."

"I like being here, but I have to head back to talk with Jessie."

"Ok, I will walk you out."

As I slowly walk home, I mentally prepare for my call with Jessie. I have just enough time to brew a fresh cup and take a seat before she calls.

"Hi, Genevieve. How are you?"

"I'm well. And you?"

"I'm well, also. I will get straight to the point. There are a few things that we need to cover before we talk about your request. First, I owe you an apology. Daniel applied for a promotion and I told him he was not management material. He took my statements completely out of context and used you to attempt to get promoted. I want to stress; I did not tell him to get married. I told him his single partying bachelor ways were not what this company seeks in management level positions. I am glad you were able to see through him before you actually got hitched. I'm truly sorry that my criticisms of Daniel put you in an awkward position."

I'm almost at a loss for words. I didn't put much stock in Daniel and Lindsay's version of the situation, but it was twisted from the truth.

"An apology isn't necessary. I'm sure that Daniel came to that conclusion all on his own. However, I was dating him before that. At least I came to my senses in time. Thank you for sharing your position."

"Second, I note that you didn't apply for any promotions for which you're qualified this year. There are two open promotions: regional manager for the east and executive manager for the east region. You are overly qualified for the regional position and perfectly qualified for the executive manager position."

I speak up at this moment, surprised that she is aware of my resume. "Aren't you the executive manager for the east region, Jessie?"

"Yes, I am for another three weeks. I'm resigning my position due to health reasons. Also, they are moving the position to Boston, and I'm not willing to move my family."

"I'm sorry, Jessie. I wasn't aware you were ill."

"Thank you, no one was aware. I have multiple sclerosis, and I have been in remission for the last year or so. With all that said, I have been tasked with finding my replacement. The position is yours if you want it. I just emailed you a list of the job requirements. The requirements for in-person meetings is slightly higher than your current one. Please review it and get back to me. As far as your request to work from home you would be able to work from home except for the required monthly meetings."

"Thank you, Jessie. I missed the deadline for the regional manager position when my grandparents died. I will review your email and get back to you early next week."

"You're welcome, Gen. I look forward to hearing from you. Have a great weekend."

"You too. Bye."

I sit in my chair floored by what Jessie has just offered me. I lean forward and pull up the job requirements for the executive position. Am I really considering this? Yes, yes you are! I'm reading the duties and the only additional face time requirement would be a one-time one week in office training and then two monthly meetings. So, one additional in-person meeting for the new position. Why couldn't I teleconference into them? Based on the information from Jessie, the move to Boston won't be complete for another six months. I should be able to convince them in the interim that I don't need to be there, since I haven't been during construction. I glance down at the salary.

Before learning about the life insurance, I would have looked at the salary first. Of course, it will be higher than I already earn. I immediately do a double take. Yikes, it's a lot higher - as in twenty-five thousand dollars higher. There is a lot for me to consider. I take a deep breath. Then, I glance over my shoulder and see Memére and Pepére's wedding photo on the shelf next to Pepére's box. I stand and run my fingers over the carvings on the box and it falls to the floor. As I turn it right side up, a letter to Joey falls out. I place it back in the box and find the folder from Collette. I recall reading something about the box in the folder.

Collette is a very organized person. While pondering my call with Jessie, I start gathering the information that she needs to proceed with the estates. I'm not at all surprised to find a folder in the top desk drawer with the majority of the paperwork I need.

"Thanks, Pep. You already did the work from me," I say as if he could hear me. That only leaves me the death certificates and final bills to add to the folder. I thumb through the papers and see the list of financial advisors. I place calls to two of them to set up consultations. I grab the box and place it on the dining table. I will take it over to Joey later today.

I hear a faint knock on the door. I see James standing there with Charley. I wave him in.

"Hi. Is everything okay?"

James is out of breath. "I'm sorry to disturb you." I smile. He is such a polite boy.

"Yes, I'm fine," he says catching his breath.

"Charley ran over here as soon as I let her out the door."

"Let me text your Dad to let him know where you are." I turn to grab my phone off the table and Joey appears at my door.

"Hey there!"

"Hi Dad," James says. "Charley ran over here straight away. I think she missed Miss Gen."

"No problem. Buddy. Why don't you get Charley some water so I can talk to Miss Gen."

"Sure. Charley, come on, Charley. Good girl," he says as he leads her to the water dish.

Joey wraps his arms around me. "I guess Charley couldn't stay away either. How was your call with Jessie?"

"I just wrapped up with her when I knocked the box off the shelf in the office. There was a letter for you inside."

"We never did talk about my letter, did we?" He grins at me knowing I recall exactly why we didn't talk about it last night.

"No, we didn't. I assume info about the box is in there."

"Just that there is a letter and a key." I gesture towards the box and he opens it pulling out the letter. As he opens it a key falls to the table. I watch him as he reads the letter. It must be short because he looks up at me and asks if I'm free for the rest of the day.

"Yes, I am. Why?"

"We're going on a field trip. James and I will head home and clean up. Can you be ready to leave in a half hour?"

"Of course!" He pulls me into his arms and kisses me gently. I hear a faint 'ewwww' from the kitchen. I pull away giggling like a schoolgirl.

"That's gross, Dad," James says.

"You say that now. Let's go get ready. We have a field trip to attend!"

"Yay! Is Miss Gen coming with us?"

"She is. Is that ok?"

"Definitely."

"We will be back in a bit," Joey says. He leans into me and whispers, "I love you" in my ear and then gently nips my lobe. I'm at a loss when he heads out the door.

The storage unit isn't very far away. Kittery is a nearby town with lots of outlet shopping and restaurants. If you need something, you are almost guaranteed to find it there. The *Self Lock and Store* was a mid-sized climate-controlled storage unit. Joey heads to the office to get directions to the unit that Pepére left the key for. After getting directions, James and I follow him to unit #34. It looks like a garage more than a storage unit. Joey uses the key, opens the lock and then removes it and lifts the door. It looks like a car and a few boxes. Joey lifts the cover to reveal a masterpiece.

"Amazing! Look at that, Dad! It's Pepére's Mustang," James exclaims.

"Yes, it is, and it looks amazing. I didn't know he still had it. He must have restored it or had it restored. Did you know, Genevieve?"

"No, I thought he sold it when they moved here."

The three of them start circling the car, gently caressing the body. It is in pristine condition, the red paint gleaming even in the dim light. Joey opens the driver door and peers inside. There is a note on the seat with his name on it.

"What does it say, Dad?"

"Pepére left the car to me along with everything else in here."

"Sweet! Can we go for a ride like now?" James asks.

Joey chuckles, "Absolutely, as soon as I find the key. Genevieve, will you join us?"

"Yes, of course," I reply. Thinking I have an idea where the key is, I walk around the car and slide between Joey and the car interior. I was not intending on grazing the front of his body nor did I plan to bend down quite so seductively to get the key, but I did, and his reaction was noticeable.

He chokes out, "Genevieve, what are you doing?"

"I'm getting the key. I know where Pepére would put it. Would you have preferred I told you where it was?" I ask sweetly, noting that James is totally oblivious to his father's tenuous position.

"No, you're fine where you are." He grinds out. I reach down and lift the floor mat, grabbing the keys and turning back towards Joey. We are so close; I can smell his cologne and if I lean just a bit forward, we would be lip to lip. Joey leans forward and presses a peck on my lips while grabbing the keys.

"Seriously gross, Dad," James says, shaking his head.

"Get in Bud. Let's go." Joey says as he escorts me back around to the passenger side of the car.

"You're sassy, Genevieve." He whispers so James won't hear.

"Only with you," I say as I sit in my seat. Joey runs around and starts the engine. He reverses out the unit and closes the door. He guides the car out to the road. James is gushing in the back seat.

"This is fantastic. What are we going to do with the car? Can we keep it? Can I have it? We don't have a garage you know. It would be better to keep a perfect car like this in a garage," he blurts out.

"Slow down, slow down. Pepére left it to me. Yes, we're going to keep it. Past that, I'm not sure about the rest of your questions. For now, let's just go for a drive." Joey calmly replies to James' barrage of questions. We drive around the area for about an hour or so before Joey parks in front of the unit again. We all get out the car as Joey reopens the unit.

"I'm going to grab the boxes and lock up. I want to take the Mustang back to the house for now. Do you mind driving my car back?"

"No, not at all," I reply. James hurriedly jumps back into the Mustang. I laugh out loud at his exuberance. Yes, Pepére's car is amazing and gorgeous but Joey's regular car isn't anything to sneeze at either. Stop, Gen! It's just a car. James isn't rejecting you. It's absolutely about the car. I shake my head inwardly and walk towards Joey's BMW. After locking up, Joey stalks towards me. He hands me the keys and says he will meet me later. He has to make a stop on the way home.

"Okay, I will just follow you."

"It's a surprise. We will meet you on your porch."

"Okay." I say, trying desperately to figure out what he has up his sleeve this time. He kisses me more deeply this time and hurries back to the Mustang. My mind is racing as I follow him back towards York Beach. He takes a turn towards the village but that could just be a decoy. I will find out soon enough.

I see Charley at the door as I pull into my driveway. *My driveway. Our driveway.* I shake that thought away and let Charley out.

JOSEPH

"Where are we going, Dad?" James asks from the back seat where he's lounging like it's his job.

"We are going to get a special treat to take back to Miss Gen's house."

"Okay. How do you know she will like it?"

"Miss Gen and I have known each other since we were your age, as I told you last week. I know a lot about her, and I would like to show her I remember."

I pull the Mustang over in front of Smyth's. I had called ahead so my order is in a cooler, ready to go when I arrive. I don't care what it costs, it will be worth it. We hop back into the car and head to her cottage. When we arrive, Charley rushes for James as he steps out the car. He bends to give her some love and ends up with doggie kisses all over his face.

"This is both awesome and gross at the same time!" he exclaims. I laugh.

"Let's go around back." When we reach the back porch, I see her lugging the last piece of furniture onto the deck. She plops down on the couch with a thud right at the top of the stairs. It isn't even placed where it belongs.

"I could have helped with that," I say, waving me off.

"I know, but I figured I could get most of it done while I waited for you and James. It took a bit more work than I thought it would."

Luckily for me, the packaging does not give away what I got for her.

"Do you need anything from inside for my surprise? Do I get it now or do I have to wait?" she asks, like an impatient child.

I chuckle under my breath, "Just napkins, probably." She scoots inside the door to get some napkins and returns with bottled water as well.

"James, here you go. This is yours." She scowls at me for making her wait longer even though I know she expects me to serve James first.

"Thanks. Can I go on the beach and eat this with Charley?"

"Sure, just stay where we can see you and don't go into the water."

"Yay! Thanks, Dad!" He runs off down the steps with Charley.

"I think he loves your dog more than he loves me," I say to Genevieve as she watches James rush down the steps.

She replies, "Charley is great and new and fun, but he will always love you, Joey."

"I know. I'm not really jealous of the dog. Here, this is yours." I hand Genevieve her favorite ice cream combination ever.

"How do you remember all of these things about me?" she asks quietly turning towards the shore to find James. She starts to lick the chocolate soft serve with chocolate sprinkles dipped in more chocolate.

"I remember everything about our time together in vivid detail. Just because I was stupid a decade ago doesn't mean that I didn't love you then or that the things we did together weren't meaningful to me. I just want to bring whatever I can into today and the days that follow to remind you too."

She stares at me, not sure what to say which is very un-Genevieve like.

"Joey, I - thank you for the ice cream and remembering so many details. I remember too but I'm having a hard time trusting my feelings this time. I jumped in with my whole heart last time and you crushed it. I know the pressures from your family were significant. I know how you feel and you have apologized more than once already. I just need you to understand that this is going to take time for me."

I look at her and try to keep the tears welling in her eyes at bay.

"I understand, sweetheart. I'm not going anywhere. Take as much time as you need. I haven't spoken to my father except for the required calls on his birthday, Father's Day, and the anniversary of my mom's death. He doesn't control my life anymore. I will tell him about us when we're ready."

She lifts her hand to wave back to James. I stand and walk over to her holding her hand on the rail. We stand there in silence so much passing between us, until James comes back up the porch with Charley. Charley is completely covered in vanilla ice cream.

"Oh no!" She says when she sees Charley. James stands perfectly still as if she is going to yell at him. She gently says, "James, dogs aren't supposed to eat ice cream. There is special ice cream for dogs."

"I'm sorry, Miss Gen. I dropped my dish on the ground and couldn't get it away from her fast enough. Will she be okay?"

"Yes, she should be fine, but let's not share people food with her again."

"I won't. I promise." He stares up at her and jumps into her arms for a hug. I swear I hear her sigh.

"Let's take him downstairs and clean him up with the hose," I say to James.

"Miss Gen, can you get us the stuff we need for a proper bath?" He asks her with wide eyes.

"Sure can. I will meet you downstairs on the side of the house." I look over at her and nod. She heads inside and grabs the necessities and we bathe Charley. Once we are done, we bring Charley inside and watch a show called *Bunk'd* on Hulu. Soon after the second episode starts, James falls asleep on the couch.

"I will just take him home," I say reaching for James but stopping before saying, "Thank you for coming with us on our road trip today. I know we didn't get a chance to talk about your call with Jessie. I can call you when I get home."

"Thank you for inviting me. My call with Jessie can wait. There is a lot for me to consider but I will tell you it isn't bad news. In fact, it could turn out very well for me."

"That sounds promising," I say, pulling her into my arms. She threads her fingers into my hair, and I kiss her until we're panting and breathless well aware that my son is literally right next to us.

"I will call you in the morning after drop off. Goodnight, sweetheart."

"Goodnight," she replies. I scoop up James as she opens the door for me.

GENEVIEVE

I watch them leave, wondering how these past two weeks have gone by so quickly. Thinking how much I truly want Joey and James to stay with me. I go into the office and pull out my laptop. I start a remodel of the cottage. I have never had anything of my own to fix up but here I am. Right now, when you walk into the front door you are standing in the living room. Straight ahead is the kitchen through the kitchen is the wraparound porch facing the shoreline. To the right of the living room leads upstairs and a doorway into the office. Behind the office is the dining room. I will take out the walls between the living room, kitchen and dining room, making it one large open space. I will update the cabinetry and have a large kitchen island with stools and a smaller dining area. I will raise the roof and create a third-floor master with an insanely large closet and French doors leading onto a secluded deck.

I furiously draw all these ideas in my floor plan app. Could I actually make this come true? I set my laptop aside and meander outside to the deck. I smell the salty air and realize I feel like this is where I should be. Can I let myself trust him completely again? What am I afraid of? Getting crushed again. But Joey is an adult now and James is fantastic! Is he is lying when he says he doesn't speak to his father anymore? No, he isn't lying. Then what is the issue? Giving my heart away again but to two people instead of one.

I stand there stewing for some time. Finally deciding I'm not going to find all the answers tonight; I head to bed. I will start anew tomorrow. I will need my strength to call Robert. I'm not sure what to say though. I check the doors and call for Charley to follow as I head to my room. I shuck my clothes off and crawl into my bed in my panties and a tank reliving the last time I was here with Joey as I sleep.

"Charley, shut up! Charley!" I shout at my dog.

"Don't yell at her. She is just doing her job while you're sleeping like a rock!" Joey's voice almost knocks me out of my bed. He has let Charley outside.

"Good morning. This is for you."

He is all showered, dressed, and smelling amazing. His outstretched hand holds a coffee, which he clearly made upstairs in the kitchen. I take the cup. The aroma of fresh coffee is amazing.

"Morning," I say. "Apparently, I was tired and so was she. She didn't make a peep until you showed up."

He leans down and kisses my forehead before taking a seat in the chair where we - *focus Gen*.

"You look ridiculously sexy right now," he says while casting his eyes down my entire body. Every part of my body heats under his gaze.

"Thank you," is all I can manage to say. I place the cup on the dresser and saunter over to him, grabbing his cup and setting it aside. I straddle him, placing myself in the same position I was a few nights ago and start to undress him.

"Genevieve."

"Yes," I reply. I continue unbuttoning his shirt only to realize he is wearing a fitted undershirt.

"So sexy," I murmur. I can feel his arousal between my legs.

"Genevieve, look at me," he grinds out. I lift my head to look him in the eyes.

"As much as I would like to finish this, I have a conference call in fifteen minutes. I just came to check on you because you didn't answer your phone. I was worried about you."

"Oh, I'm sorry," I reply, and, a bit embarrassed - I begin rebuttoning his shirt.

He grabs my wrist and I stop buttoning.

"Don't ever be sorry for showing me how you feel. I would cancel this call and let you take off the rest of my clothes, but it's prep for my meeting tomorrow evening. I can be back here in a little over an hour to finish this."

"Yes, absolutely. Yes." I nod. He lifts me off him and places me on the floor.

"Could you just crawl back into your bed and wait for me? I will be back as soon as I can."

I crawl back onto the bed, making sure to leave images of me on my hands and knees swimming in his head until he gets back here. I look back at him seductively.

"You're killing me, Genevieve!" he growls as he stalks out the door towards his home. I run upstairs to use the bathroom and come back down to my room to wait. I grab my phone and see a bunch of missed texts from Joey and one from Kelsey.

Kelsey: Hey there! How are you doing? How was your call with Jessie?

Me: Hey. I'm thinking, processing and sorting how I feel about all of it. My call with Jessie was good. She gave me two options. One is good, the other is great. I'm deciding which I want.

Kelsey: That is awesome! I'm so happy for you. I will miss you but . . .

Me: What do you mean, you will miss me?

Kelsey: I know full well you aren't coming back here girl! I wouldn't either if I could work from home from an amazing cottage with a delectable man a few doors down. Who loves you by the way? How are things with Joey? Did you sleep with him yet? Yes, I went there.

Me: Kelsey! No, we didn't but we were close yesterday. I'm afraid it is too perfect. He has been amazing and supportive through all of this. I adore James and I could easily see a future with them.

Kelsey: You know you have to do him to find out, right? I mean, again as an adult.

Me: Kels! You're too much! I'm going to beg off girl's night tonight. I'm going out with Joey and James. I hope you don't mind.

Kelsey: Of course not! Have a wonderful time.

Me: Are you sure?

Kelsey: Of course! Bye.

Me: Thanks. Bye.

I look at the clock. I flop onto the bed and scan my email. There is one from Collette asking for my banking information for the insurance company. I will send it later. I hear fast footsteps. I sit up and I see Joey standing at my doorway.

"What are you doing here already? It has only been twenty minutes." He is out of breath and not in a good way.

"It's Gwen. She's on her way to the hospital."

"Go, be with Gwen," I respond.

"Can you go to my house and wait for James?" he asks as if he has no right to lean on me.

"Of course. I will get dressed and head over there. He will be there around three forty-five, right?"

"I'm so sorry we can't finish what you started before. I have ideas swimming in my head, Genevieve. No, today is a half day so he will be back at one thirty." He kisses me with force and pulls away.

I place my hands on his chest. His heart is beating so fast. "Go, I will take care of James. Please text me with updates."

He presses a key into my hand.

"Thank you. I love you."

He runs out the door towards his car. I stand there gathering my thoughts. I glance at the clock. It's almost eleven. I pull on my robe, run upstairs, and take a quick shower. I throw on some jeans and a light sweater. I make coffee and respond to Collette.

My phone chimes with texts from my siblings and my mother. I have a voicemail from Robert. I quickly respond to my siblings who want to come to the cottage for a weekend in late October. I tell them I will check with Joey and get back to them, but it should be fine. I have no plans to answer my mother any time soon. I sit on the couch, steel myself and call Robert back. He answers on the first ring.

"Hello?"

"Hi Daddy!" I say.

"Hi pumpkin. Thank you for taking my call."

"Why wouldn't I take your call? You learned about everything at the same time I did."

"I wouldn't blame you if you didn't want to talk to either of us. How are you holding up?"

"I was more concerned about you to be honest. I didn't really know Leonard, except how the accident impacted Joseph."

"I won't lie to you, Gen. Leonard was an alcoholic, but aside from his addiction, he was a good man."

"Thank you for sharing that. No one knows anything about him other than you and — well Mom."

"How is Joseph handling this information?" he asks.

"Joseph said he doesn't care whether Leonard was my uncle or my father. Either way, Stacia is gone."

"At least someone in that family has some sense," he replies.

"What does that mean?" I ask, waiting for the other shoe to drop.

"First, I want to say, I see how happy you are with Joseph. Give him a second chance. He was a pawn in a bigger game. A game I don't believe he knew he was in. Since our meeting on Wednesday, I have learned there are more layers to why Mrs. Cavallaro didn't want you near Joseph. Apparently, during the time your mother was stepping out on me with Leonard, she was also frequenting the country club searching for a rich man to sink her claws into. One of the men she targeted was Joseph's father, Samuel. He rebuffed her efforts, but he clearly shared the events with Jeanette. When she learned you and Joseph were spending so much time together, she cast you as just like your mother and put her foot down, so Joseph followed along," he says.

"I have no words. Was she already pregnant while she was doing this?" I ask incredulously.

"I'm not sure, pumpkin. Look, none of this matters as it pertains to you and Joseph. If you love him, give him a chance. Despite the circumstances of that meeting, I could see he cares for you a great deal. As far as your mother is concerned, I have no intentions of speaking to her again unless it's through my attorney. You can handle your relationship with her as you wish."

"Thank you. I care for him too. I'm afraid to trust my feelings for him."

"That is completely understandable. Just take it slow. What are you going to do about your apartment and your job?"

"Actually, Jessie and I spoke, and she offered me a promotion to work in the Boston office."

"That is wonderful. Where will you live?"

"I haven't made a decision about the promotion, but either way she said I could work from home so I will probably move into the cottage."

"That is wonderful! I'm so proud of you! I'm glad you are going to be happy." I smile to myself. I glance at the clock.

"Dad, I have to get going. I have a work call. I love you."

"I love you, too. Bye."

I grab a few things to bring with me to Joey's - laptop, phone, purse, Charley, food for Charley. I call Charley and we head over to Joey's. As I open his door, I have a weird feeling being here alone. Charley just prances in like she owns the place.

I set my stuff on the island and step out on the deck. I doubt being here, I hear Mrs. Cavallaro's voice in my mind. *We don't allow guests like her in our home, Joseph, stay on the front porch.* My dad's revelations don't really shock me after what I learned in Collette's office. It does mean; however, it will take longer for me to speak to my mother again.

I'm in need of some baking therapy. What is the chance Joey has ingredients? I search the kitchen thinking of something I can bake with what is on hand. Not much here. Think simple, Gen. Maybe something that James can help with after his homework. Got it! I look around the kitchen for a clock but don't find one. The microwave clock isn't set. I grab my phone and set the microwave clock. It's time to wait for James. I head to the front steps with Charley on my heels.

As the bus pulls up, Charley rushes to the curb. James starts to descend the steps and Charley plants some kisses on him. I hear the bus driver ask him who I am.

James replies, "She's my Dad's best friend. I'm allowed to go with her, Mr. Kevin." I wave, the bus driver waves back and James runs towards me with his arms outstretched. I hug him and we head inside.

A NEW BEGINNING WITH YOU 137

"Hi, Miss Gen. What are you doing here? Where is my Dad?"

I pause, deciding what information I want to share with him at this moment.

"Hi James. I'm here helping out your dad. G-ma wasn't feeling well, and your Dad went with her to get checked out."

I see the panic in his eyes. He may have been young when his mother died but he still carries deep-rooted worry.

"Is she going to be okay?"

"I don't know what's wrong with her yet, but she is strong and she will be okay."

"Are you sure?" I'm not prepared to lie to him, but I don't see another option to calm him down.

"I'm sure that G-ma is strong and will fight whatever is wrong." I say as he hugs me again.

"Ok, thank you. I feel a bit better."

"Do you have homework?" I ask, knowing it will not be his favorite topic. Joey clearly has a system for James, and I will try to stick to it.

"Some, but I will do it later."

"No, you will do it now, as if your dad was here. Then we will do something fun," I expect some groaning, but I don't get any.

"Okay, Miss Gen. It will only take a little while." He pulls out his Math and English folders and gets to work. I wash and set to dry the dishes that Joey left in the sink when he rushed out earlier. I check my phone, hoping for an update but find none. I tidy up the living room. I find paperwork that probably should be in his office. I carry them to his office down the hall. His office is pretty much how I would picture it - clean lines, but comfortable. There is a medium sized desk facing towards the windows. There is a small sitting area with a leather couch and ottoman. I would normally be surprised to find it messy, but given today's circumstances, not so much. I set the papers on the chair and leave as James calls me from the kitchen.

"Miss Gen. I'm done."

"I will be right there. Do you mind if I look at it?"

"Sure."

"What are you working on?" I ask. I'm probably safe as far as the math is concerned for now. I will probably be out of my element when he's in high school. Wait! What?! That is almost eight years from now, Gen! I push those thoughts aside and focus on the page in front of me.

"For Math, we're multiplying three-digit numbers and for English we are starting to set up an essay that will be done around Thanksgiving. I had to pick my topic and main ideas."

"I'm not much of a math whiz but if I remember correctly, your Aunt Norah is."

"You know Auntie Norah?" he asks, as if that's impossible.

"Of course, your dad and his sisters were here during the summers when I was here. I spent a lot of time with all of them but mostly with your dad."

"You don't like my aunts?" he asks.

"Your aunts are great. I just got along better with your dad. I was a bit of a nerd when I was younger."

"No way! Like Sophie at school. She always has her nose in a book, and she's quiet, but she is really nice to me." I look at him. I don't think he realizes he just revealed his school crush to me.

"Sophie sounds really great! What do you say we put this away and bake something for your dad?"

"Woohoo!" he says, jumping off the stool and rushing to put his bag in the front closet.

"Where do we start, Miss Gen?"

"Before you got home, I searched the kitchen, we have ingredients for chocolate-chocolate chip cookies or brownies. Which do you want to bake, James?"

"Both!" he says emphatically.

I laugh. "Although that sounds wonderful, we can bake only one with the ingredients we have on hand."

"Hmmmmmm," he ponders. "Both are tasty choices. I would prefer the brownies, but Dad would prefer the cookies. Let's go with the cookies this time."

"Okay. Let's get started." It isn't lost on me that he said, "this time." As in, he would like there to be a next time. I think this adorable boy is charging his way into my heart too.

"Have you ever baked before?" I ask him. He shakes his head.

"Okay, step by step. First, we preheat the oven to 350 degrees. Pull out the cookie sheets and line them with parchment paper."

James is a great helper. Once we finish lining the sheets, we gather all the dry ingredients. I tell him the measurements and he measures each one out precisely.

"What's next?" he asks as if he has caught the baking bug already.

"Wet ingredients like eggs, vanilla, milk." He turns and grabs each of those items and sets them on the island. Soon thereafter, we're mixing the dough together.

"Miss Gen, I think we forgot to add something into the dough." He says with a smirk on his face.

"Like what?"

"We need to add tons of chips. The more the better." I laugh.

"We can't go too crazy but have at it." I stop him short of putting two full bags of chips into the dough. After mixing in the chips, I show James how to place them for baking explaining that they can't be too close, or they will mush together. He is a natural. He fills up his cookie sheet with uniform and precisely placed dough.

"Nicely, done."

"Thanks." He smiles up at me. He's a carbon-copy of Joey. We place the first sheet into the oven and set the timer. I tell him that we need a cooling rack but hadn't been able to find it.

"I'll get it!" He says, pulling two out of the skinny cabinet next to the stove.

"Perfect! I didn't look there. Let's lay these on the island so they are ready."

"Now what?" he asks.

"Now, we wait for them to cook, but in the meantime, we can wash the dishes. Do you have a stool?"

"Yup." He goes around the corner and grabs a flat wooden thing from the pantry and quickly unfolds it into a sturdy stool. He places it next to me by the sink.

"How about you wash, and I can dry?" I say, looking at him.

"Sure." We work together to finish up the dishes. It isn't long until the first batch is ready to cool. We start the second batch and I ask, "Do you know how to use a spatula?"

"You just slide it carefully underneath, right?"

"Yes, exactly. Just be careful not to touch the pan, it's very hot." He carefully slides the spatula under the first few cookies and moves them to the rack. He continues until he has successfully moved all the cookies to the rack.

JOSEPH

I hear laughter as I approach my front door. I peer through the sidelight of the front door and see them baking in the kitchen. Genevieve is teaching my son how to bake. She is patient, letting him do most of the work of moving the cookies to the rack. Not only did she save the day, but she's amazing with my son. Just one more reason that I can't let her go this time.

I quietly open the door. Genevieve looks over towards me. She looks amazing. Her hair is piled on top of her head. She has flour on her face and her sweater.

James rushes over to me, jumps into my arms, and peppers me with a bunch of questions.

"How is G-ma? Will she be ok? When can I see her? Is she going to be ok? I'm really scared, Dad." I squat down and place James on the floor and simply smile.

"Slow down! G-ma had an anxiety attack but thought it was something worse. She will be just fine. We can probably see her on Sunday. She is staying overnight at the hospital for observation, but it's just a precaution." Clearly relieved, after hearing that information, he keeps going.

"Miss Gen is so awesome. She taught me to make your favorite cookies today. We really need to up the ingredients we have in the pantry. Miss Gen and I have brownies to bake next time."

Just as I'm about to answer him the timer goes off.

"Gotta go. The next batch is done." James rushes over the stove and grabs the oven mitt. Genevieve is standing there just in case. She is amazing for letting James figure this out on his own. I'm watching this in awe. He places the tray on the stove and the mitt back in the drawer. She reminds him to shut off the oven, points to the stool and shows him how. He proceeds to move the cookies to the other cooling rack.

"Can I try one yet?" he asks Genevieve looking up at her with the widest eyes.

"It will have to be our secret," she says as she winks at me over his head. He takes a seat in one of the stools and she hands him a cookie. She reaches for the rack and lifts a cookie in my direction. I try to keep my composure while walking over to her. I have no words right now for how I feel about seeing her with James. She belongs here. I pull her into my arms first and then grab the cookie with my mouth. She just shakes her head at me and starts laughing as the cookie breaks and falls to the floor. Before I can react, Charley is already cleaning up the mess.

Seeing this, I turn back to Genevieve and kiss her. I whisper in her ear.

"Thank you for helping today. You look fantastic covered in flour helping James learn to bake. How did you remember my favorite cookie?"

She blushes and says, "I remember everything too. Thank you. We had a great time." I slowly let her go. I don't like the empty feeling I immediately have so I grabbed her hand.

"James, did you do your homework?" I ask.

"Yes, Miss Gen said I had to do it right away. She looked it over and then we started the cookies. Did you know she knows Auntie Norah and Auntie Kelly?"

I laugh loudly. "Yes, I'm aware."

"She said Auntie Norah is better at math than she is."

I laugh even harder at that statement.

"Yes, that is absolutely true." Genevieve takes that moment to lightly punch my arm.

"What? You said it yourself. You're not great with math."

"True. Very true," she says. I just stare at her. I need to find out if she is leaving after the gala. I need to convince her to stay here.

"Hey, Dad?" James says.

"What's up?"

"Do we have to go the amusement park tonight? Can we just stay here and have movie night with the three of us instead?" he asks very seriously, as if it's a hardship for me to stay home.

"I'm okay with it but tonight is the last night of the season. You will have to wait until the spring to visit again. Do you realize that?"

James ponders what I just said. "Yes, I understand. I want to have a movie night instead."

"Will you join us, Miss Gen?" James asks politely.

"Absolutely, I will, James." He smiles brightly and runs off to his room.

"Should we tell him it is only five-thirty and we really should eat dinner first?" she asks. I reach for her and take her into my arms again.

"We should. Does pizza work? I don't think I have Genevieve and James cooking essentials on hand for a full meal."

She laughs, looking up at me, and says "Yes and I don't think you do either." She's really tiny with no heels on. I lift her onto the island, so we are at eye level. "James is here," she says in a low sexy voice.

"I know, but I want to kiss you properly."

"We can wait until later," she counters.

"Have you changed your lingerie since this morning? Because I have been having images of your gorgeous ass in my mind all day?" I ask in a gruff voice.

"Yes, I have, but you will have to wait until later to find out what I chose."

"Genevieve, could you at least give me a hint?" I beg her.

"Nope, no hints." She smiles slyly at me but leans forward enough for me to see that her bra is sheer black lace.

"You're killing me, sweetheart!"

She winks at me and says, "That's the plan." She hops down from the island to search for dishes and drinks. She fills a glass of wine for herself and a beer for me. She seems at home in my kitchen and with my son.

James rushes back into the kitchen and we order pizza. While waiting for the delivery James scans the lists for available movies. He chooses *How to Train your Dragon*. The pizza arrives and we settle in on the couch to watch the movie.

"Good choice, James. This is a great movie," she says winking at me.

"Thanks, Miss Gen," James replies chowing on his pizza. I'm puzzled but let it go.

About halfway through the movie, we pause it for a quick break. Genevieve and I clear the pizza dishes, refill our drinks and make popcorn while James runs to the bathroom. After planting a kiss on her lips, I ask, "Why is this movie great?"

She tried to be serious but started laughing right away. She raises her hand to contain herself.

"This is a Gerard Butler movie," she says and starts laughing again.

"Are you serious?" I ask, as if that isn't possible. Meanwhile, she is googling the cast, and, sure enough, Gerard Butler is one of the character voices. We sit, eat, laugh and enjoy the rest of the movie.

The movie wraps up around seven-thirty and we clear the mess from the living room. Once we wrap up in the kitchen, James asks to go read.

"Sure." I reply.

"I will be up soon."

"Will you come too, Miss Gen?" he asks.

"Definitely," she replies smiling at James.

As soon as James is out of earshot, I say, "I think he likes you."

"Maybe. I like him too. He is adorable, smart and kind, Joey. You have done an amazing job with him on your own."

I wrap my arms around her from behind and nuzzle her neck.

"Thank you, that means a lot to me. At first it wasn't easy, and I gather that there are days coming up that won't be easy either."

"You're probably right, but you can handle anything," she says. I can't handle her not being in my life ever again. I shove the thought aside. It has only been two weeks. Two weeks!

We head upstairs to tuck James in. He is sorting through his books. He hands one to Genevieve and asks her to read it.

"Why don't you read it to me?" she asks.

"I can't read this whole book! It has so many chapters!" he counters.

"I think you can. Let's try." She sits next to James on his bed and he starts reading. The look on his face is priceless. Surprise and shock are the words I would use to describe his facial expressions as he reads down the page.

"See, you can. Keep going."

James continues reading for three pages. Then he gets stuck on a word. She calmly helps him sound it out. I sit in the chair in his room watching this unfold. James is growing attached to her and so am I. Can I just tell her that I don't want her to leave? Does she feel the same way? They read three chapters while I'm swimming in my thoughts before James called it quits.

"I'm done for now, Miss Gen. Thank you for letting me bake with you and letting me read to you. I like it when you are here." He reaches over and gives her a hug. "Goodnight."

"You're welcome. I like being here. Goodnight, James."

I approach his bed, give him a hug, and say goodnight.

"Goodnight, Dad."

I find her standing on the balcony of my room. The wind is blowing gently making her shiver. I grab a sweatshirt and place it on her shoulders.

"Thank you," she says. She turns into my arms. I waste no time lowering my lips to hers. The sun is starting to set earlier and there is not a cloud in the sky. The moon is bright, and a few stars are showing themselves.

"Thank you for trusting me with James today. I'm sure that wasn't easy for you."

I'm shocked by what she has just said.

"Of course, I trust you with James. He trusted you enough to seek you out two days after meeting you. You're amazing with him, patient and loving but firm. I can't believe you got him to do his homework on a Friday! I sometimes lose that battle myself."

She looks down towards the ground. I lift her head up. "I need you to know, I want you here. I know I cannot make up for my youthful stupidity in two weeks with flowers and cookies. I'm asking you to give me time, your time. I love you, Genevieve. Can you do that? I realize I come as a package deal now but can you give me a second chance?" I pause. I see the wheels turning in her head. "Say something, anything, beautiful."

GENEVIEVE

I stare into his gorgeous eyes and I see true emotion and lust at the same time. I muster the courage to speak.

"While I was here today, especially at the beginning, I felt out of place. I felt like I was intruding on your life with James, nosing around in the cabinets for baking supplies. I found myself cleaning up while he was doing his homework because I was nervous. As our afternoon went on, I felt like James accepted me and, listened to me. We had a great time. I want to be here too. I want to spend time with both of you. It won't be easy though," I say. He leads me over to the sitting area and sits next to me. I pause, getting ready to pour out the plans I haven't finalize in my own head yet.

Instead of coaxing me, Joey just waits with bated breath for me to continue. For that I love him more. He has known me for most of my life and knows I'm a thinker and a planner.

"I initially asked Jessie to work from home. During our call she offered me a promotion." I hear him take a deep breath. *Be patient, Joey. Hear me out.* "She offered me the position of executive manager of the east region."

"Oh sweetheart, congratulations. That's exciting! What does that mean exactly?" he asks.

"The reason the position is open is it will be based in a new Boston office, one that isn't even built yet. This is Jessie's job, but she refuses to move her children and her doctors are in Connecticut. It would require me to attend a weeklong training in Connecticut and to be available to be in Boston on short notice occasionally." I look up at him and he is listening intently. I can't read the expression on his face. I make a mental note never to play poker with him.

"As far as where I want to live, I want to live at the cottage. I want to be near you and James to see what our future holds together. I drew up some plans last night to remodel the main floor and add a third-floor master. I could never use their room as my own." I pause long enough to see that I have stunned him a bit.

"Joey, say something. I —" Before I can finish, he stands and pulls me to him, and sliding his hand to the nape of my neck and drawing my lips to his.

"Oh, sweetheart! I'm so happy for you and for us. I can't imagine a week without you ever again, but we will get through it. We can make the schedule work as long as you are here with me - with us. I would love to see the plans you have created for Mem's cottage." I glide my hands down his back and clasp them at his waist.

"I'm scared with all the change but I'm ready." He lifts my shirt and sweatshirt off me at once. Instead of throwing them to the ground, he walks me back into his room and places them on the bench at the foot of the bed. I start unbuttoning his shirt and help him shuck it off his shoulders. I add it to mine on the bench. I reach for his belt buckle and hear James screaming.

"Daaaaddd! It hurts, it hurts." He grabs his shirt and rushes off to James. I follow him after dressing but wait in the hallway. Joey is sitting next to James.

"What hurts?"

"My legs, my legs hurt," he screams. Tears are streaming down his face.

I whisper loud enough for Joey to hear me, "What can I do? What do you need?"

"It's growing pains. I need to massage his legs." he says suggesting this is normal.

"Okay." I reply. I continue to wait by the door. I notice Charley is curled up next to James. I may have lost my dog forever. I smile. You may be getting a dog after all James.

Joey rubs James' legs up and down from ankle to knee. Slowly, James' screams decrease, and he lies back down and falls asleep. Joey untangles himself from James and leads me back to his room. I take a seat by the gas fireplace.

He turns it on and sits next to me. He says, "I don't want to cut this evening short, but I have to prepare for work tomorrow before bed because I skipped out earlier to be with Gwen."

"Of course. I don't think Charley will want to come home with me. Is it okay if she stays with James?"

"I'm sure he would love that," he says.

"Stay. I don't know how long I will be but."

"I don't think that is a good idea yet. You and I have known each other for a long time but James has only known me for two weeks."

"Thank you. Thank you for being you and putting everyone else first." I stand and reach for his hand. He shuts the fireplace off and grabs my hand. It feels perfect but it's also scary as hell. I'm going to uproot my whole life in one week – change jobs, move to a new state and renew a relationship with my first love and I will gain a son. *That is insane!*

I gather my stuff and head for the door. I attempt to return his sweatshirt.

"Keep it. I like how you look in my clothes." I smile up at him. My teenage self is in heaven right now. Little does he know that I still have his sweatshirt I borrowed all those years ago.

"Breakfast at eight-thirty tomorrow? I will cook," he asks as I slip on my Keds.

"You can cook?" I ask smirking.

"I get by."

I go up on my toes, he wraps his arm around my waist, and he lifts me off the ground placing a kiss on my lips. He slowly lowers me to the ground. I raise an eyebrow to indicate I can tell work isn't the only thing on his mind. He grins, tucks a few stray hairs behind my ear and kisses my forehead.

"Goodnight, Joey."

"Goodnight, sweetheart."

He follows me outside. I look back and say, "I will be fine. It's just two houses over."

"I know, but I want to watch you as long as I can." I swoon a little.

When I reach the landing of my stairs, I turn and blow him a kiss, heading inside before I rush back there and prevent him from getting any work done. I chuck my shoes into the corner and strip off my jeans and tee. I fall onto the couch and text Kelsey.

Me: Hey girl. How is/was your date? We need to chat about work and stuff.

I'm not expecting an answer right away, but the three dots appeared quickly.

Kelsey: Hey! We went to an early movie. I just got home. He has to work in the morning.

Me: Awesome! I'm going to take the promotion Kels.

Kelsey: That is fantastic! I'm going to miss you. Please make sure there is a room for me.

Me: Always. There will always be a room for you. Love you.

Kelsey: Love you. So do you have any details to share?

Me: Details? I have no clue what she is hinting at.

Kelsey: Yes, sex details.

Me: We were headed that way a little while ago, but James woke up with growing pains. I relayed my day to her including Gwen, James and Joey.

Kelsey: I'm so happy for you. New job, new house, new man and son. Things are looking up love.

Me: Thanks. They seem to be looking up for you as well.

Kelsey: I'm cautiously optimistic. I'm going to crash. TTYL

Me: TTYL

I email Jessie and take the promotion. I will do my best to make sure I have to go to Boston as little as possible. I walk back to where I had dropped my clothes, pick them up and lock up. I set an alarm so that I don't scare Joey again and crash into my bed. I would have liked to finish what Joey and I were starting when James woke up. I fall asleep with the sounds of the waves crashing on the shore and images of Joey's abs floating in my head.

I wake up before my alarm on Saturday morning at five-thirty. That seems to be the waking hour for me here. I dress in some workout gear and complete a Pilates workout. I grab a cup of coffee and enjoy it on the deck. I hear laughter and barking to my right, where I see James and Charley playing on the shore. He waves and heads further down the shore with Charley. Since James is awake, I rush to get dressed and head over for breakfast.

I knock on the door and let myself in. I see Joey shirtless in the kitchen holding a cup of coffee with his back to me. My heart rate increases tenfold. Holy moly — he's hot! He must have earbuds in or is lost in thought because he doesn't hear me enter. I walk up and wrap my arms around him, spreading my hands over his chest. He turns into my arms and kisses me.

"Morning, sweetheart. You're early."

"Morning. I saw James and Charley on the beach and figured you were up too. Do you want me to come back later?"

"Of course not! That isn't what I meant. You're welcome here anytime. I want you here all the time. I would have preferred you stayed here last night, in fact.

"Oh," I say.

"What are you cooking? Can I help?"

"Nope, you can't help. If I recall, the last time you cooked the food wasn't edible." I smile remembering what transpired that night.

"True but the cheesecake was delicious!"

"Yes, it was." He hands me a cup of coffee.

"Thank you. Just sit there and look gorgeous. I will cook." He points towards the island stool. James and Charley run into the house. Although James is fairly clean, Charley - not so much. She jumps on me and plasters dirty paw prints on my jeans.

"Charley!" I shout. "I'm sorry, Miss Gen. We were having fun and Charley got dirty."

"It's fine, James. Charley likes getting dirty. I will clean her up."

"James, why don't you go clean up and get dressed."

"Ok, Dad," James rushes off.

I round the island and search for a towel. I start searching and I hear a low growl and it isn't Charley.

"Genevieve, you're killing me," he says.

"What? I'm looking for a towel." It honestly hadn't occurred to me that I was bending down right in front of him. Once I realize it, I quickly grab a towel and wet it in the sink.

He says, "I'm perfectly okay with it, except we're not alone right now. At any other time, I would have shut off the stove and dragged you to my bed to make love to you. We will need to settle for a kiss for now." He pulls me into his arms, so we're touching from lips to knees, unfazed by the mess Charley is making. Joey kisses me deeply.

I take a small step back, noting my effect on him and smile widely while I seek out Charley. I clean her and the mess on the floor. I'm careful not to bend down with my ass towards Joey. While putting the towel away, he says "That burgundy bra is see-through. Do the panties match?" I blush, noting that facing him was just as enticing considering the deep Vee of my shirt. James' footsteps echo down the stairs.

"Oops! I was trying to be good." He laughs and starts plating breakfast. Just as we are sitting down to eat, Joey's phone rings. He excused himself and took the call in his office. It was a short one.

"Everything okay?" I ask.

"Yes and no. Mrs. Jones is ill and can't watch James today," he tells me.

"I will do it," I say, at the same time James asks, "Miss Gen, will you stay with me?"

We all laugh.

"You will?" Joey asks.

"Sure, we had a great time yesterday, but first Aunt Kelly will be here with some dresses for me."

"Are you going to the gala with Dad, Miss Gen?" James asks.

"He invited me. Are you okay with that?"

"Absolutely, ok. You will have a great time."

"Thank you, James," I respond. We finish eating and clean up the breakfast dishes. James rushes off to his room, saying something about a Lego set.

Joey turns to me "Thank you. I appreciate your help. Are you sure you are okay with staying here?"

"Of course. Why wouldn't I be?"

Choosing his words carefully, Joey says, "I'm very glad you want to spend time with James, but I don't want you to feel obligated to do so."

"Joey, I want to spend time with both of you. I will be sticking around here for a while," I say looking up at him and seeing recognition in his eye.

"You took the promotion? You took the promotion! I'm so happy for you. I'm so glad you will be moving here." He lifts me up and spins us in a circle, holding me tight. I look at him.

"I gather you're happy with this decision," I say grinning.

"Happy doesn't begin to cover it." He's beaming.

"I will have to go to training for a week. I don't know when that will be, but yes, I will be moving into the cottage permanently," I say. I slide down his body as he sets me on the floor. Purposefully, I don't step back right away. For the moment we are alone, and I want to savor the feeling of him so close to me - especially knowing he is leaving for the rest of the day.

"I should get ready for work. Come with me," he says grabbing my hand and leading me upstairs. We pass James' room where he is building a Lego set with approximately 750 pieces. The booklet shows he is on step fourteen. We look in on him. Joey tries to keep going,

"Wow, that is quite a project, James," I note, standing in the doorway.

"Thanks, Miss Gen. I love Legos. This is part of the City set. There are a bunch of sets that make up an entire City. One day I will have them all!"

"You're welcome." Joey all but yanks me away from the doorway.

"Sorry, I didn't mean to pull you away but we don't have much time before Kelly arrives," he says.

"Okay."

He guides me to the bench and walks into his closet. He comes out moments later, buttoning his shirt, with a pair of dress slacks on but not buttoned. His chest and abs make me drool. I'm mesmerized as he walks around the room getting ready. I had thought he looked good in casual wear, but a suit is even better. My thoughts flash to an image of him in a tux next weekend. I'm instantly wet. I sigh deeply.

"What was that for?" he asks as if he doesn't already know.

"Nothing," I say hoping he will drop it, but he doesn't.

"Sweetheart, what was that for?"

"I want to take that suit off of you and do naughty things to you," I respond, staring him in the eyes.

"As much as I would like you to, I have to go to work," he says, leaning down to kiss me.

I hear the doorbell ring and someone shouting.

"Hey, the party is here!" It must be Kelly making an entrance just like when we were younger.

James yells, "Yay! Auntie Kelly is here!" and takes off down the stairs - the Legos all but forgotten. Joey finishes dressing and reaches for my hand. We reach the bottom of the stairs as Kelly is bringing in a second set of garment bags.

She smiles when she sees us walking down the stairs holding hands. Kelly throws the bags over the couch and rushes over to me. She pulls me into a tight hug.

"It's so great to see you!" she shouts. Joey hasn't let go of my hand but clears his throat as if to say, *Hey! I'm your brother, and I'm standing right here!*

"Good to see you too, Kel," he snaps at her and she laughs him off.

"Hi, Joseph," James snickers off to our left.

"I'm here for Genevieve not you," she says, winking at him and letting go of me.

"I love you too, Kel." Joey smiles and walks past me towards his office.

"I'm so excited to see you, Kelly!" I say. "Thank you for helping me with a dress. I wouldn't even know where to start."

"I'm happy to help. Plus, with the press at the event, my dress will be all over the papers on Sunday morning," she replies. That revelation hits me straight in the chest. I'm a private person, more than ever since learning about my uncle. While I know Leonard is my biological father, Robert is my dad and always will be.

"Press?" I ask.

"Of course. The papers cover the gala each year. It will be easy peasy. They will take a quick photo of you and Joseph and ask who you are wearing."

"Oh, okay." I say. Deep down I'm still concerned. I will have to talk with Joey about this part later.

"Okay, ladies, I have to get going. Genevieve, can I talk to you in my office?"

"Sure. I will be right back Kelly," I say, following Joey.

"Did you clean up in here yesterday?"

I answer cautiously, "Sort of. After you left, there were papers on the ottoman. I brought them in here in case they were important. Why?"

"You didn't have to but thank you. I noticed after you'd left but didn't get a chance to ask you yet. Thank you again for staying with James. I will be back late. If you can get him to bed by eight that would be great."

"Okay, no problem."

"Please feel free to go to sleep, too. You don't have to wait up for me."

"Okay," I reply.

"I will be back later tonight. I love you." He kisses me and leads me back into the living room.

"Bye, James. Be good for Miss Gen. I love you."

"Bye, Dad. Love you too!" he replies and takes off to his Legos.

Joey bids Kelly goodbye and kisses me again before heading out the door. I stand there a moment reveling in my feelings before facing Kelly.

"So - you and my brother - back on again, huh?" she asks, laughing.

"It certainly wasn't on purpose," I say, before relaying the last few years of my life to her. She simply listens as we start trying on the gorgeous dresses.

"My brother was right. You're gorgeous and have filled out since I saw you last in a good way."

"Thanks, I think," I say quietly.

She laughs. "I mean you're gorgeous and not awkward anymore."

"Oh, Thank you."

I model dresses for Kelly, each one in amazing jewel tones like deep purple, cobalt, and emerald green. Each one as luxurious as the one before. Once I try on the emerald green dress, however, I know it's the one. The dress is emerald silk with a wrapped waist and V-neck. I walk out into the living room and Kelly jumps for joy.

"That is the *one*! You look stunning! I dare say my brother will be tongue tied when he sees you in that dress." Kelly is smiling from ear to ear.

"Thank you so much! Now I just need shoes."

She quickly replies, "No, you just need to pick a pair." She has laid out six pairs of shoes that will match the dress. "You can wear any of these and still be shorter than Joseph, so go as high as you can handle."

"I feel like a princess. You think of everything!" I hug her and try on a pair of sky-high sparkly heels that match the dress perfectly.

"Perfect," Kelly exclaims starting to repack the rest of the shoes. "Here, take this bag and box to put them in. I will go check on James while you change."

I head into the bathroom and change back into my jeans. I place the dress carefully into the bag. This is amazing. I'm excited to attend the gala now that I will be properly dressed. Thank god for Kelly! I grab a bottle of water and then browse the fridge and pantry for baking and dinner options. Kelly and James come downstairs.

"Miss Gen, I'm starving," he says rubbing his belly.

Kelly and I both laugh.

"Let's go grab some lunch with Auntie and then get some baking ingredients, what do you think?"

"Yay!" he exclaims, running to the foyer and hastily putting on his shoes. I grab James' booster out of Joey's car and Joey's scent wafts towards me. I miss him already.

We take two cars and meet at a small café that is open year round. Kelly and I order sandwiches and James orders a kid's staple - chicken fingers and fries. James leads the majority of the conversation, ranging from Legos to his upcoming birthday. After eating, Kelly bids us farewell and heads home. I peek at my phone once we are in the car and see some notifications, a few junk emails and texts from Joey and Kelsey. I tell Kelsey indicating that things are going well, then look at Joey's text.

Joseph: Thank you again for staying with James. I hope he is behaving.

Me: You're welcome. I'm happy to help. He is great, Joey.

I'm not expecting an answer, so I placed my phone down but I quickly get a response from him.

Joseph: How was dress shopping?

Me: It was wonderful. Kelly is very talented. Her gowns are beautiful. Thank you for thinking of her when you invited me.

Joseph: You're welcome. What are you up to now?

Me: We went to lunch with Kelly and now we're going shopping for baking supplies.

Joseph: What are you making?

Me: Don't know yet, it's up to James to decide.

Joseph: I will seek it out when I get home. I have to go back in now. I will see you later.

Me: See you later.

James and I head to the market to grab more baking essentials. When we get to the baking aisle James asks,

"What are we going to make, Miss Gen?"

"We have two options: apple crisp or sugar cookies with all the fixings."

He brings his index finger to his lips and says,"hmmmm, both are great choices. Let's go with the apple crisp." We walk up and down each aisle. As I rattle off the ingredients, James grabs them and adds them to the cart.

An elderly lady passing by touches my arm and says "Your son is adorable. It's wonderful you're teaching him about baking and budgeting. Both are necessary for survival. Good food is a great start for everyone."

At first, I think I should correct her, but I simply reply, "thank you" and she goes on her way. No one needs to know that I'm his father's girlfriend. *Girlfriend?* Yes, girlfriend. I took the job and I'm moving in a few doors down. Suddenly, I feel happy and warm all over.

"What else do we need, Miss Gen?" James asks expectantly.

"Apples, lots of apples and cinnamon and we're on our way."

We grab the remaining items and check out. The cashier compliments me on how polite and helpful my son is. I thank her as well offering no further explanation. When we reach the car, I can see James is upset.

After hopping into the back seat, he asks, "Why did you tell her you're my mom?"

I'm treading lightly here. "I'm not trying to replace your mom, James. From what your dad has shared with me, she was a strong, hardworking woman who was taken from you too soon. I just didn't want her to ask us a bunch of questions that might have been difficult to answer. In the future, if you would prefer, I correct someone who thinks I'm your mom, I can do that."

He gazes at me and says, "I want to think about it for a while."

"Okay, James. When you are ready to talk about it more, you let me know." The rest of the ride back to the house is quiet. However, once we're unpacking the ingredients, James starts buzzing about the baking. He doesn't mention the mom stuff. After peeling, cutting, and setting up the toppings, we make six individual apple crisp dishes and bake them.

"Are you hungry?" I ask James.

"Not really. Can we watch a movie before I go to bed?" I glance at the clock and reply, "Sure, we have plenty of time for that, and for some Lego building if you're up for it."

James rushes over and hugs me. I'm grateful he isn't upset about the store. He decides to play with Legos first. We spend about an hour and a half on the Lego City project. James indicates he is done with the Legos for today and wants to watch a movie. We leave his room and prepare the apple crisps for movie time and Joey's return. James scrolls through the available movies and selects *Cars 3*. We grab seats and settle in to watch. Once the movie is complete, James heads to his room with Charley closely behind.

"Miss Gen, will you come say goodnight?"

My heart swells a bit.

"Yes, change and brush your teeth. I will be right up," I respond. I quickly wash the dishes, place them to dry and recheck the front door and head upstairs to find James already changed and in his bed.

"Miss Gen, if I decide I want to, can I call you Mom? If I call you Mom will you die too?" *Oh James.* I do my best to keep my emotions in check and figure out what to say. I sit on the edge of his bed and reach for his hand. Charley has her head on James' ankles.

"As I said earlier today, your mom was a wonderful woman who died too soon. Whether or not you decide you want to call me Mom, I will be here for you. Whether or not, your dad and I get married someday, I will be here for you." James nods his head and throws his arms around my neck.

"Thank you. I love you, Goodnight."

My eyes tear up, but none fall.

"Goodnight, James. I love you too." I'm scared out of my mind about trusting your dad again, but I won't ever leave you, sweet James.

I leave James' room and walk straight to Joey's. It is about eight-thirty, but it has been a long day. I begin to wrap my head around the fact Charley is a traitor who is changing her allegiance to James. I'm okay with it. Realizing I didn't plan to sleep here tonight, I search in Joey's dresser for a shirt to sleep in. I find one from Northwestern and peel off my jeans and tee placing them on the bench. I open the French doors and take in some salty air. I hope James is content with my explanation earlier. I make it a point to tell Joey. I sit outside a bit longer.

Leaving the balcony, I search for paper to leave Joey a note. I look inside the night table and find a small pad of paper. I write a note asking him to wake me when he gets home.

I check on James. I approach the threshold of his room and Charley picks up her head. James is sound asleep. I pad back to Joey's room and turn on the TV. I opt for *Good Bones* on HGTV. I love the mother-daughter team and their remodeling projects.

JOSEPH

I have never wanted to get out of a work function more than I do tonight. I'd much rather be home with James and Genevieve. I'm so happy she decided to take the job and move into the cottage. I'd prefer she moves in with us but I understand that she thinks it's too soon. That makes me love her even more. I'm so happy to have her back in my life and I will not mess it up this time.

Realizing I'm not listening to the high roller I'm supposed to be schmoozing into a donation to the club, I refocus my attention on him, garnering a new sponsor after walking him through the steps to complete his donation. I quickly tally my night and decide I have been here long enough. I exit the large conference room and duck into my office. I pull my tie off and undo the top button of my shirt. I grab my bag, keys, and a coffee and head for the exit. I have somewhere better to be.

As I set the coffee on the roof of the Mustang, I spill it. I quickly reach inside, hoping there are napkins in the glove box. When I open it, a bunch of napkins fall to the floorboard, as well as an envelope with my name on it. I grab the napkins and clean the coffee spill, then I sit in the driver's seat and open the envelope. Inside there is a letter and a ring box. I don't dare open it before reading the letter.

3/28/2019

Joseph,

If you're reading this, I have moved on to a better place. I have cherished every moment that you, James and I have spent together over the last five years. Your visits were the highlight of my week. I want you to have the Mustang and use it. Create more memories with James.

My darling, Corinne, and I have discussed your intentions for our Genevieve. Aside from each other, she is the bright spot in our world, and she deserves your whole heart. If you get a second chance to love her, don't squander it. Enclosed is Corinne's engagement ring. I purchased it many, many years ago, using every penny I had. My hope is that you and Genevieve find your way back to one another.

Edmund

I open the box ever so slowly. Inside is an elegant diamond ring set in filigree-lined platinum. I close the box and stare out the window, lost in my thoughts. Has Genevieve even looked through Mem's jewelry? She probably hasn't been ready to yet. I put the car in gear and point myself back towards Genevieve and James. I replaced the ring box in the envelope and slide it back into the glove box. I'm deep in thought for most of the ride home. Should I simply give it to her? How would she feel if I proposed with it? It's her ring, whether she marries me or not. I can't keep it from her. I still have the ring I bought for her over a decade ago. I take a short break from my thoughts to focus on the road and realize that I'm about ten minutes from home.

It's a little after eleven when I pull into the driveway. I note Charley is a very bad guard dog. She hasn't even budged from wherever she is when I enter the house. Yet, Kelsey had said she was barking at her place. I leave my shoes in the foyer. I decide to put the envelope in my office for the time being. I lock it in the desk drawer. I find a note on the island from James.

"Here Dad, we made this for you. Love, James and Miss Gen." He has even left a spoon for me. I take a bite of the apple crisp on the island and it melts in my mouth.

Genevieve isn't on the couch. She must be asleep, or she would have come to greet me. I take the stairs two at a time and pause at James' doorway. I shake my head when Charley lifts hers, acknowledges me, and lies back down in her place. I approach my room and hear the television. Looking to the right, I note that she couldn't find a Gerard Butler movie and has settled for HGTV. I chuckle softly. I look to my left and I'm taken aback by the sight of her. She is sound asleep in my bed. The white sheets are tangled low around her tan, toned legs. Her auburn curls are spread on my pillow. She is wearing one of my college shirts tied at her waist, exposing her abs and a pair of barely-there burgundy lace panties. I'm frozen in place. She looks like she belongs here. I want her here always. In this moment, I realize that I will never hurt her again. She may gut me, but it will be her choice this time. I should have fought harder for her all those years ago. The thought makes my heart heavy. I hope Corinne and Edmund know their granddaughter's heart and I truly have a true second chance with her.

I finally get my feet to move and I sit on the edge of the bed. I place a soft kiss on her forehead. I sit there taking her in, the curve of her nose, the small lone freckle on her ear but she doesn't stir. I kiss her again and she stirs.

"Hi, sweetheart. You look sexy as sin in my bed wearing my shirt." Sleepily, she smiles.

"Hi. Thank you. What time is it?"

"A little after eleven. Go back to sleep, I will go to the guest room."

"No, I will move. I won't kick you out of your own bed." She tries to get up, but I gently hold her still.

"We need to talk about a few things anyway," she says, sitting up against the headboard.

"Is James okay? I just checked on him, he seemed fine." Joey asks quickly.

"Why don't you get comfortable. I promise everything is fine, but James and I talked about a few things. Also, he said a few things you need to know. It isn't bad." I lean forward and kiss her. She threads her fingers into my hair while I finish unbuttoning my shirt. I pull back and strip off the rest of my clothes, adding them to hers on the bench. Wearing only boxer briefs, I climb into my bed and pull her closer to me so that we are lying facing each other. My shirt has moved higher on her torso exposing more of her creamy skin. I gently caress her side as she starts to speak.

Her wide emerald eyes bore into mine as she relays her day with James to me. She cautiously tells me about the elderly woman in the store, the cashier, and the feelings James shared with her.

"I'm so grateful he opened up to you. Thank you for being there for him. How do you feel about it?"

"I was honest with him. He is smart, kind, and looks just like you did when you were young."

I lean forward to kiss her. She smells like lavender and vanilla. I want to keep her here in my home. In my bed. She moves even closer to me. I slide my hands down around her perfect ass and she hooks her leg over mine. I glide my hands up her back and under her shirt delighted to find she isn't wearing a bra. I reach back down and attempt to lift the shirt over her head, but it gets stuck. I laugh at myself as she reaches down and undoes the knot. I gather the fabric and lift it over her head. I gaze down at her. She is perfect.

"You're gorgeous," I say.

"You aren't so bad yourself," she replies, wrapping her arms around me. Her breasts are pressed against my chest. We lie there kissing and touching. The feel of her hands on me is driving me crazy. She reaches for my underwear, but I stop her.

"I need to leave those on for now, or this won't last as long as I want it to. I want to go slow, so very slow." Her green eyes stare back at me with passion and desire. She drags her hands over my erection and back up my abs and chest.

"Genevieve," I say. I roll to my left, pinning her beneath me. I grab her hands and hold them above her head.

"Leave your hands there," I command. I see a momentary pause of uncertainty.

"Do you want me to stop?" I ask her.

"No, I'm just - please don't stop," she pleads. I work hard to calm myself and take this slowly despite how badly I want her. How badly I need her. I kiss my way across her chest stopping to lick both of her nipples. Soft sighs escape from her lips. Her hips are moving under me, making it difficult to remain focused.

"Joey," she moans. I kiss her painstakingly slowly, moving over her belly and to her left hip. Her reaction leads me to believe the spot near her left hip is an erogenous zone for her. I glance up at her. Her eyes are closed, and she is biting her lower lip. Hot-so-hot is the first thing that comes to mind.

I glide my hands down her thighs to her toes and ever so slowly back up the inside of her thighs. I see goose bumps as she shivers. Instinctively, she opens herself to me. I place a few light kisses on her inner thighs and brush my tongue up her folds. She mumbles something that is unintelligible except for my name. I continue licking and nipping until she comes on my tongue. I blaze a path with my mouth back up to hers. She has her gaze towards the windows. I turn her chin so that she is looking at me. I see tears in her eyes.

"Talk to me, sweetheart," I say, choosing not to acknowledge the wetness in her eyes. She knows I see it though.

In a whisper, as one tear falls, she says, "I have never felt like that before except with you. I want you. I want to feel you inside me again." I gently kiss the tear away, slide my hand around the nape of her neck into her hair, and kiss her senseless. Her hands crawl down my back to my boxers. In a few quick movements, she tosses them on the floor. I gaze down at her and see unfiltered desire in her eyes. I had heard her very clearly, but I keep checking as I shift between her legs. Go slow as if this is the first time. I remind myself because it might as well be for her. I reach for the night table and she shakes her head whispering "I have an IUD." I nod and look into her eyes. I make a small movement forward into her. I feel her tense and then relax taking a deep breath. I push forward again and again until I am fully surrounded by her tightness.

"Joey," she says. I start to move, and she moves with me. I thrust forward and she responds. Our mouths are locked together. Her nails dig more deeply into my back as she gets closer to orgasm.

"Let go, sweetheart," I say, against her mouth. Her head falls back, she says my name, and falls over the edge. I follow her over. I take my time calming myself, burning each second of this moment in my mind. It's better than the first time only because we didn't know what we were doing then. I shift off of her. Her eyes are on mine. Her hands are on either side of my face as she pulls me closer to kiss me. She licks her way around my mouth before crashing her mouth onto mine. Soon thereafter, I move to get up.

"Don't go yet," she says.

"I will be right back. I'm just getting a towel for you." I hurry to the bathroom and wet a towel with warm water for her. I see my reflection and realize I'm truly happy again, not because of what just happened but because she's back in my life. I need a plan to regain her trust fully and completely. Having made love to her is a huge step in the right direction.

I rejoin her in the bed and use the towel to clean her up. Once I'm done, she grabs my shirt from the bench, as if to leave.

"Stay with me," I say, patting the bed.

"Are you sure?" she asks.

"Yes," I reply simply. She turns, drops my shirt back to the floor, and presses herself against me. I wrap my arm around her waist and pull her even closer, feathering kisses on her neck and ear. She draws lines on my arm with her finger.

GENEVIEVE

I'm lying here in Joey's arms in his bed. The experience was so many things, all the things! There has been so much upheaval in my life these past six months. I had given Joey my whole heart all those years ago, completely and unapologetically, and he broke it into a million little pieces. Am I ready to give it to him again? Is it too soon? But I love him. I always have and always will. He is the love of my life. He is why I didn't get married. Things are different now. His mother is gone, and he appears to have put his foot down with his father. I sigh and realize that Joey's breathing has slowed. He has fallen asleep. I whisper, "I love you, Joseph James Cavallaro," knowing full well he can't hear me. I deeply sigh again, reach for my phone, and set a silent alarm for five in the hopes I can slip out before James wakes up. I snuggle deeper into Joey's arms and fall asleep.

It feels like I have only blinked when the alarm starts going off. We're in exactly the same position we were when we went to sleep. After shutting off the alarm, I rotate in his arms and caress his face.

"I love waking up with you," he says before even opening his eyes. His hands slide down my body, waking up every nerve ending along the way.

"Bonus points for you being naked too. Inquiring minds want to know, I want to know, do you always sleep naked?"

I laugh quietly. "I usually sleep with a small amount of clothes, like a tank and panties only sometimes naked. I love waking up with you too, but we need to get up. I'm not ready to explain this to James yet. Are you?"

He frowns, "I know in my head you're right and that we should be downstairs by the time he wakes up, but I don't want to let this moment go yet. I want to make love to you again," he says, pulling me on top of him. He opens his sleepy eyes to gauge my reaction to his suggestion.

I bite my lower lip and ask, "What time does James get out of bed? Do we have enough time?"

"There is always time," he replies.

"Such a guy answer, Joey" I respond. He smirks at me as he rolls us both over so that he's hovering over me. He presses his lips to mine, and I realize I don't want to win this argument. In no time, we're furiously touching, kissing, and grinding. He pushes deep inside me and I feel full and sated as we both tumble over the edge again. He lowers himself next to me and traces the curve of breasts while we come down.

He jumps out of bed like a rabbit and reaches for my hand. He rounds the bed and gently pulls me to my feet. I follow him to the bathroom. I haven't been in here before. I'm seriously in love with this bathroom. There is a double vanity with Carrera marble counters. The marble is white with grey veining. The shower is huge. It has two showerheads plus a rainfall showerhead in the center. The tiles match the vanity counter and are laid in a herringbone pattern. As if that wasn't enough, there is a huge soaking tub, too.

"Earth to Genevieve. What are you thinking?"

"This bathroom is insane, babe!"

"You didn't ogle it last night?" He asks as if that were impossible.

"No, I didn't even come in here. I was either on the balcony or watching HGTV in your bed."

"It's seriously messing with my head that you were on the balcony in only panties and my shirt last night."

I smile and look up at him. "No jealous response required. No one was on the beach and your shirt untied is long enough to be a dress on me. I wasn't out there very long."

"Good to know," he says, reaching in to turn the shower on. He walks to the closet and pulls out two large plush towels, placing them on the rack. He opens the door and gestures for me to enter. I don't think twice. I stand under the rain showerhead for a little longer than necessary. He wraps his arms around me. Even though time was short, I draw my hands down his chest and abs, and around his waist up to his shoulders. After a lot more exploration and a notable reaction from Joey, he moved under one of the other showerheads.

"I love your shower! I might never leave!"

He laughs. Although I want to stay in here and make love again, we need to maintain our cover for James. Joey quickly finishes washing and leaves the shower. I suppose I should do the same. I take a quick shower and step outside. Joey hands me the remaining towel. It is warm. I stare at him.

"What?"

"I repeat, your bathroom is insane! A towel warmer, just what every girl needs." I say luxuriating in the warmth of the towel.

"Do you have a toothbrush, I can use?"

He pulls a brand new one out from under the sink and hands it to me. I rip it open and add the paste. I pad back into his bedroom and find him standing naked in front of his dresser. Seriously, Gen! Take it easy. It hasn't even been half an hour and that was after ten years of nothing! From the looks of him, he is ready to go again as well. I gather my thoughts and tuck them away. It just occurred to me that I don't have anything clean to wear.

"Do you have another shirt I can wear?" I ask. "I don't have anything clean here." I watch him put on boxers and a pair of shorts.

"I'm sure I have a shirt, but that is about it. Once I'm dressed, I will run over to Mem's and grab you some fresh clothes."

"Just a shirt is fine. I will wear these jeans and change after breakfast."

"Are you sure? I don't mind and I can be quick." He winks at me.

I laugh. "I'm sure you can, but I think we have already pushed our time a little." At that moment, Charley comes trotting into the bedroom.

"See, we're out of time." I smile at him and finish getting dressed.

We head downstairs and I let Charley out. Aware of the limited sleep we both had last night, Joey wisely starts making coffee. I watch him make our coffee and can't help but remember last night and this morning. I'm in deep already. It's happening so fast.

We sit at the island drinking our coffee. James plods down the stairs looking for Charley.

"Good morning, Miss Gen and Dad. Where is Charley?"

"Morning," we say in unison, laughing.

"Charley is outside."

"What do you say we go out for some breakfast and take a trip to the Nubble Lighthouse?" he asks both of us. James immediately rushes back up the stairs. I place my cup in the sink and turn to leave.

"Don't go yet. I want to put these few minutes alone with you to good use," Joey says, planting his lips on mine.

"I think we used our alone time last night and this morning well," I say, smiling up at him. We go from kissing to steamy very quickly. I place my hand on his chest and slowly take a step back. He immediately pulls me back into his arms. I sigh and sink deeper into his arms. Soon thereafter, he slowly releases me. As I step away, his expression is hard to read.

JOSEPH

While gathering her stuff she says, "I will take Charley with me to the cottage to feed her. I will change as well. I can be back in twenty minutes or less. Does that work?"

I wait too long to answer.

"Joey, are you okay?"

"Yes, I'm sorry. I was thinking about what James said to you yesterday and how he didn't even blink that you are here this morning."

"Okay, I will be back in a little while," she says, going up on her toes to place a short kiss on my lips before heading for the door.

As she turns the knob, James asks, "Dad, what kind of clothes do I need? I watch the front door close and shake my head as I walk upstairs.

"Will these work?" James asks as I step into his room.

"Yes, those will be fine," I respond, James begins putting on his clothes.

"How was your day with Miss Gen?" I ask, wanting to leave it open to see what he is willing to discuss with me.

"She picked out a dress with Auntie Kelly. I saw Miss Gen walking by with a bunch of different ones on. I saw purple, green, blue and white flash by my door. I don't know which one she picked. We had lunch with Auntie and then shopped for baking ingredients."

"Wow! You were busy," I say.

"The lady at the store told Miss Gen her son was very polite, and Miss Gen didn't say she wasn't my mom."

"How do you feel about that?" I carefully ask him.

"I know I just met her, but Miss Gen is awesome! She's fun, she bakes, she's nice to me, and I love her. Is she going to leave us? You said she was on vacation. Is she going to live with us? Are you going to marry her? I would like her to be my mom someday."

"Genevieve is awesome. I'm so glad that you love her. As far as your other questions, I love her too. I have loved her for a very long time. Miss Gen was offered a new job and she will be moving here soon, but she will need to go away for about a week for some training. I would like to marry her someday, so yes, we would live together then."

James leaps into my arms and says, "I'm so happy, Dad. She makes you happy, too!"

"She does, James. She does." I stare at my son, slightly taken aback by his observation. He has no issues expressing his feelings for Genevieve despite the loss of his mother. I might be doing something right, or it could just be how amazing she is.

"Let's go. I'm starving!" he says, grabbing my hand and trying to drag me downstairs.

"Hold on. I need socks and shoes first."

"Okay, I will be downstairs." He rushes down the stairs.

I walk into my room and let out a deep sigh. Not only am I in love with her but my son is, too. While I want her to live here, I understand she wants to live at Mem's. We should talk about her renovations. I'm not a fan of her sleeping on the enclosed porch alone. I mindlessly grab some socks and head downstairs. I find James reading aloud from the book he started with

Genevieve. I sit next to James and listened. I hear the doorknob twist and see Genevieve return dressed and ready to go with fresh coffee.

"All set?" I ask her. "Yes, I'm hungry."

"Me too!" James says, leaving his book on the ottoman jumping from the couch.

"Where is Charley?"

"Charley is at the cottage. We can't bring her to the restaurant," Genevieve states.

"Let's eat." James shouts as he jets out the door to the car.

I happily accept the coffee, place a kiss on her forehead, lead Genevieve to her side of the car and open her door.

"Thank you."

We sit at a quaint café that I have never been too and eat insanely decadent breakfast dishes. James' pancakes are piled high with all kinds of fruit and whipped cream. I catch myself staring at Genevieve. She is perfect. Busted! She looks over at me and smiles. I need her smile in my life every day, but I can't rush it. We wrap up our breakfast and drive towards the Nubble Lighthouse. Genevieve and I used to come here on occasion once we were old enough to drive. She always said she wondered what it looked like inside.

As we wind over the road towards the point, I see a sense of calm come over her. Immediately, I feel a pang of guilt. It's my fault she left and had never returned until now. James has been here a few times a year but mostly for Dunne's ice cream. If I recall correctly, it was called Brown's when we were kids, and it was further down the road than it is now.

She hurries out of the car and closes her door too quickly for me to do it for her.

"I was going to get that," I say to her.

She replies, "I'm sorry. This place is so magical to me and I didn't realize how much I missed it until now." I pull her into my arms and block out the snickers coming from right beside us. We walk hand in hand towards the rocks and look at the stately lighthouse. I look down at our hands between us. They are a perfect fit always have been. We soak in the salty air and watch the waves crashing for a bit on the rocky outcropping. James is already itching to leave. I ask him to sit on the rock with the Nubble placard to take a quick photo. He resists, but I want to keep a record for him. I have one from each of the other times we visited here. He asks Genevieve to join him and she does. I take their photo. I am so happy he is as taken with her like I am. A sweet couple offers to take a family photo of us. In this moment, I completely understand why Genevieve handled the cashier as she did. I don't want to explain our family dynamic, but on the flip side, I want us to be a family. I gratefully accept their assistance and join Genevieve and James on the rock. The gentleman asks us to say 'cheese' and takes a few photos. I thank him and we walk back to the car.

"Could you send those to me?" Genevieve asks when we get to the car.

"Of course." I reply. As I scan the photos, I see one of just Genevieve and I as I moved towards the rock. Not only can I see my future clearly, but I see she feels the same way. I just need her to say it to me out loud.

"Ready to go?" I say noting she is looking at her phone.

"What's wrong? Is it Collette? Kelsey?" I ask grabbing her hand.

"No, it's Jessie. She wants me to be there tomorrow at noon to start the training."

"Oh, sweetheart," I say, reaching for her hand.

"I know you don't want to give up your vacation, but you earned a promotion. You knew you would need to leave eventually."

"I know you're right, but I was hoping I would be able to have one more week. Jessie has arranged to train me herself so I will be in Rhode Island, but I will not be here with you and James." She pouts.

I can't stand that look on her face.

"Genevieve, we can do this. I will miss you terribly, but we made it ten years." She slowly looks up at me.

"We can make it a week. Let's go grab Charley and take a walk on Short Sands. I also want to see the plans for the cottage you created. We, and by we, I mean you, can whip up dinner and then we can tell James."

"Okay." She says quietly. She responds to Jessie and asks Kelsey if she can stay with her, then she gazes out the window as we wind our way down the hill. The ride to the cottage is largely silent. Either James feels the tension or is simply not paying attention. I pull into her driveway-our driveway - no, it 'll always be hers regardless of whether I own part of it. James rushes to the door. He opens it and Charley bounds out down the stairs and towards the shore.

"Can I go with Charley, Dad?" he asks.

I nod and say, "Don't go in the water and stay behind Mem's cottage so we can see you."

"I will." He shouts, already halfway to the shoreline, with Charley running circles around him. His laughter soothes my dad-heart. I find Genevieve in the kitchen making coffee.

"Another cup?" I ask.

She turns to me, "I'm not sure what else to do. I can be packed very quickly. The rest of my stuff is in Kelsey's storage unit. I will need to arrange to have it brought here."

I stalk over to her, kiss her speechless, and softly say,

"Breathe, sweetheart." I see her eyes well up, but just as quickly, I see her shove her emotions back down. I decide not to mention that I have seen them.

"Let me get you the plans while I gather a few things to pack," she says. She walks into the office and brings out her drawings. She places them on the counter. I can feel her heat and I smell vanilla and something new today.

"You smell different. New lotion or perfume?"

She finally smiles for the first time since the email from Jessie.

"I ran out of my regular one. The backup is vanilla and cinnamon. You prefer the lavender?"

I lean down to her and place a few kisses on her neck.

"I love them both." I say, as I kiss my way into the V of her shirt. She sighs and turns towards me. I pull away when I hear footsteps on the porch, and I believe I hear her whine. James and Charley bound into the house and plop down on the couch. I turn my attention back to the remodel plans.

"Wow, these are surprisingly detailed."

"Thanks. If I'm going to spend money, I want it to be perfect, but I don't want to change their room at all." she says, looking out towards the water. "Is that crazy?"

"No, of course not. This was their home and you want to preserve it, but also make it functional for you. I believe they wanted you to have this home and they would be fine with whatever you decided to do with it, sweetheart. I don't know anything about remodeling, but this master suite you designed is perfect and you rearranged this floor while adding function as well. Have you reached out to any contractors yet?"

"No, I was just doodling a few days ago and this is what I came up with?" she replies.

"If this is doodling, I can't imagine what it would look like if you had time."

"Thank you. I'm adding towel warmers like yours though. A girl could get used to having those." I smile down at her.

"You can use my towel warmers anytime you would like."

She laughs.

"I'm going to just assume that comment is about the actual towel warmers."

"Genevieve, it's going to be awful being away from you next week. I want you with me- with us all the time. I'm saying you can use the towel warmers, the kitchen, the shower, my balcony - all of it, any time you want. I would give you your own key if the front door code wasn't already set to your birthday."

"Joey, really? All this time."

I kiss her lips lightly.

"Yes. All this time. My code to the house has always been your birthday. I picked it when I was ten or so," I respond.

"I don't know what to say," she replies.

"The words are on me this time. I meant it when I said I would apologize every day for the rest of my life. I should have stood up for you, for me, for us — but I'm doing it now. We will be here for you when you finish your training. I love you, Genevieve. I always have."

She reaches for my face and starts to speak, "Joey, I -"

"Dad, Charley just puked on the floor!" James yells from the living room as if he were in the next county. Damn it! Why does she always get cut off just when I feel like she may tell me she feels the same? I drop my head resigned to the fact our discussion is over for now, I reach for the towels while she chases down Charley to clean her up. Once Charley is cleaned up, we head out for a walk on the beach. We turn left towards the cavern. I don't think it's a conscious decision. Genevieve and I both simply turned that way. We are walking hand in hand with James and Charley off to our right near the water. They are splashing and having fun in the freezing water.

I recall it having taken longer to walk to the cavern when we were younger. To be honest, I haven't been here since I left for college. There were too many memories with Genevieve here. I have never even brought James here until today.

"What's wrong?" she asks me. She must feel the tension radiating off of me.

"I was thinking about the last time I was here," I reply. As if she could read my mind and knows it was with her.

"Oh," she says.

"Genevieve, I don't think you understand. The last time I was here was right before I walked away from you. I have not once come back here in the last ten years." I think I may have shocked her. She stops walking and looks up at me, speechless. Although she is a thoughtful and purposeful decision maker, staying quiet is not her strong suit.

"Really?" she asks almost too quietly. I barely hear her.

"Yes, I have not been back here without you. It was our space and I couldn't bring myself to draw those memories back to the surface knowing I didn't have a chance in hell with you. I thought about coming here after a few of my talks with Memére, but it just didn't feel right." Tears are creeping down her cheeks.

"And now?" she whispers. I slide the pad of my thumb across her cheek to wipe her tears away. She leans into my hand.

"Now," I pause, reaching for her hands bringing them to my mouth to kiss them, "Now I want to walk in there with you and start over. I know the past is part of us, but nothing bad ever happened here. We were just us here. Will you join me?" She nods her head and follows me into the cavern.

GENEVIEVE

I follow Joey into the cavern, and I'm flooded with memories of us. All of them are wonderful except the last one. I stand tucked under his chin, his arms around me, mine around him, taking this place in again. Like him, I haven't been back here. I had loved it here. I could get away and spend time with Joey here. I was myself here. I was only truly myself with Joey. James is running around in awe of this place. His reaction is like a flashback to when we first found it. I lift my head and see that Joey is having a tough time being here.

"Do you want to leave?" I ask. He shakes his head no. I release him and call James over. I reach for his hand and take him further into the cavern to explore, giving Joey time to handle his guilt, or whatever he is feeling at this moment. Joey takes a seat on one of the rocks and I continue to lead James further away.

I'm not sure how long James and I are exploring but Joey joins us. He reaches for my hand and intertwines his fingers with mine. I look at him questioningly. He nods at me, indicating he is fine and talks with James about this fantastic place.

"It's pretty cool, right?" Joey asks.

"Dad, when did you find this place? It's so awesome!" Joey shakes his head and tells him that we found it together when we were ten or so. Astute as ever, James says, "But you don't come here anymore."

"Not until today." Joey replies. I look at him and he smiles at me. Oh, how I have missed his smile. James indicates he's hungry. I check the time and it is a little after three. I decide I should tell James about work.

"James, I have something I need to tell you." He comes over and sits next to me. Joey is holding my hand for support.

"I have to go back to Rhode Island tomorrow morning for training," I tell him.

"Already?" he asks, "I thought you had one more week here!"

"I thought so too, but because of the promotion, I need to go back sooner than planned. I will be back one week from right now. I have decided to live at Mem's cottage after my training and to work from home like your dad."

James looks up at me and I see a mixture of sad and happy emotions crossing his face.

"Hold on, did you just say, you have to leave, but when you're done with training, you're moving here?" he asks me.

"Yes, I will be moving here."

James leaps up and throws his arms around my neck hugging me with all his might.

"I'm so happy, Miss Gen! I love you and I'm glad you are going to stay."

"Me too. I love you, James," I reply. Joey squeezes my hand as I respond to James. James lets go of me and heads out of the cavern.

"Thank you," Joey says, as we stand to follow James.

"For what?" I ask.

"For walking with him so I could handle being here again. For loving him. For giving me a second chance. For telling him you need to leave for a while. I was dreading that conversation. He is going to miss you. Hell, I'm going to miss you so much."

"Thank you. I will miss you too. I will talk to you every day. I never wish to speed up time, but I hope this next week flies by. I will meet you for the gala and come back for good next Sunday," I say, looking into his eyes.

James is standing at the entrance of the cavern ready to head out. Joey raises his finger, indicating he needs a minute. We are standing face-to-face in our spot. So many emotions are coursing through me and between us right now. I slide my hands up his chest and around his face. I rise up onto my toes and lightly brush my lips on his.

"I love you," she whispers as if my life just changed. Deep down I know it changed the moment I handed James his ball on the beach two weeks ago.

"I love you, Genevieve. I always have, and I always will. I plan to show you every single day for the rest of my life. Let's go. The sooner we face this week, the sooner it will be over."

We stroll back to Mem's cottage. My emotions are raw and mixed right now. I still can't wrap my head around the fact the cottage belongs to me or that I'm putting my heart back out there for Joey and James. Charley and James skip up the steps and head inside. James asks to help me cook dinner. Lucky for him, I only have ingredients for my favorite comfort food — mac and cheese.

We start bustling around the kitchen setting water to boil and slowly mixing the cheeses. Joey watches us intently. I catch his eyes and mouth, "Are you ok?" and he simply nods yes. I know he's in his head, deep in thought about something. It's the same look I saw the last day we were together, so long ago. Get it together Gen. It doesn't have to be bad.

Joey comes into the smallest kitchen ever to gather the place settings. We collide as I'm preparing to drain the pasta. The heat of his body near mine makes my whole body tingly. He puts his hands on me to steady us and takes it to a whole new level. I'm keenly aware we're not alone. Luckily, the water only splashed on the floor. I pour out the remaining water and set the pot on the rack. Joey scoots behind me to get towels to clean the floor. For the love of all things, his whole body grazes mine. It's clear I'm not the only one fighting with my libido right now. It doesn't take much for heat to pool between my thighs. I look at him. Whether the collision was intentional or not, I see the same desire I feel staring back at me through his eyes.

Joey dries the floor while James sets the table. Joey grabs drinks and we sit to eat. We eat quietly until James asks if Charley can stay with him while I'm training.

I answer him as gently as I can.

"I'm sorry, James. Charley must come with me. She has a vet appointment on Wednesday for her physical. Her boarder was going to bring her in for it while I was away, but Kelsey picked her up early for me." James makes a sad face but goes right back to his dinner.

"Once she gets her physical, I'll have time to find a vet for her here."

"Okay, Miss Gen. I understand," he says, bringing his plate to the sink. He washes his hands and heads to the couch. Charley is hot on his heels as soon as he stands. I have lost my dog for good now. I sigh.

Joey and I finish eating and clean up the kitchen. I turn to him." I need to pack. Can I stop by when I'm done? Why don't you take Charley with you, so I have an excuse to come by in a little while?" I wink at him.

James and Joey leave with Charley and I dive into packing. I don't have a lot here yet, but I pack a few extra things like the folder from Collette, their wedding photo, and the keepsakes in the office making sure not to forget the sign with Memére's favorite saying 'Saltwater Cures Everything'. I will only be gone for a week, but it's all I have to remember her now. I still haven't been through Mem's jewelry box. That is the only item remaining in their room untouched. I climb the stairs and pause at their doorway. It will always be their doorway. I remove the box from the long bureau and carefully pack it as well.

Surprisingly, it only takes an hour to pull together my things. I send a text to Kelsey.

Gen: I will be at your condo no later than ten. I meet with Jessie at noon. See you soon.

I lock up and walk to Joey's. I lightly knock on the front door. I look inside and see that no one is downstairs. I turn the knob, but it's locked. I input my birthday, 0504, into the keypad and hear a faint click. I try the knob again and step inside. Oh Joey! My heart squeezes. I slide out of my shoes and note that Charley must be upstairs. I hear James and Joey talking.

JOSEPH

"I'm going to miss her," James says.

"I will too."

"Can she live with us when she gets back?" James asks innocently. I would love for her to move in with us too. I answer him simply hoping to move on from these thoughts for the time being. "Miss Gen wants to live in Mem's cottage when she comes back."

"I really like when she is here, Dad. She makes it happier." I look at my son and realize he loves her almost as much as I do. "I completely agree with you, and I hope someday in the future, we will live together. Goodnight James."

"Goodnight, Dad."

I descend the stairs and notice her shoes by the door, but I don't see her. I find her on the main floor deck, looking at the sky. I push the door open and she turns and steps into my open arms.

"That didn't take long," I say.

"No, I didn't bring very much stuff with me. Can you handle something for me while I'm gone?" I ask.

"Of course. What do you need?" I smile.

"I need there not to be training."

He chuckles.

"What do you need that I can actually accomplish, sweetheart? Getting rid of the training isn't in my repertoire."

She rolls her eyes at me. "I know. Just wishful thinking. Could you contact the internet company and increase the speed at Mem's? I think they only have basic and if I need to mirror my office computer, I need more than that."

"Absolutely. Just send me the account info."

"Thank you." She steps back just enough to look up at me.

"I don't want to go but I need to."

I pull her back into my body and kiss the top of her head.

"I know, sweetheart, I know. I don't want you to go either, but it must be done. I will meet you on Saturday before the gala. Gwen booked a room for us."

"Good." She replies.

"Is something else bothering you?" I ask her.

"Yes. No. It dawned on me while I was packing that not only will I have to see Daniel tomorrow, but once Jessie shares the news, I will be his boss."

"You handled Daniel and Lindsay very well at Kelsey's. I have no doubt you can do it again."

"You always know what to say," she says tightening her arms around me.

"I should go."

"Stay with me," I implore her.

"I want to spend as much time with you as possible. Just sleep in my arms tonight."

She looks up at me with so much emotion in her eyes and simply says, "Yes."

I unwrap my arms from her, intertwine my fingers with hers, and lead her to my bedroom. I notice she slows at James' door and peers inside. As we enter my room, we strip off the majority of our clothes. She sets an alarm on her phone and climbs into my bed. I round the bed and join her. I drape my arm around her waist, gently snuggling as close to her as possible. The scent of her surrounds me. I want this every single night. I place a few kisses on her neck and shoulders.

"Goodnight, Genevieve."

"Goodnight, Joey."

GENEVIEVE

I wake before my alarm goes off. I'm nervous about being late. Before I move, I take stock. I'm tangled in bed with Joey. He's warm and I feel loved and protected. This is really happening. I told him I loved him yesterday in our spot. I was utterly floored by the revelation that he hasn't been back there. I have no doubt he's being genuine. I could tell by his reaction.

"Good morning, beautiful. You're thinking very hard." How does he always know? It's as if he hears my thoughts.

"I know you, that is how I know." I turn to face him.

"How are feeling?" he asks.

I wish I did have to go but . . . "

He frowns as if that wasn't what he was asking. It dawns on me what he means.

"Oh, that kind of feeling. I'm sore but in a good way. I should get going. I can't be late." I move to get dressed. He places his hand on my arm and I'm still for a moment. I stand and pull on my clothes.

"Thank you for staying with me last night," he says.

"Thank you for inviting me," I respond. He starts to get up.

"Stay there. It's early for you to get up." I sit back down on the bed on his side and lean forward to kiss him.

"Drive safely. Text me when you get to Kelsey's, please." I steal one more kiss.

"I will."

I walk to the door and take a quick look back at Joey. He looks amazing all mussed up in the morning. Despite his pull on me, I walk into the hallway to find Charley waiting for me and let myself out.

A few stray tears fall as I collect my clothes from my cottage and head for my car. I glance back at the cottage. Don't worry, Gen. A week isn't that long. As I start my car and begin to pull away, I glance to my left to see Joey watching me from his porch. I park and run into his arms for one last kiss. This right here is what I thought would happen a decade ago.

"I love you, Genevieve."

"I love you, Joey." I walk back to my car knowing if I don't, I will never leave.

The drive back to Rhode Island is uneventful. Charley sits on watch out the passenger window for me. I pull into the visitor's spot at Kelsey's. I look at my phone and see a text from Joey.

Joseph: I miss you already. Have a wonderful last week at the office. Your home office awaits. I love you.

Me: I'm at Kelsey's. I miss you too. Thank you. I can't wait to decorate it! I'm giddy about it. I love you.

Hopefully, Kelsey is awake. I don't know if she worked last night. I have a little over an hour to get ready for work. I pull out my key and slide it in the lock. Everything is quiet. She must have worked last night. I throw my stuff in her guest room and set up Charley's food and water bowls. I take a quick shower and get dressed for work. I peek in her room and she is still sleeping. I'm surprised Charley and I haven't woken her. I make a fresh cup of coffee and leave her a note. I take a deep breath and head into the office for a countdown week. One wake-up down, four to go.

I arrive a bit later than usual, so everyone is in already. Some greet me and say congratulations while others simply say hello and walk away since they know I didn't get married. I walk straight to my office. As I approach the door, the pool secretary, Susan, starts rattling off the messages I've received. She hands me some packages I've missed, and details other information I need. As she sums up, she whispers, "I'm sorry about your wedding."

I reply, "Thank you. It was my choice and for the best. I will be at my desk until my meeting with Jessie at noon."

I walk into my office and close the door. It's walled with glass, and I decide to turn on the privacy shading for now. I toss my bag and purse on the side chair and sit to work. I quickly and efficiently sort through the messages, noting which ones require a call back and which ones don't. I realize that I don't know who will be replacing me and make a note to ask Jessie. I glance at my email and sink back into my chair. I have been gone for two weeks. My inbox contains 347 emails despite my away message. I refresh my coffee and start from the oldest first. After a solid forty minutes, I have culled my inbox down to just under two hundred emails saving only three of those I reviewed requiring my attention. I hear a faint knock.

"Come in," I say.

Jessie steps into my office, "Good morning. How are you? You look as if the cottage agrees with you," she states.

"Thank you, Jessie. It does." I decide to leave out any mention of Joey and James. Jessie and I aren't that kind of co-workers.

"Who will be replacing me?" I ask her.

"Right to the point. I like that. I was actually coming here to talk to you about your training and a few other matters, including that one."

"Sounds good," I say, gesturing for her to sit in the free side chair.

"The other executive managers and I were directed to streamline the copyediting department company wide. We need to lay off two staff editors here. Your staff editor position will not be filled, and we will be laying off one additional person. I'm telling you this out of courtesy; it has already been decided that Daniel will be let go on Wednesday.

"Oh," I say, very quietly.

"I will make sure you're offsite when he is informed, and we will announce your promotion on Thursday. As far as your training, you're scheduled to meet with HR and security to update some paperwork early this afternoon. I will forward you a list of your new duties. I need you to draft a memo with all of your open manuscripts, the hours needed to complete the editing, and whether you have a preferred editor to assign to each based on the subject matter."

"Thank you, Jessie especially for making the transition easier for me regarding Daniel. He will not take my promotion or his lay off well. I will attempt to steer clear of him as much as possible."

"You're welcome." She stands and leaves my office.

Immediately thereafter, Susan appears at my door with a large bouquet of flowers. I know by looking at them Joey sent them. She places them on my desk and hands me the card.

"These are wonderful," she says, turning to leave. I scan the card. "Thinking of you. Wishing you were here. Joey." Well, today is starting off with a bang. I grab my phone from my purse and see messages from Kelsey and Maggie as well as a voicemail from my mother which I simply delete. I'm not ready to hear anything she has to say. I tell Maggie that she can use the cottage in a few weeks.

Kelsey: Hey girl. Sorry, I didn't wake when you arrived. I worked until close last night. See you later.

Me: No problem. I will see you when I leave work today.

Then I send a message to Joey.

Me: Thank you for the gorgeous flowers. You didn't have to do that.

As if he is waiting for me to respond he texts back almost immediately.

Joseph: Every day is a reason to celebrate. Promotions are a big deal. I'm so happy for you.

Me: Thank you. I will call you after work.

Joseph: Okay.

I check the time. I have over an hour to tackle the emails. I set a reminder so that I'm not late and jump in. I search the inbox for key words and mark those to save for later. The rest I delete. This narrows the inbox down to a manageable thirty-two emails requiring my attention. The alarm sounds and I head to HR.

My time at HR takes up the rest of the day. Perfect! I grab my things, close my office door, and head to Kelsey's. Before I pull out of the parking lot, I call Joey. He doesn't answer so I leave a quick voicemail. I find Kelsey and Charley chilling on the couch. I collapse next to Kelsey and Charley crawls into my lap. Maybe she is still my dog. Nah, just an opportunist. James isn't here. I push that thought away.

Kelsey and I chat about my work, her work, Michael (which is not going well), and Joey.

"So how was it?" She asks.

"I don't know what you are talking about, Kels?" I blush, knowing full well what she wants to know. I am stalling trying to figure out what I am willing to share.

"Gen! You did! Come on, girl! I know it has been forever! Give me details!" she shouts.

"Kels, it was perfect. It was worth waiting for," I tell her. I'm hoping against hope that she will drop it.

"That's it? That is all you are going to share?"

I decide to turn the tables on her, "Yes, that's all I'm going to share. What about you and Michael? Give me some details, too."

"I haven't slept with him and I don't plan to."

"Let's eat!" she says bouncing off the couch towards the kitchen. Luckily, her second job is at a high-end restaurant and bar. She always has great food to eat. We sift through her take out dishes and settle in front of the TV for an episode or two of *Friends*.

JOSEPH

This is more painful than I thought it would be. Watching her drive away is crushing despite knowing she will be back. I feel renewed guilt for having left her. I turn and walk back into the house. I muddle to the kitchen and make coffee. James plods down the stairs, ready for school.

"Morning," I say.

"Morning, Dad. You aren't dressed yet."

"No, I'm not. I'm going up now. We need to leave in fifteen minutes. Grab some breakfast and pack your bag."

"Got it." he says.

I head upstairs and dress for the day. I don't have any appointments or conference calls, so I dress more casually than usual. James and I head outside to wait for the bus as if nothing has changed. Except everything has changed. I have a heavy feeling in my chest, and it sucks! James jumps on the bus and waves goodbye. I grab a water and head to my office. I grab my phone and text Kelly.

Me: Thank you for helping Genevieve with a dress for the gala. She had a great time with you and James.

Kelly: Anytime. She's amazing, Joey.

Me: She is, Kelly. I'm in deep all over again. Part of me wishes I was stronger the first time around but then I wouldn't have James.

Kelly: I'm happy for the both of you. I know you were in an impossible spot.

Me: Can you tell me what her dress looks like? I want to get her some jewelry for the gala.

Kelly: No, I won't tell you, but I will shop for jewelry to match the dress and send you a link to pay for it. What do you want to spend?

Me: Thank you so much! Just find what will match and I will pay for it. Love you.

Kelly: Love you, too.

I set my phone aside and focus on my inbox. Today should be light based on the event on Saturday evening. Instead of reading emails, though, I find myself rereading Edmunds letter and staring at Corinne's ring I pulled out of the drawer. She should have this ring. While I appreciate their sentiment, I want her to wear my ring. The ring I have been holding onto for the better part of a decade. I lock them back in the drawer and order flowers for Genevieve. I also set up two more surprises for her while she's training.

I clear out my work inbox and focus on my personal one. There are two about the gala and one from Collette. I handle the details about the gala and then review Collette's. Why is she emailing me? I wonder, but it's nothing major. She needs my personal information for the estate to properly transfer the cottage and the car to me. I respond and see a new message from Kelly.

She has given me two options - earrings and a ring or a necklace and a ring. The necklace looks like a V made of clear crystals and the ring has an Asscher-cut emerald with smaller diamonds on either side. Neither tells me anything about what Genevieve will be wearing although I was secretly hoping it would. I opt for the necklace and the ring. Lucky for me, I still have her class ring, so I know the correct size. I pay for the gift and arrange for delivery at our hotel in time for the gala.

I see the note Genevieve gave me with the internet account number for Mem's. I reach out to the company and upgrade the service at the cottage. It will be complete by Thursday.

I'm getting restless, so I change and go for a quick run on the beach. I turn to the right towards the village and follow my usual five-mile route. I end near Village Perk and buy a water to cool down.

The barista, Keeley, has my water ready for me. She motions me over to the pickup counter. It is not crowded today. Most of the tourists have been gone for a few weeks. "How are you Joseph? It has been a bit since you came in."

"I'm well. Thank you. And you?" She reaches for my hand. "I'm good as well. I was wondering, now that tourist season is over, would you like to have dinner with me on Thursday?"

"Thank you for the offer, but I have a girlfriend."

"Oh. No, problem. It's just I have never seen you with anyone."

I turn to walk away feeling like there has to be a better way to let her down. I turn towards the house. I will make it home just before James. I sit on the front porch waiting for the bus. Kevin, James' bus driver, waves me over.

"I just wanted to make sure everything is okay. Last time I dropped him off, James said the woman waiting for him was your best friend, so I let him go with her."

"I appreciate your concern for James. Her name is Genevieve and we've been friends since we were seven. She's moving back here this weekend."

"Perfect. Have a great evening, Joseph," he says.

"You too."

James jumps off the bottom step of the bus.

"Hi, Dad. How was your run?" he asks." "You need a shower. You stink."

I laugh.

"My run was great! How was school?"

"School was okay. Sophie's seat was moved next to mine today."

"Oh, who is Sophie?" I ask.

"Miss Gen didn't tell you about her. She's a girl in my class. She's quiet and reads a lot, but I like her."

"No, she didn't tell me, but I'm glad you like Sophie. She sounds a lot like Miss Gen was when she was younger." We open the door, and James immediately starts his homework.

"I will be back down in ten minutes."

"Okay." James replies. I leave James at the kitchen island doing his homework. I open the door to the shower and succumb to flashbacks of Genevieve's luscious curves with water raining down her creamy skin and perfect breasts. It hasn't even been a whole day, Joseph. Come on. I make quick work of showering and head back downstairs since taking matters into my own hand isn't an option right now. James is staring at a worksheet.

"Dad, I don't get this one." When I join him at the island and take a look at the paper, he says, "I think we should call Miss Gen. She helped me with my English homework on Friday."

"I would love to do that, bud, but she can't take personal calls during training. Let's give it a try, and if we can't figure it out, we will call her when she's finished for the day." He frowns but reluctantly agrees.

"Can we call her later anyway? I miss her. It's brighter here when she is around."

"Yes, we can. I miss her, too." My son's observation is keenly correct. It's brighter and happier when she's around.

GENEVIEVE

Kelsey must be working too much. She only makes it through one episode of *Friends*. I grab the dishes and clear them, then I text Joey to see if he's free to talk.

Joseph: I will always be available for you.

I try not to let the past creep into my feelings right now.

Me: Thank you again for the flowers.

Joseph: You're welcome. I'm going to call you; James wants to talk to you. Okay?

Me: Of course!

I walk into the guest room and close the door. I try and fail to silence my phone, but I answer it as quickly as I can. I had been expecting Joey, but James is on the other end of the line.

"Hi, Miss Gen. How was your training? The teacher moved Sophie right next to me in school. I'm near her all day now. I was having trouble with my English, but we figured it out. We were going to call you for help, but I think we got it."

"Wow, James! You had a busy day. Do you like having Sophie closer during the day? Of course, you and your dad figured it out," I say.

"Thank you. I do like that she is closer. Most of my classmates aren't nice to her because she is always reading. I have to go to bed since I have school tomorrow. Goodnight Miss Gen. I love you."

"Goodnight James. I love you, too." James hands the phone to Joey.

He asks, "Can I call you back in fifteen minutes or so?"

"Sure."

I set the phone aside to figure out my clothes for tomorrow and then pull out Mem's jewelry box. I take a deep breath and open it. Everything looks in order — her gold leaf brooch, the gaudy crystal bracelet she wore on every special occasion, her wedding band and Pepére's wedding band and her watch. I pull her watch out and place it on my wrist. She wore this everywhere. It's a simple silver face with black strap. I add it to my outfit for tomorrow. My phone rings.

"Hi!" I say.

"Hi, Gen. How are you?" Instantly, I knew it wasn't Joey on the other end of the phone.

"Who is this?" I ask.

"Really? We were engaged, and you still don't know who this is?" Daniel asks smugly. I wish I could just hang up the phone.

"I was expecting someone else. What do you want Daniel?" I ask, even though I truly don't care.

"I want you back in my life. I messed up. You were the best thing that ever happened to me." I listen with my mouth agape. He *what*? Is he out of his mind?

I compose myself and reply, "Daniel, you chose Lindsay. You lied to me repeatedly for the better part of a year! You used me for a promotion that you didn't even get! You took her on our honeymoon. I don't want anything to do with you." I hear him swear under his breath.

"But your mother said you were single and ready to get back together with me."

"Did she now? Well, I haven't talked to my mother about anything of substance for the better part of three years. Unlike you, I didn't have a backup plan waiting for me after the rehearsal." I pause and realize my mother using Daniel to get to me. I muse that even though I didn't know at the time, Joey was waiting for me. My heart swells. I'm miserable here without him.

"What did she offer you?" I ask.

"What do you mean?" he retorts.

"What did she offer you to find out how I'm doing?" He pauses for a little too long.

"She wants to know what you're going to do with the cottage and the money. She said you're rich now." Of course, she does! *How does she know about the life insurance?*

"Daniel, I will spell this out for you only one more time. I don't want to talk to you ever again. The information about my inheritance is none of your business. You can tell my mother you failed. We're not together anymore. We will never be together again. Don't contact me again. Do you understand?" I yell. Kelsey cracks open the door.

"Yes," he says. "Are you really rich?"

"Goodbye, Daniel." I promptly block his number in my phone and fall back onto the bed with a thud. Kelsey sits next to me on the bed.

"I'm sorry I woke you," I mumble, sitting up. She pulls me into a hug. "You didn't. I was going to the bathroom and heard you yelling."

"Apparently, my mother contacted Daniel to get the scoop on me since I won't talk to her."

"That conniving witch!" Kelsey says.

"I have a better word for her," I mutter. My phone rings and Joey's gorgeous face pops up on the screen. Kelsey excuses herself and heads to bed.

"Hi, Joey," I say, still calming myself down from my call with Daniel.

"What happened?" he asks noting my agitation. I relay the conversation with Daniel and the happenings of my day.

"I'm proud of you, sweetheart. You handled that well." he says.

"Thank you. How was your day?" I ask. He tells me the details of his day including his conversation with Keeley and Mr. Kevin and his lustful thoughts in the shower.

"Well, our shower time was short but full of delicious sights and touches," I say, hearing a groan come through the phone.

"You're killing me, sweetheart. I'm counting the days until I can have you in my shower again."

"So much for sleeping tonight. I will be dreaming of your hands and mouth on me in your luxurious shower!" I say coyly.

"That makes two of us!" Joey replies. We exchange goodnights and I turn out the lights and go to sleep. As I had expected, my dreams are filled with Joey's panty-wetting abs and skillful hands.

The next two days fly by. There are two bright spots. First, Joey sends me a box of taffy from a local candy shop, the Goldenrod, which Kelsey and I greedily inhale after work. She fills me in on the goings-on at her jobs. I know Kelsey's big dream is to run a special events bakery and that these jobs are small stepping stones to get there. The second bright spot is that by one in the afternoon on Wednesday, I'm out of work for the day. I'm grateful I will not be present when Daniel gets laid off. I will probably see him tomorrow or Friday. I stop by Helen's on my way to Kelsey's. I will have just enough time to change and take Charley to the vet.

I quickly change and get Charley to the vet. She is given a clean bill of health. I had texted Joey earlier, but he hasn't responded yet. Upon my return, I find Kelsey sprawled out on her couch. I grab her hand, check her fingers, and announce that we need manis and pedis right away. She agrees, and we're out the door again in ten minutes. The salon we use is run by an amazing woman named Estella. She embodies every grandmother, Nona, and Nana in one spunky package. Plus, she always fits us in. We spent more than an hour having our hands and feet scrubbed, massaged, and prettied up. During our time at the salon, Kelsey and I chat about Joey.

She says, "You've got it bad. You haven't taken his sweatshirt off since you got here except to go to work. You're sleeping in a t-shirt I have never seen before, so I'm assuming it's his. It probably smells like him too. Spill."

"I do. I have it bad. I'm terrified that it's happening so fast. But it isn't as if I just broke up with Daniel. I knew months ago that marrying him was a bad idea. I'm a planner, Kels. You know that. It just took me too long to see he wasn't the one for me and apparently a cheater as well. Joey is none of those things. He's kind, funny, an amazing father, and so hot! Yes, he crushed my teenage heart into a million little pieces, but now I know why and I forgive him completely. The problem is, I'm afraid to give him my whole heart again. The even bigger problem is that James has already stolen it." I sigh, Kelsey sighs, and so do the manicurists.

JOSEPH

Today has been a complete nightmare. Two of the vendors for the gala have backed out and I don't have any leads on replacements. I have reached out to Gwen and to everyone else I know except Genevieve, whose text from hours ago I haven't responded to yet.

Me: I'm so sorry I didn't respond earlier. There have been a few problems with the gala.

Genevieve: How can I help?

She really always does put others first.

Me: Do you happen to know anyone that can bake? Before you volunteer, not you. A photographer by chance?

Genevieve: I would do it for you, but I was going to suggest Kelsey. I don't know a photographer though.

Me: Really? She bakes! Is she available?

Genevieve: I will ask her. What do you need?

I list the items I need, and Genevieve says she will call me back soon. While waiting for Genevieve, I handle the issue with the photographer. Luckily, I find a replacement. Fifteen long minutes later, Genevieve calls me back saying Kelsey will handle the gala desserts. I almost literally do a dance of joy. I chat with Genevieve about her day and then collapse into bed.

GENEVIEVE

I wake up smiling. Today's the day! I'm ready for this promotion. The announcement is scheduled for ten this morning. Surprisingly, Kelsey is already up in the kitchen, and it's a mess.

"Morning" I push out as she hands me coffee. "You're the best. What are you doing up? Didn't you work last night? What time did you get here? Charley was barking his head off around three."

She looks up covered in flour. "I did work. I got home at two. I was knocked out by three. I called in sick for today and tomorrow for the gala preparation. Thank you so much for recommending me."

"Of course, honey. You will rock it and will have one more stellar event on your resume. One step closer to your very own company."

"You're the bestest bestie ever! You're as excited for me as I am. I love you!"

"Love you too."

"You're going to be late for your announcement if you don't leave now."

I squeeze her, careful not to get flour on my clothes, and rush out the door. I haven't been this nervous about going to work since my first day. My palms are sweaty, and my mouth is dry. As I enter the building, Susan hands me my messages and tells me she put a delivery my office. My phone chirps in my purse.

Joseph: Congratulations, sweetheart! I'm so happy for you.

Me: Thank you so much! I'm excited about the new job.

As soon as I finished responding I open my office door. I literally walk into a flower shop. There are roses everywhere, covering every surface in every color. I send off a message to Joey.

Me: Oh Joey! You didn't have to buy every rose in Rhode Island.

Joseph: Yes, I did. You deserve them and more. Congrats again. I can't wait to see you on Saturday. I love you.

Me: I can't wait to see you either. I love you.

I stand in awe of my office and hear a knock on my door. Jessie walks in and notes all the flowers. "Wow! Those are amazing! Are you ready?"

"Yes and no. Thank you for having confidence in me. I won't let you down," I say, as she leads me to the conference room. Jessie commands the attention of the room and announces the restructuring, her resignation, and my promotion. Applause erupts, and I'm bombarded with well wishes and good luck sentiments. I say a few words to indicate my excitement.

The rest of the day is a flurry of work as I set out my plan for my staff. Wow, *my* staff. I say to myself. I set up two in-person meetings for tomorrow and head home. I plan to gather my stuff from storage and pack it in my car. Joey and I exchanged texts during the day. He asked me to call James because he is asking for me. My heart swells at the thought. I miss James too. I call Joey but ask for James.

"I see how it is," he says.

"Don't be jealous," I retort. "I can and will talk with you later." Joey passes the phone to James.

"Hi James. How are you? How was school?" I ask.

"School was great. I really like having Sophie next to me. I miss you. When will you be back?" he asks.

"I will be back on Sunday around lunch time," I reply.

"Ok. I love you. See you then." I hear a thud and then Joey's laughter while he picks up the phone.

"I guess he's done chatting. You got more out of him than I normally do. He really likes Sophie."

"Yes, he does. Thank you again for the flowers. They're fantastic! I brought some to Kelsey's. I will bring the rest tomorrow."

"You're welcome. I miss you. I'm glad I will see you very soon."

I sigh. "I miss you too."

This Friday is even better than every other Friday because I'm only one day from seeing Joey again. Kelsey is already baking up a storm as I leave for work. I'm glad the vendor fell through. This is a big opportunity for her. I head to work with a skip in my step. I feel like things are falling into place. My workday is going along just fine until Daniel knocks on my office door.

"Can I come in?" he asks. In an effort to minimize the exposure of our failed nuptials I let him take a seat.

"What do you need?" I ask.

"I wanted to congratulate you on your promotion. I'm sure you heard I was laid off." I nod. He continues, "I want you to know I was wrong for the way I treated you. I realize you won't believe me, but I never meant to hurt you. I was trying to get ahead. You look amazing. What's different?"

Since we are at the office, I remain as calm as possible. "I want to be clear; I'm never going to get back together with you. Good luck finding a new job. I look different because I'm happy now. Please leave my office and don't contact me again." He stares at me in shock but nonetheless stands to leave. He turns back as he reaches the door, then shakes his head and walks out. I let out a deep breath that I didn't know I was holding.

I handle my last two meetings and make two trips to my car with the flowers. I leave one vase with yellow roses on Susan's desk. They're her favorite. I return to grab the last of my personal items and bid farewell to the office staff. I peek into Jessie's office. She waves me in even though she is on a call.

"Heading out?" she asks, after wrapping her call.

"Yes, thank you again Jessie. Good luck with your health."

"You're welcome. You earned it. Thank you." I turn and walk towards the elevator, box in hand. I walk to my car ready to tackle my new job but first I have to get to a real first date in forever where I get to wear a fabulous gown. When I arrive at the condo, Kelsey is still working in the kitchen. The counter, table, and island are all covered in baked goods or parts of decadent goodies.

"Do you want a hand?" I ask after I finish bringing in the flowers.

"Yes, please."

I change and jump in to help. Kelsey and I fall onto the couch at eleven. She has been baking, frosting, and prepping for sixteen hours.

"I'm exhausted but so excited," she says.

"I'm so happy for you, Kels!" Things are looking up for both of us. "We should get some sleep," I say.

I text Joey goodnight and crawl into my bed.

JOSEPH

When I left her for college, I thought it was the right thing to do. I truly thought my parents would cut me off. Now I know I was wrong — so very wrong. I crushed her heart and yet, by some miracle; she's giving me a second chance. My father plans on attending the gala tomorrow evening. I hope he will be gracious. I have double checked with the remaining vendors and everything is in place. Kelsey has jumped headlong into this opportunity. I'm looking forward to seeing her work. I have checked on the delivery for Genevieve and I have packed. I plan to spend the rest of the evening with James. I know he will have a blast with Norah, but I will miss him just the same. I'm looking forward to a real date with Genevieve even though it may be awkward for her. I send her a quick text letting her know I will call her later. James and I settle in to finish his Lego City project. After about two hours of building, we rush the kitchen for some snacks. After an Oreo dunking contest, we watch an episode of *Bunk'd* before James goes up to bed.

"Dad, can I call Miss Gen?" Sure. I will bring up my phone. After getting ready for bed, I hand James my phone and he calls Genevieve.

"Hello," she says. It must be on speaker because I can hear Kelsey in the background.

"Hi, Miss Gen! How are you? How is Charley? I miss you both. I wanted to say goodnight."

"Hi, James. I'm doing well. We miss you too. We're preparing desserts for the gala. Are you excited to spend time with Auntie Norah?" Genevieve asks.

"How did you know I was staying with Auntie Norah? But yes, I'm excited."

"Aunt Kelly told me when I picked out my dress," she replies unsure why it was a big deal.

"Oh, okay. I'm going to sleep now. Love you, see you soon."

"Goodnight James. I love you too," she responds.

I jump on the phone. "Can you hold on or do you need me to call you back?"

"Can you call me back?" she says.

"Of course, I love you," I say, with a smile on my lips simply from hearing her voice. "Love you back." She replies and hangs up. I settle James into his bed and listen to a chapter or two of his reading. I'm so glad he gave it a try with Genevieve.

I amble to my room and take in the beach sounds from the balcony. I grab the remote and watch some SportsCenter before turning in. Hours later, I wake in the chair. I have missed a text from Genevieve, and my neck hurts. I shut off the TV and curl up in my bed.

I don't usually get nervous the day of the gala. It isn't the speech. I give simple remarks and read the biography of the worthy recipient. This year is different though. I have a date. I have never brought a date to the gala, thinking it wasn't the best choice given my relationship with Stacia. I rise from bed and take a shower. I will dress at the hotel. Gwen will be here in about two hours to travel to Rhode Island with me. Despite my intention to, Genevieve and I haven't really talked about the logistics of getting ready or coming back on Sunday other than that I would leave a key for her at the front desk. I can't wait to see her. I check my bags one more time and start downstairs for coffee. I peer into James' room. He is still sound asleep. Hopefully, he will wake up before I have to leave.

After setting my bags by the couch, I grab a cup and sit out on the deck. When I was away at college, I missed the ocean the most. Nothing beats living near the shore. Having Genevieve back in my life and living on the shore is more than I could've ever hoped for. I just need to show her every day that I will never hurt her again to earn her trust again. I will tell her and show her every single day until she believes me. I gaze out at the ocean and let my feelings settle. Norah should be arriving anytime now.

Just as the thought crosses my mind, Norah steps inside the front door. I wave and walk inside.

"Good morning," I say to her.

"Good would have been at noon," she replies.

"I appreciate you rolling out of bed early for me," I quip.

"I love you too," she says smirking. She grabs my cup and drains the rest of my coffee.

"Of course, finish my coffee."

"Like I said, dear brother, it's early on a Saturday for me," she says dropping her bag at the foot of the stairs.

"Genevieve, huh?"

"You sure jump right into it despite your lack of coffee. Yes, Genevieve. You know the whole story, Nor. I believed Mom and Dad were serious in their threats and she suffered for it. I would love to go back and change things, but the reality is if I did, I wouldn't have James and well, that world doesn't sit right with me either. I'm lucky enough to be getting another shot with her, and I won't mess it up."

She looks up at me. Norah is the shortest of the three of us.

"How are you going to handle Dad tonight?" Blunt as always.

"I hope he will be gracious. He knows I started seeing her. We shall see."

Norah says, "I always liked her. Until I knew the full story, I never understood why you let her go. Happiness looks good on you, big brother."

"Thanks, Nor. I'm happy and James is as well. Charley may play a small part in it though."

"Who's Charley?" I laugh. "Charley is Genevieve's dog, who James has taken a liking to."

"I see," she replies.

James rushes down the stairs and wraps his arms around Norah from behind. "Hi, Auntie! How are you?"

"Hi James. I'm pretty good, and you?"

"Hungry, very hungry."

Norah and I laugh, and we hit the kitchen for some breakfast. I whip up some pancakes for them and wash the dishes while they eat.

"Can you bake, Auntie Norah? We stocked the house full of stuff for Miss Gen to bake with me tomorrow. Maybe we can get a head start."

"Miss Gen can bake, huh?" Norah asks him.

"Yes, she's really good at it, too," he says, as if that's the best quality ever.

"I'm sorry, James, but Auntie can only make box brownies."

Joy appears in his eyes.

"Perfect! We have those since Dad can't bake either."

Norah and I both laugh. We talk about their plans for the sleepover tonight and about house rules. I'm sure Norah will break as many as she can with James. Gwen arrives at eleven to pick me up.

"Hi, G-ma!" James says as she comes inside.

"Good morning, James! Hi, Norah." She hugs James. I gulp the rest of my coffee and circle the island to hug him too.

"Have a great time with Auntie. I will be back tomorrow around lunch time," I tell him.

"With Miss Gen and Charley, right?" I smile. My son is enamored.

"Yes, with Miss Gen and Charley."

"Perfect! I miss them. Love you, Dad. Have fun," he says, wrapping his arms around me and promptly turns all his attention to Gwen.

"Bye, G-ma. Have fun at the party for Mom."

"Goodbye, James. Thank you. I love you."

He replies in kind and waves her out the door. Gwen hands me the keys and gets into the passenger side of her car. I put my bags in the trunk and hang my tuxedo in the back seat. The ride to Providence is mostly quiet, other than some small talk. Although this is the third gala, Gwen is introspective each time.

GENEVIEVE

I'm up with the sun today. It's very early so I try to go back to sleep but to no avail. I'm even awake before Kelsey. I get up and practice some yoga poses. I quietly pack my things in the guest room into two bags, one for the gala and one to stay here. I will grab the stored items when I pick up Charley tomorrow morning. I throw on jeans and a tee. I will get ready at the hotel after helping Kelsey with dessert station set up. She has been adamant that she has it covered but I want to help.

Kelsey strolls out of her room just as the coffee finishes brewing. We exchange curt acknowledgments and drink our coffee. Once the magic potion reaches her brain, Kelsey runs through her set-up plan. She wants to be at the hotel by one. She estimates it will take two hours to place and organize the stations. That should give me more than an hour to get ready. We pack both cars and double check that we didn't leave anything behind.

We pull into the Biltmore service lot and park side by side. After stepping out of the car, before she goes into work mode, I place my hand on her arm.

"I'm so proud of you, Kels! This event is a big step for you. You've worked very hard. It will show and you will kick ass!"

"I love you, girl! You're my biggest supporter. I'm grateful for the opportunity." Over the next hour, we roll and carry the decadent desserts into the kitchen. Arranging them is a time-consuming task, but Kelsey is in control and making things happen. She kicks me out of the kitchen a little before three. I walk towards the front desk, taking in the beautiful lobby.

The clerk greets. "Good afternoon, Miss. Welcome to the Biltmore. How can I help you today?"

"Good Afternoon. I need to pick up a key left for me by Joseph Cavallaro." The clerk starts typing on a computer.

"Your name, Miss?"

"My name is Genevieve Harpin."

"Thank you. Here is your key to the suite. A package was delivered for you as well. Have a wonderful stay." I take both the key and the package and thank the clerk. As I turn for my bag, a tall, gorgeous, blue-eyed brunette who has overheard the exchange introduces herself.

"Hi, I'm Francesca Huntington. Are you here for the gala?"

I reach out my hand towards her.

"Genevieve. Yes, I'm here for the gala."

"So, you must be the current flavor of the month," she says as if it was a known fact that Joey doesn't settle down.

"No, I'm Joseph's girlfriend," I reply waiting for some witty retort that never comes. My reply indicates that I'm aware of his former dating habits. She appraises me.

"Wait, your name sounds familiar. You're the one that got away."

I look at her, surprised.

"I'm sorry, what did you say?" She guides me away from the desk.

"Joseph was honest with me when we started dating about seven years ago. He said he let the love of his life get away and that she could never be replaced. I knew from date one, we had no future." I nod, dumbfounded by her words. I was doing math; Francesca must have dated Joey right before Stacia. She continues.

"Joseph's description of you pales in comparison to the real thing. He didn't do you justice when he said you were stunning."

"Thank you," I reply, unsure of the appropriate response for that type of compliment, especially considering I had just finished prepping dessert stations with Kelsey.

"Take care of him. He's a good man. I'm glad the two of you found your way back to each other."

"Thank you. I will see you tonight," I say, in shock while I watch her walk away.

I take a few moments to settle my thoughts and proceed to the suite which is huge. I'm not sure why Gwen would book something so large for one night. There are two bedrooms and two bathrooms. Perhaps it comes with the gala planning. I set my things on the bed and grab a water from the sideboard, which also holds a fruit tray and packaged snacks like pretzels and nuts. I reach for the package that was waiting at the concierge. It's elegantly wrapped in silver paper with an arabesque design.

Genevieve,

I hope these work with your dress. I will see you soon.

I love you, Joey

There are two boxes. I open the slim one first. Inside is a necklace with crystals set in a V shape, which will compliment my dress. He didn't see my dress. Kelly must have told him. The smaller box was a ring box. I open it and see a beautiful emerald ring. I immediately try it on, wondering if it will fit. Of course, it fits. How does he remember my ring size? I text Kelly.

Me: Did you tell Joey what my dress looks like?

Kelly: Of course not.

Me: Then how did he know these would work?

Kelly: Oh, the jewelry. He asked me to tell him, but instead I gave him a few jewelry options. Which one did he pick?

Me: You're the best, Kel! He picked the ring and the necklace.

I snap a quick picture for her.

Me: Thank you, Kel.

Kelly: You're welcome. I will see you later.

I stare at the ring a bit longer and then place it back in the box. I haven't really talked to Joey about when he will arrive, so I decide to start getting ready. I take a long shower making sure I exfoliate and moisturize. I style my hair with half of it up and loose ringlets around my face and apply my makeup. Once I'm comfortable, I step out of the bathroom and search for something to eat. I make a small plate from the fruit tray and finish it quickly. I peek at the clock and realize I should finish getting ready. I wonder where Joey is. I unzip the garment bag, lay my dress on bed, and gather the rest of my outfit. I pull on my dress, shoes, and the ring. Hopefully, Joey can help me with the necklace when he arrives. The lock of the suite door clicks, and I step into the main room.

JOSEPH

I step into the suite, and I'm stopped in my tracks. She is breathtaking in that dress. The emerald color brings out her eyes and her auburn hair. I stare at her unable to speak or move. She walks towards me, slowly starting to smile at me. I take my time memorizing her in this moment.

"Hi," she says stopping right in front of me. After a few more moments of just taking her in, I'm finally able to say, "You look stunning, Genevieve."

"Thank you," she says just before sliding her hands around my face and bringing her lips to mine. After a few minutes, I pull back but continue to hold her in my arms. The heat from her body is searing my hand resting on her back.

"I missed you so much. Not seeing you, not holding you for a week has been pure torture," I tell her.

"I missed you, too. Thank you for the ring and necklace. You don't have to buy me things."

"I know. I wanted to. As much as I would like to stay here holding you, I need to get dressed. I was held up in the ballroom. Kelsey knocked the desserts out of the park, by the way." I reach for her hand and lead her to the bedroom. I sit her in one of the chairs and scurry into the shower. Despite my lustful thoughts of stripping Genevieve out of that dress and despite wondering what she is wearing underneath it, I resist the urge to take matters into my own hands. I hurriedly shower and towel off. I walk back into the room with a towel tucked at my waist. I find my tuxedo laid out on the bed. I swear I hear a low moan when she returns with the cufflinks and shoes.

"You need to put on that tux, or we will never leave this room," she whispers in a strained voice, running her hands across my chest and down to the top of the towel. I stop her from removing the towel altogether. I place a soft kiss on her lips, wrap my arms around her, and walk her out of the room.

I unwrap myself from her body and say, "I will be right out. If you stay here touching me like that, we will be very, very late for this party, and that's not an option."

Not ten minutes later, I open the door to find my gorgeous girlfriend in exactly the same spot I left her. "What are you thinking?" I grin, thinking I know the answer.

She replies honestly, "Before you opened the door, I was wondering how long we need to stay at the gala before leaving. I want to be alone and naked with you. Now, I'm thinking that tux takes your hotness to another whole new level."

I smile at her and say, "We have to stay until the presentations are over and we need to dance at least once before leaving. So, I'm thinking we could be back here before ten." A smile breaks out on her face lighting up the whole room. I can't imagine going back to a time without her in my life.

"I can work with that. Can you put this on for me?" She hands me her necklace. I take it from her, place a hand on her waist, and slowly turn her back to me. I move her hair onto her shoulder and caress her exposed skin with my lips.

"Joey," she sighs. My hands cross her face to clasps the necklace around her neck. I drag my hands down towards her waist, leaving a trail of heat from my fingers on her back. She turns in my arms and I place a light kiss on her forehead.

"Ready?" I ask.

She takes a deep breath and says, "Yes."

I reach out my arm and she takes it. She grabs her clutch on the way out and we ride to the ballroom alone in the elevator. I take the opportunity to hold her close to breathe her in. I feel her trembling in my arms.

"What's wrong?" I ask, afraid to hear the answer. Afraid she will not attend the gala with me.

"I'm just nervous. Not only is this our first real date in a long time, it's a really big deal for you and your family. Your family will be here, and Stacia's family will be here." I press every single button that is not illuminated to slow this ride to the lobby.

"Genevieve, I love you. I want you here by my side for the gala and every day after today. The only opinions that matter are mine, yours, and James' and he loves you." Even with the sparkly heels, she needs to look up at me. Her eyes glisten.

"Genevieve, will you accompany me to the awards gala?" I ask her once more, giving her the chance to stay in the elevator.

"I would love to, Joey."

The elevator opens and we walk towards the ballroom. Now, I truly hope my father is gracious tonight. We pause at the ballroom entrance and pose for the obligatory photos. Genevieve dutifully answers all the questions about her gown and its designer. She handles it perfectly. The ballroom is decorated in navy and white, the colors of Johnson and Wales. The ballroom is pretty full already. I lean close to her and whisper in her ear, "We're at table two." I see her shiver from my closeness and smile inwardly. As we approach the table, I see my father. He greets the two of us cordially. I also see Gwen, her husband, Jeffrey and their son, Scott. Kelly is there chatting with them. I leave Genevieve with Gwen and Kelly to go get drinks. I overhear chatter about dresses, jewelry, and fantastic shoes punctuated by laughter. I procure a drink for each of us and cut into their little group.

We are served the first course, and we eat in silence. I'm drawing circles on Genevieve's thigh with my fingers. The staff clears the plates, and I whisper I need to leave.

She nods and whispers, "I will be fine." in my ear. I give my father, who is sitting at our table, a look silently imploring him to behave, as I leave my seat to give my remarks.

GENEVIEVE

Joey walks towards the stage. He's confident and assured as he ascends the steps. At the dais, he begins his remarks about the scholarship recipient Brittany Jones. Joey describes Brittany as embodying many of the same qualities that Stacia possessed. Qualities that he hopes to pass on to their son. I reach over and grasp Gwen's hand.

She says, "she would've liked you very much. You're wonderful with James. Thank you."

I nod at her and mouth, "You're welcome."

Once Joey's remarks are complete, Brittany walks the stage to accept her award. I excuse myself to the restroom. Kelly joins me. Kelly gushes over how I look in the dress she designed.

"Stop it," I say, blushing.

"You look amazing, Gen. I'm thankful my brother contacted me."

"I am too. I never could have found a dress like this in time."

Kelly leaves to take a call. I notice that she doesn't have a date tonight, but that is a discussion for another time. Francesca enters the restroom while I am washing my hands.

"Hello again, Genevieve. That color is perfect for you," she says.

"Hello to you, as well. You look beautiful."

She places her hand on my forearm.

"Thank you. I saw you and Joseph earlier, in line for photos. You're a gorgeous couple. I have never seen him look at anyone the way he looks at you. I wish you both the best."

"Thank you. Enjoy the rest of your evening."

She leaves. I sit on the chaise pondering what just happened then I stand and exit the restroom. I see Joey talking with Francesca. She kisses him on the cheek and walks back towards the ballroom. He approaches me, taking my hands in his.

"I was looking for you. I heard you spoke with Francesca."

"I did. How long did you date her?" I ask him.

"We went to a few functions like this for the club, but we were never dating."

"Yesterday in the lobby, she told me what you said about me before your first date with her." I relay what happened to him. "Is what she said true?"

"Every single word," he replies, stepping closer to me placing a kiss on my temple.

I hear someone clear their throat. Samuel Cavallaro is standing off to our right.

"Can I have a word with you both?" He asked. Joey looks at me and sees silent acquiescence in my eyes.

"Of course," he replies to his father. I jump in before he starts to speak.

"Mr. Cavallaro, I have recently learned why your late wife did not want our families, especially Joseph and I, spending time together." I take a breath before continuing but he raises his hand and cuts me off. Joey tightens his grip on my hand. I squeeze it three times and gaze into his eyes. He turns his attention back to his father.

"Joseph, your mother and I felt we were guiding you as best as we could. I see now that we were wrong. I have never seen you so happy. I would never begrudge you the happiness I had with your mother. Genevieve, we judged you based on your mother's abhorrent choices which was misguided. On behalf of Jeannie and myself, I sincerely apologize. I hope you both can forgive us and find your way back to each other."

"What changed your mind?" Joseph asks Samuel, holding my hand even tighter.

"I see a great difference between the women I deemed worthy and Genevieve. Also, I spoke with Robert about the estate meeting and some other issues from the past. It made me realize how short-sighted your mother and I were. I'm deeply sorry. Goodnight." He reaches his hand out and Joey takes it. Samuel turns and walks away.

Joey doesn't move for a long moment. I simply wait for him to speak.

"Will you rejoin me in the ballroom? I need some time to think this all through."

I intertwine my fingers with his.

"Anything you need."

We stand still for a moment longer before he leads me into the ballroom. We take our seats at the table, with Samuel noticeably absent. Kelly and Gwen are staring at us with concern. I indicate everything will be fine and they continue their meals. The music has swiftly changed from the soft jazz that played during dinner to more popular dance songs. Joey is still glued to his chair. I can only imagine the turmoil going on in his head. I turn in my chair so that I'm facing him. He swivels his eyes to meet mine. I stand, reaching out my hand. When he takes it, heat travels up my arm. I lead him to the dance floor mostly because it will be more appropriate for him to put his hands on me but also so we will have a little more privacy if he needs to talk. I take the chance to press my body to his. Awareness courses between us.

The feeling of his strong arms around me is one I will never tire of. He tucks me under his chin as we move as one to the music. Luckily, a second slow song plays, and we sway to the music. The closeness of him is doing things to me. My body tingles where his hands are. All my senses are in the mix. He looks so sexy in this tux; I want to strip it off him. His heart beating fast. I lift my head to meet his piercing blue eyes. They gaze deeply into mine.

"Are you ready to leave?" I ask softly.

"Yes," he says, in a low breathless tone. We say our goodbyes to those family members still at the table.

We ride the elevator to our suite. All of a sudden, I'm nervous. As if he has heard my thoughts, he reaches between us and twines his fingers with mine. Joey hasn't uttered anything of substance since our encounter with Samuel. Up until then, I had a pretty good idea how the rest of the night would turn out. Now, I have no idea what to expect.

JOSEPH

The thoughts in my head are a mess. My father, I have no words. Do I want to know more details? Honestly, I'm not sure at this moment. I open the door for Genevieve and follow her inside. Once the door closes, I pull her back to me.

"I'm so grateful for you. I appreciate you coming here tonight. I know it was hard for you."

"I would do anything for you. Though, it scares me how much I feel already. Deep down, I don't think I ever stopped. I . . ." I press my lips to hers and kiss her until we both need air. I reach down, scoop her off her feet and walk to the bedroom. She kisses her way up my jawline from my chin to my ear while in my arms. I set her on the tufted bench and kneel to unstrap her shoes. She pushes my jacket off my shoulders, and it falls to the floor. She focuses on removing my bow tie. Once it's loose, she starts working on the buttons of my shirt. Waiting to unzip that dress is taking so much restraint. She feathers kisses across my chest while unclipping the cuff links. As much as I want to take this slowly, I need to see her. All of her. I grab her hands and pull us to our feet. She stills. I turn her around, holding her against me for a brief moment. I push her hair over to her left shoulder. I grip the top of her dress's zipper pulling it down and following it with light kisses down her back. I notice now that she isn't wearing a bra. How did I miss that all night long? The realization only makes me harder. I slide the straps of the dress down her arms, and it floats to the floor. I look down and see the sheer black thong she is wearing. I graze my hands over the back of her thighs, over her perfect ass, and around her body to cup her breasts. Her head falls back onto my chest. I kiss the top of her head while kneading her breasts, plucking her nipples into tight peaks. Her hands are gripping my outer thighs. Through my pants, I can feel the heat radiating off of her. I slide my left hand down her belly and between her thighs only to find her thong soaked through. She opens herself for me, and I take this chance to plunge two fingers inside her. Sweet, unintelligible moans come out of her mouth. I move my fingers in and out, drawing circles on her clit with my thumb until she comes on my hand. After she tumbles over the edge, she makes quick work of my belt and pants. I hook my thumbs through the sides of her thong, and she steps out of it. We walk over to the bed and fall onto it. I look down at her. It hits me in the chest that I want her, and only her for the rest of my life. I can't change the past, but I can absolutely secure the future. I slowly slide deep inside her. She's tight around me. We move together until we both rush over the edge. We lie together coming down. Her left arm is across my chest and her left leg across mine. My right arm is around her and she fits perfectly.

I move to get off the bed.

"Stay with me," she whispers.

"I need to get something," I say, walking to my bag and placing the package from Edmund on the bedside table. I climb back into bed. She looks at me confused.

"I need to say a few things," I say. She nods.

"As you know, I've been alone for the better part of seven years. I never imagined you would come crashing back into my life. Let alone that my son would bring us together. Four days before I left you," he chokes out, "I bought you an engagement ring with every penny I saved from the previous two summers. I planned to give it to you that night. As you know, it didn't work out as I planned." Her eyes are filled with tears. One falls down her cheek. I sweep it away with my thumb.

"Edmund and Corinne were very supportive of James and me when they moved back here. As you know, he left me the Mustang." I reach over for the package.

"He left this for me in the glovebox of the car. I found it last Saturday after work." I hand her the letter with shaky hands.

"Please read it."

She reads the letter. Tears fall from her eyes, wetting the paper as she looks up at me. I hold her hands in mine and press on even though her tears are shredding my heart.

"I love you. I have loved you since I was eight years old. I want to spend the rest of my life with you, but I want you to wear my ring." I hand her the box.

"I appreciate their confidence in me, in us, and I'm hopeful they're right about us. However, this belongs to you whether we get married or not." She opens the box and stares at Corinne's ring for what feels like an eternity. She attempts to speak a few times before words finally escape her lips.

"That is why I didn't find it in her jewelry box. You bought me a ring?"

"Yes." I wait for her to continue. I realize I just put myself out there for her. She could crush me.

"Thank you for giving this to me now. Not having them here is difficult for me. A love like theirs is what I wish for myself. I want you. I love you. I always have and I always will." I crush my lips onto hers pulling, her on top of me. The sheets are tangled around us. We make love for the second time tonight, but the emotional shift this time is obvious. Now, we're on the same page as we were our very first time at the cavern.

GENEVIEVE

Did that really just happen? Details from the last day slide around in my head, Francesca, Gwen giving me her blessing to help raise James, and Samuel. Joey bought an engagement ring for me over a decade ago. I open my eyes and see his gorgeous face lying next to me.

Yes, it did happen. I want this. I want us. I want to wake up like this every single day. Trying to move as little as possible, I note the clock reads six thirty. I brush my lips across his. A knowing smile breaks out on his face.

"Good morning, beautiful."

"Good morning. Should we order some breakfast?" I ask, sitting up to reach for the menu. Joey pulls me back down to him.

"Not yet. I want to savor you a bit longer," he replies, with a devilish grin on his face. I smile back succumbing to his charms. An hour later, Joey orders enough breakfast for an army. While we are waiting, we take a long shower and dress to head home. We eat in companionable silence. I'm sure there is so much he wants to say but doesn't know how.

"How are you feeling?" I ask him. I leave it open on purpose. He looks at me, pondering his response.

"The gala was a huge success. I'm glad I created it for James. As far as my father, although I'm grateful he apologized to you, I didn't need it. I know I want to spend the rest of my life with you. For us, I'm grateful that you are understanding and willing to give us a second chance. I love you, Genevieve."

"I love you."

We finish our meal and pack up to leave. I hand the keys to Joey as we descend in the elevator. The ride to Kelsey's is quick. I use my key to enter her condo. I don't see her anywhere, but Charley is lounging on the couch. I motion for Joey to stay as I check her room.

I return to the living room and say, "She isn't here. Can you pack up Charley's bowls in the kitchen? I just need to grab one bag here. The rest is in the storage area."

Having grabbed my bag, I meet Joey in the kitchen. He is on the phone with Norah checking in. They are out getting some supplies for a craft project. I leave a note for Kelsey. telling her she rocked the gala last night and that I will call her later today. I secure Charley's leash.

At the storage unit, we add the rest of my things to the car. We leave towards home around ten in the morning. I love the sound of that. *Home in Maine.*

Once we get to Massachusetts, it starts pouring. It's so heavy; we must drive slowly on the highway. At one point, we consider pulling over to wait it out. Despite the awful weather, we're enjoying each other's company and laughing at each other's song choices. At least we still agree on our favorite sports teams. We argued over who the starting quarterback should be and whether our team should replace the front four.

JOSEPH

We reach the state line just before two in the afternoon. It's still pouring but the winds have lessened. We will arrive at the cottages soon. We round the corner near my cottage and see a police cruiser blocking the road. I pull over and park the car. Before Genevieve can say anything, I 'm running towards my house, worried about James. I know in my head that he's fine since I just talked to Norah.

I stop in my driveway and turn towards Genevieve. Charley is hot on her heels.

"Genevieve, stop. Please, baby, stop!" I yell, holding my hands up. This is going to shatter her. She doesn't register my statement until she reaches me.

"Nooooo!" she screams at the top of her lungs. I wrap her in my arms to keep her from crumbling to the ground. Tears are streaming down her face as she fights to get closer. I'm holding her as tightly as I possibly can without hurting her. There are emergency vehicles in her driveway; the firefighter is using the jaws of life to pull someone out of a car. There is a massive tree through the roof of the cottage.

"Their room, no, their room. It's destroyed," she wails, burying her head into my chest and gripping my shirt with both hands. I can only imagine the pain she's in right now. In reality, it's just a house, but to her it embodies every good memory she has ever had - especially of Memére and Pepére. She was starting over there. Starting over with me. After what seems like an eternity but is closer to five minutes, a police officer in a tailored suit walks towards us as the ambulance pulls away.

"Captain Ramirez," he says, reaching out his hand.

I shake it. "Joseph Cavallaro."

"Is this your house?" he asks me.

"It's hers. She inherited it from her grandparents who died a few months ago," I reply.

"That explains her reaction." Captain Ramirez says. He turns to Genevieve. "I'm sorry for your loss." She nods but doesn't say a word.

"Joseph, the driver struck the tree which ultimately fell on the cottage. The fire department will cut the portions of the tree near the power lines, but the rest will be handled by her insurance company. The power to the house has been shut off. My report will be ready in a few days." He reaches into his pocket and hands me a card.

"If you or Miss?"

Despite her current state of shock, she rasps, "Genevieve Harpin."

"If you or Miss Harpin have any questions, please contact me directly. Do you need assistance with somewhere to stay tonight?"

"No, thank you, Captain Ramirez. I will be fine." He walks back towards his car.

She looks up at me with sad hollow eyes. Her face is puffy and blotchy. Even so, she's still the most beautiful woman I have ever seen. Just six hours ago, those same eyes were beaming with hope and light for us.

"Let's go inside," I say. She nods against my shoulder. I let go of her and drop my hand to hers, intertwining our fingers. I step towards my door, but she doesn't come. I wait, and eventually, she takes a few deep breaths and follows me into my house. Charley rushes in as soon as the door opens. Norah and James aren't back yet. I guide Genevieve to the couch and make some coffee to warm us up.

I hand her a hot cup of coffee. As I sit next to her, she looks at me and quickly looks away as if she's trying to find the right words.

"Can I stay here until the cottage is fixed?" She asks.

"Genevieve, you're welcome here for as long as you need or want." I answer, wondering why, after all we shared the past few weeks, that's even a question in her mind. I chalk it up to her current state of mind. I take our cups, set them aside and wrap her in my arms.

Norah and James return from shopping. Charley hustles over to greet them and James pour on some extra love. I see the last emergency vehicle pull away as Norah walks in. I move my car into the driveway and start unloading Genevieve's boxes. While he pets Charley, James is bending Genevieve's ear about his time with Norah. Even though she is devastated, she hangs on his every word. After a few trips inside including one upstairs where I put her boxes at the foot of the bed, Genevieve notices what I'm doing. She rises from the couch to help.

"I will do it," I say, "I have one more trip left." Although the boxes aren't labeled, I think the one I'm holding belongs in the office. After I set it down, I hear James talking to Genevieve.

"I'm sorry about your cottage, Miss Gen. It was cozy there."

"Thank you, James," she whispers in reply.

Without missing a beat, he shouts, "You should stay here with us. It's so much happier when you're here. Right, Dad?"

I approach the living room. James has a huge grin on his face.

"Right, what James? I was just going to tell you that I invited Miss Gen to stay with us because we're happier when she is here."

"Yes, she's welcome to stay, and it is happier when she is here. I agree with you." Genevieve blushes but says nothing. Her wide eyes stare at me with an emotion I can't place – hope, maybe.

Norah takes that as her cue to leave. I walk her to the door. "Be careful, big brother," she says, "he loves her too. Don't screw it up."

I laugh, "Squarely on team Genevieve, Nor?"

"I'm squarely on team Cavallaro, and well, she makes you happy. She should be on the team, too. I love you both."

"She does make me happy. She always has. Thanks, Nor." We hug and she walks out to her car.

I lean against the door gazing at them on the couch. I had already concocted a plan when I found Corinne's ring. Now, I just have to reorder a few things - first, ask her to move in and then ask her to be my wife, instead of the other way around. I will need to enlist some help to pull it off properly.

James continues sharing his escapades with Genevieve. Suddenly, he takes a quick conversational turn and asks about the gala. I jump in sharing the details of the evening and telling him about Brittany. After hearing about the gala, James goes to his room to continue his Lego City.

Genevieve looks at me.

"How is this going to work? Where should I set up my work stuff? Where should I sleep? This is a bad idea. What about James? This is really, really fast."

"Sweetheart, breathe. I love you. One question at a time." I encircle her in my arms, tucking her under my chin. I kiss the top of her head. I feel some tension leave as she relaxes a bit.

"First, James invited you to stay here. Based on that, he's fine with it. Second, it may seem a little fast, but only because we took a long break. The time we spent together doesn't count any less because it was a long time ago." She lifts her head from my chest and looks into my eyes. Tears threaten to fall. It shreds me when she cries. "Third, for your work stuff, we can make the spare bedroom into an office or we can reorganize mine and share it.

Lastly, you will sleep with me. Without you, the past week has been awful. Waking with you in my arms is the only way I want to start my days."

"Are you sure? I don't know how long it will take to fix the cottage."

"Absolutely, sure. I was sure about us when we were seventeen. I'm more sure about us now. Let me be here for you. Let me hold your hand and help you through this."

I see the wheels turning in her head.

"I will."

"Where do you want to start?" I ask her.

"Let's decide what to do with the office."

I reach for her hand and she slides it into mine. We stand in the office. I'm thinking about how to rearrange it. I don't need that much space.

"I can shift my things to the right half of the desk, and you can use the left until we can get a desk for you here." I point towards the client-side of his desk, where two chairs sit. If I remove the chairs another desk will fit.

"Works for me," she says and leans in to kiss me. I will never tire of her soft supple lips on mine. Her stomach rumbles, and we both break out in laughter.

We scour the kitchen for ingredients, but apparently Norah and James ate all the food in the house over the last two days. So, we order takeout for dinner.

Once we finish dinner, we head up to James' room. After three chapters, James settles in for the night. Charley has officially adopted James as his master. Genevieve just smiles as her dog snuggles up on his bed. She slowly shakes her head. Genevieve and I walked to my room — our room.

GENEVIEVE

I'm not sure what to do with myself right now. I have so much to unpack and I hadn't even planned on unpacking here.

"Stop overthinking it, sweetheart," Joey says. He sits beside me, rubbing his hand up and down my back.

"How do you always know?"

He smiles.

"As I said the last time, I can read your mind, I may be rusty, but I remember everything. We will get through this. Does it suck that a tree fell onto Mem's cottage? Yes. Does it suck that you're here now? No, not at all."

I lean into him using the strength he has given me.

"Thank you for knowing what to say to pull me out of my head. I know I was going to make changes to the cottage, but I wasn't planning on starting tomorrow. I guess now I am."

"That's my girl!" He kisses my forehead and stands up. "How much dresser space do you need?" He points to the tall bureau near the balcony doors. "That one is empty, it's yours. There is a closet to the left of the sitting area that is also empty."

"I'm in awe of this room. You built it for two even when it was just you. Smart, very smart. Plus, that bathroom is to die for." I wink at him and start placing my clothes in the bureau.

"Can I help?" he asks.

"Sure, the garment bag has some clothes you can hang in it." He scoops up the bag and opens the closet door. I know full well I'm never going to want to leave here even after Mem's cottage is fixed.

"Oh Joey," I murmur under my breath not meaning for him to hear me.

"What, sweetheart? he responds stepping out of the closet.

"Nothing," I sigh, continuing to fill the bureau with my clothes. We unpack the majority of the boxes. I set Memére's jewelry box on the bureau leaving my hand on top for a brief moment. A tear falls down my cheek.

Joey surrounds me with his arm and whispers, "It will get easier. That feeling doesn't go away but remembering will get easier on you. I promise."

I turn to him, rise on my toes, and press my lips to his.

"Which side of the bed do you want?" he asks.

"Which side do you use? Are you a starfish in your own bed?" I smirk at him.

"What?" he asks incredulously, as if he doesn't have a clue what that means.

"Do you sleep like a starfish when you are alone?" I say, scurrying away from him and jumping onto the bed to show him what I mean.

Laughing, he says, "No, I prefer the side by the door." He slowly lowers himself next to me on the bed as I pull back my limbs. He cradles me in his arms, kissing my shoulders and neck.

"What time do you get up for work?" he asks.

"I have been waking up at five here with no alarm. Normally if I set an alarm, I get up at six, workout, and then get ready for work. What time does the bus come in the morning? Do you run in the morning?"

"James gets on the bus at seven forty-five. I run in the morning if it works out with my call schedule for the day."

"Let's set the alarm for five thirty to be on the safe side," I say. Joey rolls over towards the night table and sets the alarm. He turns back towards me and pulls me closer.

"Goodnight, sweetheart. I love you."

"Goodnight, I love you."

I sleep so soundly with Joey. I first noticed it the night after the meeting with Collette. I glance over at the clock and it's just before five. I study his face for a few moments and slip out onto the balcony. Oh, how I missed this while I was training and all the time before that. I enjoy a few more quiet moments, take a deep breath, and turn back inside to take on this day. I find Joey standing in the doorway staring at me.

"Good morning. How did you sleep?" he inquires.

"Morning. I slept well, and you?"

"I did, too. Are you ready, Miss Executive Manager?"

I smile.

"Yes, I am." I step into his arms knowing, without any reservations, I want this every day for the rest of my life regardless of how fast it seems or if it's crazy that I'm already feeling this way. Deep down, I know, I never stopped loving him.

"I love you," I say.

He replies the same way and we start our day together.

GENEVIEVE

TWO MONTHS LATER

Settling into my new job and living with Joey and James has been wonderful. The first week or so was rough, with us sharing one desk, but once I got enough space, I didn't mind sharing the office. The renovation to my cottage is moving along though it's taking longer than I anticipated. If I'm being honest, though, I don't care how long it takes. I don't want to move, even when it's done. The trick will be getting Joey to let me stay. Today is Tuesday, and my workload is light. I'm enjoying a second cup of coffee on the deck. Fall is almost over, and it has been getting chillier, so I grab one of his sweatshirts even though I have my own. I text Kelsey to check in on our weekend plans.

Me: Hey there!

Kelsey: How are you, girl?

Me: I'm well. I don't know how I'm going to move out of here when the renovations are finished. Morning coffee on this deck is heavenly.

Kelsey: So, don't. Have you told Joey yet?

Me: No, I haven't said anything. It's really fast, Kels.

Kelsey: I don't blame you but you're happy, in love, and settled.

Me: Thanks. I'm all of those things for the first time in my life. How is Michael?

Kelsey: You're welcome. I'm happy for you. Not sure about him, Gen.

Me: Will I see you on Friday?

Kelsey: I will be there with bells on. I miss you girl. Love you.

Me: Yay! Miss you too. Love you too.

I pad back into the kitchen for a fresh cup to bring to the office. I'm pleasantly surprised to find a sweaty post-workout Joey in the kitchen. Holy Moly! I mean, he has a drool-worthy body but that same body covered in sweat. Wow! In my mind, I check my calendar. I have enough time. I saunter over to him and pull his mouth to mine. I whisper for him to meet me in the shower and take off running up the stairs. I hear an audible groan and my name, but he beats me to the top of the staircase all the same.

JOSEPH

I have spent the last two months reveling in Genevieve's presence. Our house has settled into a simple easygoing rhythm. We added another desk to the office so now we both have enough space to work. She and I tradeoff who picks up James from the bus so the other can work a bit longer. She has slowly added little touches to our home to make it more comfortable, like a blanket or pillow here or there. The renovations at her place have started but are taking a bit longer than she would like. Her anxiety about the delay makes me nervous that she wants to move out when it's done. Her plans are amazing, though. The new kitchen will be an open floor plan with plenty of seating. Selfishly, I want the renovations to stretch out as long as possible. I have almost completed step two of my plan and although the order is reversed, I don't want her to leave.

Today is one of the best days of the year. It's James' birthday. He has opted for a party with his friends at the laser tag place one town over. I greet all of the parents and children, including Sophie. She's a cute little girl with bouncy, blonde curls and big, blue eyes. James is shocked she came, but he takes her hand and leads her inside to get their gear.

The scoreboard shows that both James and Sophie are eliminated fairly quickly. James and Sophie spend most of the time removed from the other party guests. My son is very intuitive. He must have known it was hard for Sophie to come though she did anyway. Otherwise, the party goes off without a hitch.

Genevieve leans close to my ear. "They're so sweet," she says. The closeness of her sends dirty thoughts through my mind.

"They remind me of us," I say, looking over at her. Her smile tells me she has been thinking the same thing.

Two days after the party, I finally receive the call I have been waiting for. Now, there's just one more detail to attend to for my weekend with Genevieve.

Me: Everything else is in order.

Kelsey: What do you need for Saturday?

Me: Could you bring me a few mini versions of her favorite desserts, please. You're an amazing friend, Kelsey.

Kelsey: No problem and thank you. I'm so happy for the two of you. I'm glad you found your way back to each other.

Me: Thank you. Me too.

James is spending this upcoming weekend with Gwen, but she is picking him up on Friday instead of Saturday. Genevieve has no idea what I have in store for her.

Since Genevieve moved here, Kelsey has been coming up for girls' night at least once a month. I'm so glad they can continue that tradition. Kelsey seems to prefer coming here. James and I make ourselves scarce if they are going to be home. When Kelsey comes by on Friday, I head out for a run, and when I return, they're unsurprisingly watching *P.S. I Love You* with of course, Gerard Butler. I laugh to myself. I place a kiss on her forehead and hide out in our room until Kelsey falls asleep. Around midnight, I feel her slide into our bed and curl her arm around me.

"Movie over?" I ask her.

"Yes," she whispers against my neck.

"Would it be wrong to make love to you on girls' night?" I ask, spinning to face her.

"There is never a wrong time for that," she replies reaching for my shorts and pulling them off in one swift motion. I laugh and roll over, caging her underneath me. I pause, thinking about tomorrow and how this is the last night she will be my girlfriend.

"Are you okay?" she asks. I may have stared at her a bit too long.

"Yes, more than okay." I crush my mouth to hers.

Morning light streams through the French doors. She wakes up with the sun refreshed and ready for anything. It's only six but she is on the balcony swimming in my sweatshirt.

"I like seeing you in my clothes, but I'd rather you in no clothes at all." I grin at her.

She replies, "I'm aware of your preferences, but we aren't alone right now."

She frowns at me and drags me back to bed. Around seven, we make a move for some coffee and breakfast. Kelsey takes off right after breakfast to prepare for a shift at the Bistro.

GENEVIEVE

"Do you have any plans today?" I ask Joey.

He looks at me, trying to hide his giddiness. "Yes, I have planned the whole day for us. At my request, Kelly sent over a dress for you."

"Where are we going? I need a dress?" I ask.

"Don't worry, it will be amazing. It's something you mentioned wanting to do when we were younger."

I pout hoping it will persuade him to share details. "Nope, not going to work. I will hold strong against your feminine wiles even though most of the time they reduce me to a pile of mush. Go, get ready; we need to leave at one."

"Don't you need to shower? Do we have time to share the shower?" I say with a glint in my eye.

"There's always time," he replies. Once again, he beats me up the stairs. After we shower, Joey points me to the garment bag that I swear wasn't there when I woke up. Kelly has sent over a gorgeous tea-length dress with a crisscross neckline in a deep purple color. I immediately grab my phone and text her.

Me: Thank you, thank you. It's gorgeous!

Kelly: You're welcome. Have a great date.

I glance at the clock and realize I have spent too much time gazing at the ocean. It's solace and peace for me, always has been. I hurry back inside and finish getting ready. Joey smiles amused by me scurrying around.

"I'll be downstairs." He smiles as he leaves the room.

"I need five minutes. I just need to find shoes." I find a pair of shoes and walk downstairs.

"You look amazing!" He grins at me.

"Thank you. Kelly's dresses are amazing. The color is gorgeous." I smile at him. Even though it's past lunch time, Joey has made us both a cup of coffee for the road. How far away are we going?

"The coffee isn't a clue about the length of the car ride, sweetheart." Again, it's as if he is reading my mind. "I know you love coffee in the car regardless of the distance to be travelled."

"I love you for paying attention." I grab my purse and indicate I am ready to leave.

JOSEPH

I open her car door and gawk at her amazing legs as she settles into her seat. This is just a date, no need to worry about anything yet. Later, maybe. No worrying required. Of course, she will say yes.

I take the longest possible route to the Nubble. There are only two ways to get there from the cottages. She will know soon enough that it's our destination, but she has no idea what I have up my sleeve.

We pull into the parking lot. I glance over at her and see the same calm serene look she had when we came with James. I ask her to wait for me to get the door for her. She simply nods. I round the car and open her door. Immediately, she notices there is a boat docked over to the side near the rocky edge. I offer her my arm and guide her towards the boat.

"No way! Are you serious?" A huge smile breaks out on her face and she kisses my cheek. "How did you . . . how did you even remember I wanted to do this?"

"Sweetheart, I told you before, and I will tell you every day until my last breath. I remember every detail of you and our time together." I smile looking at her. "Are you ready?"

"I have been waiting for this chance since I was twelve years old. I'm so excited. In case I forget later, I've had a wonderful time so far today. I love you." She places a soft kiss on my lips.

"You're welcome. I love you." We walk towards the boat. I reach for her hand to steady her as she boards. Apparently, that calls for some fanfare, as a bunch of tourists applaud.

We are greeted by a member the York Parks and Recreation Department. Her name is Lucille and she takes us over to the island. It's rare for people to visit the actual lighthouse. My donation, however, was hefty. The sheer joy I see in Genevieve's eyes makes it worth every single penny. Although the lighthouse is automated now, she reads the history of the lighthouse and climbs the tower to see the view. We stand and watch the sea. The view is spectacular. If we didn't have an amazing spot at the cavern that was ours alone, this would be the perfect place to propose.

After our amazing visit to the lighthouse, we leisurely drive back to the cottage. On the surface, I'm calm, cool, and collected but on the inside, I'm freaking out. I'm absolutely sure, she will say yes, but the last time I planned to propose everything went to hell. No panic is required. We're both adults now. Get it together, Joseph!

We let Charley out and walk from my cottage towards Short Sands beach away from the cavern. We walk slowly in the shallows, hand in hand. On the return trip from the far side of the beach, we let Charley back inside, grab a jacket for Genevieve, and continue our walk to the cavern. Moments later, we arrive.

"Joey, this is amazing," she says, taking in the twinkling lights and dining table. Kelsey and Gwen have also set up a sitting area, with pillows on a fluffy blanket. "You didn't have to go to all this trouble."

"I wanted to." I smile at her taking in the utter perfection of her smooth skin and emerald eyes. The jewel-tone purple dress Kelly sent her is perfect.

Even though I know this is a public space, I wanted this time to be just for us. With a little help from my friends Gwen and Kelsey, the cavern has been set up for a romantic dinner for two. Gwen prepared a full meal for us, from the salad to Chicken Piccata. Captain Ramirez even blocked the cavern off for me. If Genevieve has any idea what I'm planning, she doesn't let on. As we eat our dinner, memories flash in my head, and I'm sure they do in hers.

We talk about everyday things like the cottage renovation and work while enjoying the meal. After eating, we walk deeper into the cavern like when we were young. The sheer glow on her face makes all the planning worth it. I guide her back to the table and pull out the desserts that Kelsey made.

"How did you get all my favorites? Wait, is Kelsey here?" she asks looking around the cavern. I smile.

"She brought them last night," I tell her.

"Oh, makes sense." That is the end of her questioning; she digs into the desserts with gusto. She's absolutely oblivious to the anxiety roiling in my head and my belly. Everything is different now.

I take a few deep breaths and find her gazing at me. I stand, circle the table, and get down on one knee in front of her chair. Her hands immediately cover her mouth.

"Genevieve, I bought this ring for you when I was a young man. I was barely able to care for myself, but I knew we would have a great love story." I open the box holding my original Asscher-cut engagement ring set in platinum. Her eyes well up with tears but she doesn't utter a word.

Opening a second box, I say, "I designed this ring the day I found Edmund's note in the glovebox. It gave me the courage to fight for you, for us." I show her the halo of ten diamonds, one for each year we were apart, and I fit them together. Tears fall down her face, and I haven't even asked her anything. I reach up to her face and sweep away a tear. She turns her head and kisses the inside of my palm. I continue to hold her left hand in her lap.

"It has taken us a long time to get back here. Genevieve, I have loved you since I was young. You came back into my life and made it brighter. I didn't realize how dull it had become until James found you on the beach. I love you, Genevieve. Will you marry me?"

"Yes, Yes! I love you and I can't wait to be your wife." I slide my rings onto her finger and lift her off the ground. I hold her, kissing her until we are both panting. I spin us around and sit in her chair, cradling her in my lap. Her arms are immediately around my neck our foreheads pressed together. We sit in silence, enjoying the moment.

"Do you know what day today is?" She asks softly in my ear.

"Maybe?" knowing better than to suggest something wrong.

"It's her birthday."

"Oh, sweetheart. I didn't plan today knowing it was Mem's birthday but I'm glad I chose today."

"Me too. How soon do you want to do this?" she asks between each soft kiss she gives me. I pull back to look into her wide eyes.

"I would marry you right now, if I could."

"Would you mind sharing our wedding date with them?" she asks.

I don't even have to think about my response. "No, it would be an honor to follow their example. When is it?"

"Next Saturday."

EPILOGUE

GENEVIEVE

"Do you, Joseph, take Genevieve to be your lawfully wedded wife?"

"I do."

"Do you, Genevieve, take Joseph to be your lawfully wedded husband?"

"I do."

"By the power vested in me by the State of Maine, I now pronounce you husband and wife. You may kiss your bride."

Cheers and applause surround us as we kiss for the first time as husband and wife.

"I love you," I whisper in his ear as he pulls me up from the dip.

"I love you, Mrs. Cavallaro."

"I could get used to that Mrs. Genevieve Cavallaro." I smile and we walk down the aisle between our friends and family. James walks with us holding my hand.

He looks up at me and says, "I'm glad you are officially my mom now. I love you."

With tears in my eyes, "I love you, James. I'm happy to be officially your mom, too!"

I'm amazed that we were able to pull this off in one week. Everything I dreamed of when I was younger, we were able to make happen from the beachfront wedding to the calla lily and purple dahlia bouquet. Kelly is the most amazing sister- in-law/designer/seamstress on the planet. She created the most spectacular gown for me and hooked up Kelsey and Gwen with gorgeous dresses for the occasion.

Despite the short notice, everyone was able to make it except my mom. Her choice, nothing, I can do about it. I know she received the invitation because she signed for it personally. I checked.

Joey and I are mingling with our guests. Kelsey is pulling double duty; she baked our cake and now is watching it like a hawk until it is time for us to cut it. Her cobalt blue dress makes her eyes seem a deeper blue.

KELSEY

I'm so happy to be here. Gen is finally happy after all these years.

"Hey there! How are you? You look gorgeous." I say to the blushing bride.

"Thank you. So, do you. That blue is amazing on you," Gen replies.

"Thanks. Let me know when you are ready to cut this cake."

"Give me about thirty minutes and we will be ready."

"Sounds good," I reply. The cake will be fine without a bodyguard, I decide, and move towards the bar.

"Can I have a glass of Cabernet Sauvignon, please?" I ask the bartender. I feel a presence before I see him to my left. A disgustingly gorgeous man in a grey tailored suit stands next to me. I glance over at him and he smiles at me. His eyes are deep brown like dark-chocolate and those dimples — oh my!

"Good evening. Are you a friend of the bride or the groom?" he asks me.

"I'm the bride's best friend, Kelsey," I say, reaching my hand out.

The moment his hand slides around mine, sparks seep from my fingers to my toes and surround me.

"William Ramirez. It's a pleasure to meet you, Kelsey. Enjoy the party."

"You too," I reply. In all my years of shaking hands, I've never felt anything like that. Too bad I live in Rhode Island because I want to feel that some more.

ACKNOWLEDGMENTS

First and foremost, I would like to thank my husband for pushing me to leap out of my comfort zone and give my dream a shot.

I would like to thank my team of early readers—Jaclyn Salmon, Barbara Chabot, Julie Scarpa, Susan Kantor and Melissa Elliott. Your input was appreciated and helped make this novel better.

I would like to thank Ashlee Sasscer Nassar for the amazing cover design.

UP NEXT

Don't miss the next book in the York Beach series coming soon!

Taking a Chance on Me (Kelsey and William)

http://bit.ly/TCMYB_Kindle

Did you love A New Beginning with You?

Thank you for taking the time to read it. I hope you loved it!

If you liked this book or another one of my books – please consider

posting a review. A short line or two will be perfect!

I appreciate your support and feedback.

I love hearing from my readers. Drop me a message

or comment on these platforms:

Visit me on Social Media or online to learn about my newest releases:

Facebook (http://fb.me/NicoleVidalAuthor)

Instagram (http://instagram.com/nicolevidal_author)

Amazon (https://www.amazon.com/Nicole-

Vidal/e/B082DJHPXP?ref_=dbs_p_ebk_r00_abau_000000)

My website (www.nicolevidal.com)

Pinterest (http://pinterest.com/NicoleVidal_Author)

Goodreads

(https://www.goodreads.com/author/show/19827329.Nicole_Vidal)